REQUIEM FOR A WREN

By the same author in Pan Books

MOST SECRET
THE CHEQUER BOARD
LONELY ROAD
A TOWN LIKE ALICE
NO HIGHWAY
RUINED CITY
AN OLD CAPTIVITY
PIED PIPER
PASTORAL
LANDFALL
ON THE BEACH
SLIDE RULE
IN THE WET
SO DISDAINED
WHAT HAPPENED TO THE CORBETTS
MARAZAN
ROUND THE BEND
THE FAR COUNTRY
TRUSTEE FROM THE TOOLROOM

NEVIL SHUTE

REQUIEM FOR A WREN

UNABRIDGED

PAN BOOKS LTD : LONDON

First published 1955 by William Heinemann Ltd.
This edition published 1971 by Pan Books Ltd,
33 Tothill Street, London, S.W.1

ISBN 0 330 02672 0

Printed in Great Britain by Cox & Wyman Ltd.,
London, Reading and Fakenham

I shall never be friends again with roses;
I shall loathe sweet tunes, where a note grown strong
Relents and recoils, and climbs and closes,
    As a wave of the sea turned back by song.
There are sounds where the soul's delight takes fire,
Face to face with its own desire;
A delight that rebels, a desire that reposes;
    I shall hate sweet music my whole life long.

The pulse of war and passion of wonder,
    The heavens that murmur, the sounds that shine,
The stars that sing and the loves that thunder,
    The music burning at heart like wine,
An armed archangel whose hands raise up
All senses mixed in the spirit's cup
Till flesh and spirit are molten in sunder —
    These things are over, and no more mine.

A. C. SWINBURNE

CHAPTER ONE

THERE WAS a layer of cumulus, about seven-tenths, with tops at about five thousand feet as we came to Essenden airport; we broke out of it at two thousand and we were on the circuit downwind, with the aerodrome on our starboard wing. I sat with my eyes glued to the window looking out at Melbourne, because this was my home town and I had been away five years. The hostess touched me on the arm and drew my attention from the scene, and told me to fasten my safety belt. I had not seen the sign light up.

'Sorry,' I said.

She smiled, and then she said quietly, 'Would you like any help down the gangway, sir?'

I shook my head. 'I'll wait till the others are all off. I'm all right if I take my time.'

She nodded and moved on, courteous and efficient. I wondered how she knew that going downstairs was the tricky part; perhaps that was a feature of her training, or perhaps the hostesses on the machine from San Francisco had told her about me at Sydney. I turned back to the window to watch the approach to the runway and the landing, and I remained absorbed in the techniques till the machine came to a standstill at the terminal building and the engines came to rest.

While the other passengers got off I sat at the window trying to see who was there to meet me. It was likely to be my father. I hadn't given them much notice, for I had only telegraphed the time of my arrival from Sydney when I landed there the previous evening and it was barely two o'clock now; moreover, they weren't expecting me for another four days and we live a hundred and twenty miles from the airport. The wing hid a good part of the enclosure but I saw nobody I knew. I wondered if I should have to go into town to the Club and telephone home from there.

I followed the last passenger down the aisle to the door, and thanked the hostesses as I passed them. I made slow time down the steps but once on the flat I was all right, of course, and walked over to the enclosure. Then I caught sight of a face I knew. It was Harry Drew, our foreman, come to meet me. It was a warm, summery spring day and Harry was very smart. He is a man about forty years old, with dark, curly hair and a youthful figure. He was wearing an opulent-looking American shirt without a jacket on that warm day, a brown shirt buttoned to the neck and worn without a tie; his brown-green grazier's trousers were clean and newly creased and held up with a brand-new embossed belt with a large, shiny buckle. He caught my eye and half raised his hand in salutation.

I passed through the gate and he came to meet me. 'Morning, Harry,' I said. 'How are you today?'

'Good, Mr Duncan,' he replied. 'We didn't expect you till Friday.' He took the overnight bag from me.

'I came along a bit quicker than I thought I would,' I said.

He was clearly puzzled, as they all must have been, by my telegram. 'Did you come on a different ship?' he asked. 'We thought you'd be flying from Fremantle, arriving Saturday morning.'

'I didn't come that way,' I said. 'I had to stay in London a bit longer. I flew all the way, through New York and San Francisco to Sydney.'

'Come the other way round?'

'That's right,' I said. We passed into the airport building. 'How's my mother, Harry? She's not here, is she?'

'She didn't come,' he said. 'She gets out most fine days, but sitting in the chair most of the time, you know. She don't go away much now. Three months or more since she went down to Melbourne.' He paused by the newspaper stand. 'The Colonel, he was coming down to meet you, but we had a bit of trouble.'

'What sort of trouble?' I inquired.

'The house parlourmaid,' he said. 'Seems like she committed suicide or something. Anyway, she's dead.'

I stared at him. 'For God's sake! How did it happen?'

8

'I don't really know,' he said. 'It only happened this morning, and I left about half past ten to get down here to meet you. She took tablets or something, what they give you to make you sleep.'

'She did it last night?'

'That's right, Mr Alan.'

'Who found her?'

'She didn't come down to her work. They get down to the kitchen in the house about six or quarter past and have a cup of tea. When she didn't come down Annie went up to her room about seven.'

'Old Annie found her?'

'That's right. She was dead. The Colonel rang through for me to go up to the house, 'n soon after I got there Dr Stanley, he arrived. I suppose the Colonel telephoned for him. But there wasn't anything he could do; she was dead all right. So then they got on to the police, and just about then your telegram came from Sydney saying you'd be coming in today. The Colonel, he couldn't leave home with all that going on to come down here to meet you, so he said to me to take the Jaguar and come instead.'

I stood by the paper stand while the crowd milled around us. It was a muddle and a mess, and I was deeply sorry for my father and mother. My father was over seventy and my mother not much less, and neither of them in the best of health. Too bad that they should have a nuisance of this nature thrust on them.

'What did she do it for?' I asked. 'In trouble with some man?'

He wrinkled his brows. 'I wouldn't think so,' he said. 'Coombargana's a small place and not so easy to get away from unless you've got a car of your own, which she hadn't. She couldn't have been going with one of the lads at Coombargana and have no one know about it. I wouldn't think it was that.'

'How long had she been with us?'

'About a year. Maybe a bit longer. English, she was.'

I nodded; she would have been. English or Dutch or German; an Australian house parlourmaid is rare indeed. 'Well, I wish to God she'd picked another day to do it,' I

9

remarked. He grinned, and we went out to where the motor coaches stand to claim my luggage.

The Jaguar was two years old but it was still fairly new; as they grew older my parents were staying more and more at home. They had the Buick, too, which they still used a lot, that they had got through Singapore before I went away to England. We put my suitcases in the boot and Harry said, 'Will you drive, Mr Alan?'

I shook my head; I wanted to be able to see the country-side on this my first day back in my own country. 'You take her. How long did it take you to get down here?'

'About two hours and a quarter. I was afraid I'd be late.'

Our Australian main roads are straight and good and rela-tively empty, but even so an average of over fifty was good going. 'You've had dinner?' I asked.

He nodded. 'I got some tucker while I was waiting for the plane. Do you want to go in to the city before going home?'

I shook my head. 'Let's get going and find out what the form is about this trouble at home.'

He nodded, and we got into the car and drove out of the airport. He made for the Western Highway by a short cut through suburban roads I did not know; there had been much building on the outskirts of the city since I left. I did not talk to him till we were clear of the houses and making good time on the highway out to Bacchus Marsh, but then I began to question him about the property.

'Let's see,' he said. 'It was after you went away that the Colonel sold the hard land up on Baldy Hill to the Com-mission, for resumption? Five thousand two hundred acres he let go, for the soldier settlers. All the bit on the far side of the road, from the crossroads up to Sinclair's place.' I nodded. 'They cut it up into eleven lots, with eleven houses; there's chaps in seven of them now and four houses still finishing.' He dropped to forty for a moment behind a trailer truck and then accelerated past it and up to seventy-five again. 'I was sorry when the Colonel decided to do that,' he said, 'but thinking it over, maybe he was right. What's left is all good land, and we've got enough.'

'That leaves us about thirteen thousand acres?'

'Thirteen thousand three hundred and eighty-seven,' he replied.

'What are we running on that now?'

'Thirty-seven thousand, eight hundred and forty Merinoes all told,' he said. 'That's counting this year's lambs, of course. Six hundred and eighty-two Herefords.'

I nodded, indexing the figures in my memory. This was my business from now on, and everything that I had known and been in Europe was behind me. 'Finished the shearing?' I inquired.

'Finished last Friday week,' he said.

'How did it run out?'

'Good,' he said. 'We sheared seven hundred and sixteen bales this year.' A bale of wool contains three hundred pounds in weight, and at the prices that I knew were current it was worth about a hundred and sixty pounds, taking an average of the grades. Our wool clip must have been worth a hundred and fifteen thousand pounds or so, and then there would be the sales of cattle and of lambs on top of that. Take away the costs of running the property, say thirty or forty thousand pounds, and we were still left with an income of over a hundred thousand pounds for tax. It had been like that for several years.

'That's all right,' I said. 'How many did we shear last year?'

'Six hundred and seventy-eight bales, Mr Alan,' he said. 'It's the improved pastures doing it. We sowed another five hundred acres last autumn, across the river, from where we make the firebreak by the marsh up to the main road, Phalaris and Sub Clover.'

'Up to where Harrison's place is?'

'That's right, only Harrison's not there now. He got another property over by Ararat. His place was resumed.'

As we went on into the Western District through Bacchus Marsh to Ballarat he told me all about the property. My father had been ploughing back much of the profits into the land and saving the rest for death duties. He was determined to improve the carrying capacity of the property by mechanization and re-seeding paddocks and pasture conservation.

Silage was made in a big way for winter feed, a novelty since I was at home last, and there were now four big diesel tractors on the place, one of them a crawler. Horses were still used by the boundary riders but draught horses had vanished from Coombargana, and my father drove all over the property in a Land Rover instead of riding on a horse as he had always done when I was young. That suited me, for artificial feet are something of a handicap upon a horse. There was a great deal for me to learn about the property before I could unload some of the work from my parents, and I was quite keen to make a start. First of all, it would be necessary to clean up this infernal business of the house parlourmaid, however.

We passed through Bacchus Marsh and up over the Pentland Hills. On that fine, sunny, warm October day the air was like wine, with all the glistening glamour and the scents of spring. The view was superb from the top; I could see right over to Geelong forty miles away, and the blue curve of the bay as it swung round to Queenscliff and the Heads. Over to the west, ahead of us, the long blue ridge of the Grampians was already showing up over the horizon, over a hundred miles away and twenty miles or so past Coombargana. We dropped down off the hills at eighty miles an hour on the way to Ballarat, and there were the long gorse hedges all in bloom that the property owners in that part affect, mile after mile of them, scenting the countryside in the warm sun as we drove on into the Western District.

This was my own country, and I was glad to be home. When I had come home before I had disliked it all, and fretted bad-temperedly till I got away again. That was in 1946 when I had come out of hospital in England, stumbling along insecurely on my dummy feet. On board the ship I had tried to do too much and had fallen a couple of times in the rough weather of the Bay; after that I had stayed in my cabin most of the time, angry and frustrated. When I had come home it was all too easy and too pleasant for me in the Western District. The wartime restlessness was still on me and the European sense of strife and urgency; I could do little that was effective at Coombargana with my disability, and my father was still active and well capable of getting along without me. I stuck it for three years, because it seemed to me that now that Bill was dead and Helen married I ought to be at home learning to carry on the property, but it didn't work out well. By 1948 I was safe on my feet and able to get about quite normally, but I was thirty-four and life was slipping past me. I could not face burial alive in Coombargana at that age after all that I had been and done during the war, and I began to feel I should go crazy if I didn't get away from it to England again, where things were happening. I think my parents understood, because they made no objection when I suggested that I should go back to Oxford for a year and finish taking my degree. That was five years ago.

What I didn't realize then was that it wasn't England I was really fretting for. It was my lost youth.

I came back this time with a quieter mind, my youth behind me and all packed away. I was thirty-nine, middle-aged and mature, able to realize and to appreciate that it was not only in England that important things went on, that there were things of consequence and value going on even in my own country. Even the job that I had spurned before, the job of running Coombargana to turn out more meat and wool each year, now seemed to me to be worth doing, not one that would impress the world or get me a knighthood, but a job within my powers and worth doing in a gentle, unsensational way. I owed it to my parents to come home for they were getting tired and old, and sometimes rather ill, and now that I was home I was glad that I had come.

We drove into the suburbs of Ballarat and went trickling along like a twenty-year-old Austin Seven. I turned to Harry by my side. 'This bloody parlourmaid,' I said. 'You say she was English. Do you know if she had any relations in Australia?'

'I never heard she had, Mr Alan,' he replied. 'Your Dad might know.'

'Did my parents get her through a registry office?'

He shook his head. 'She turned up in Forfar at the Post Office Hotel one day, by bus from Ballarat I think it was. Working her way round the world, with a rucksack on her back – hiking, you might say. She worked in the hotel with

Mrs Collins for a week or two. Then she come out with the postman one day for the ride. Your parents had a Polish married couple but the man was always on the grog, 'n your Dad gave them the sack. Then this girl came along and offered herself for the job, and your mother took her on.'

'How long ago was that?'

'Let's see,' he said. 'It was wintertime. August, I'd say – August a year ago.'

I thought about it for a minute. 'Do you know where she went for her holiday?'

'I don't think she took one – not whilst she was working at Coombargana.'

'What was her name?'

'Jessie Proctor.'

He weaved the Jaguar skilfully through the traffic of the town and drove out down the Avenue of Honour and turned off on to the Skipton road. 'You may find your parents kind of upset,' he said presently. 'She was the best help they had in the house since I've been at Coombargana. I think they liked her, too.'

'They did?'

'I think so, Mr Alan.' He paused, and then said awkwardly, 'I thought you ought to know, case you might say anything rough about her, not knowing.'

I nodded. 'Thanks for telling me.' We drove along in silence while I thought this over. 'If she was happy in the place whatever made her go and do a thing like that?'

'I dunno, Mr Alan,' he replied. 'I dunno what makes girls go and do the things they do.'

I sat silent, thinking all this over. If my mother had grown attached to this girl it made things so much the worse, and nothing was more likely if she was a decent girl. My mother was now crippled with arthritis and could not get about very much, so that she met few people and perhaps was rather lonely, which was one of the reasons why I had come home. In a big house like Coombargana that must be run with indoor servants, unsatisfactory servants can be a continual worry and a nuisance to a woman in my mother's state of health, and they had had a long succession of married couples who had come for a few days and departed without notice because the place was too isolated, or had quarrelled with Annie our old cook, or had got drunk, or had stolen things. If in the end a girl had turned up who worked happily at Coombargana and made no trouble it was very likely that my mother would have grown to depend on her and might even have treated her more as a companion than as a servant. An English girl working her way round the world would be a well-informed person, possibly even well educated. She might have been a great comfort to my mother.

We passed through Skipton while I sat in silence thinking of these things and many others, and ran on into the undulating pastoral landscape that was my own place, a country not unlike Wiltshire in England but without the people, so that you can stand on almost any hill top and look all round the horizon and see nothing but the pastures and the sheep, with no sign of man except perhaps one fence in the far distance. There are shallow lakes and trout streams, seldom fished because they are too distant from the city, and most of the homesteads are located beside permanent water anyway so that anyone who cares for fishing can catch a trout with fly or worm within a few hundred yards of his own home. A lonely country for those who are not interested in the land, and bleak in winter when we usually get quite a lot of snow. In summer, a country in continual danger from grass fires, so that we spend much time and energy in planting wide strips of green crops such as rape for firebreaks. A summer fire that gets out of control in my country can wipe out all the pasture feed and fifty thousand pounds' worth of sheep in a couple of days. A country with not much mental stimulus outside the land, so that those who dislike us and call us the wool barons say that we all sink to the mental level of the sheep, and get to look like them too.

We came to Forfar, which is our village and about six miles from Coombargana, a little place of one long street straggling on the highway. Not much seemed to have changed there; there were a couple of new stores and electricity had reached the place while I had been away. For the rest it was unaltered; I saw Tom Hicks the garage owner at his pumps and waved my hand to him, and then we turned off on the gravel road to my home.

Presently we came in sight of the house, backed by tall pine trees that shelter it from the west, with the river curling round before it. Coombargana is my home and I would not willingly live anywhere else, but architecturally I will admit that the house isn't everybody's cup of tea. My grandfather, Alan Duncan, built it about 1897. He was born at Ellon between Peterhead and Aberdeen in 1845, the son of a small farmer. He came out to Australia when he was twenty years old to make his fortune in the goldfields of Ballarat, but gold was already big business by the time he got there, and he soon tired of working for a wage in a mine. Within a year he had moved farther out to farm, and took up land at Coombargana with the first settlers. By the time he was fifty he was running sheep on thirty thousand acres, and able to afford what he called a gentleman's house.

He made a trip home in 1895 to see his relations, and while in Ellon he went to see the Queen's house at Balmoral; I doubt if he saw the Queen. He returned to Coombargana with a picture postcard of Balmoral Castle and set himself to build a house like that, but on a smaller scale. There was no architect in the countryside to help him and the only materials that the builder could produce were a peculiarly ugly red brick, and concrete. The house that evolved was a castle that looked like no castle has ever looked before, yet inside it was comfortable and well designed; a good house to live in. It was like that till his death in 1922; I remember it well as a child. When my father inherited he took down eleven little spires that ornamented the battlements and started to grow creepers over it to tone it down a bit, but the possums used the creepers as a ladder to get into the roof. My father had the creepers removed and painted the whole thing cream in colour, which did away with the hot look in summer anyway. In 1938 my parents spent some months in England and my mother came back all steamed up about the modern décor, and painted all the outside doors and window frames crimson.

Well, that's Coombargana. It's my home, and I like it.

We crossed the river by the wooden bridge and swung round towards the house, and passed in to the drive between the great mossy concrete gate pillars. The place was well cared for, because my parents keep two gardeners going all the time, the enormous macrocarpa hedges neatly clipped in rectangular forms, the drive and the gravel sweep up to the house freshly raked and free from weeds. There are many better houses than Coombargana in England, but not many so well kept. The beds of daffodils were bright in the sunlight, masses of them, and behind the japonica bushes the camellias in bloom made a brave show of colour.

The Jaguar drew up before the door and I thanked Harry and got out. The red door opened and my father was there on the steps to meet me. I knew, of course, that he would be older but I had not visualized him in old age; one always remembers people as they were when last you saw them. My father was thinner than he had been and his face had a white, pallid hue I didn't like at all, but he was the same old Dad.

He said, 'Hullo, Alan. You're back earlier than we thought.'

'I know,' I said. 'I got hung up in London and had to miss the boat. I flew through America.'

'So that was it!' he said. 'We thought you must have flown. How did you get the dollars to come through America?'

I grinned. 'There are ways and means.'

He laughed. 'Well, come on in and see your mother.' Harry was unloading my two suitcases from the boot. 'Stick them just inside the door, Harry, and I'll get John to take them up presently.' He turned to me. 'I'm not allowed to lift anything now.'

'I can manage them,' I said. 'I can take them up, one at a time.'

He hesitated. 'Would you rather do that?'

I nodded. 'I like doing everything I can.'

'All right.' He said no more about my disability, but told Harry to put the car away. We went together into the great hall.

'You're looking very well,' he said.

I grinned. 'Wish I could say the same of you, Dad. You're not looking too good.'

'Ah well,' he said, 'we none of us get any younger, and this has been rather a trying day. I expect Harry told you about the trouble here?'

I nodded. 'I was very sorry to hear it.'

'We'll talk about that later,' he said. 'Come on and see your mother. I kept her in bed today.' He paused, and then he said, 'Did I tell you that we sleep on the ground floor now?'

I was surprised. 'No.'

He nodded. 'Your mother can't manage the stairs alone. It was either that or putting in a lift. We turned the billiard room into our bedroom with the gunroom as my dressing-room, and put the billiard table up in what used to be our bedroom. It's worked out quite well. Matter of fact, I like it better.'

He led the way into the old billiard room. They had re-decorated it, and with the french windows opening on to the lawn it made a sunny, pleasant room. My mother was sitting up in bed, not very much changed in her appearance. I went over and kissed her. 'Back at last,' I said. 'You're looking very well, Mum.'

She held me for a moment. 'Oh Alan dear,' she said, 'it *is* nice to have you back. But how did you get here so soon?'

I told her my story about being held up in London and missing the ship, and complimented her on the arrangement of the room. My father went out and Mother asked me about Helen, and I spent a few minutes answering all her questions about my sister in London.

Helen was the youngest of us; she had gone to England in 1946 when she was twenty-four, avid to get away into a wider world, like many young Australians. In England she had gone all arty and crafty and had picked up with a chap called Laurence Hilton who worked for the BBC and put on plays for the Third Programme. She married him in 1947 and had not been home since; they had one child, rather an unpleasant little boy. I had tried to like Laurence and to get alongside him but we had very little in common. Privately I thought him a phoney and I suspected that he had seen Helen coming because, of course, she had a good bit of money behind her. However, she seemed happy with him and had adopted most of his views, including the one that Australia was a cultural desert that no decent person would dream of living in. His earning capacity, of course, was quite inadequate for the life they wished to lead. They have a very pleasant little house in Cheyne Walk overlooking the river where they entertain a lot of visitors from ivory towers, and Coombargana pays.

I annoyed Laurence very much one day by referring to my father as a patron of the Arts. I'd probably have annoyed my father too if he'd known.

I gave my mother a roseate, expurgated account of Helen and Laurence and their way of life, stressing its importance and the reputation that Laurence Hilton was building up in the artistic world. My father came in again then pushing a tea trolley, for my parents live and eat in the English way with dinner at eight o'clock in the evening. There was trouble about the tea, because my father had brought the wrong sort of cups and had forgotten the tea strainer and the hot-water jug, and my mother sent him off to get them.

'We're all a bit upside down today,' she said sadly. 'We haven't had to do this ourselves for so long.'

'I know,' I said. 'Harry told me. I was very sorry to hear about it.'

'Yes,' my mother said quietly, 'it's been a very great blow to us, Alan. I'm so sorry that it had to happen on the very day that you come home.'

'That's all right,' I said. 'I'm glad in a way it did happen now, if it had to. Dad doesn't look too fit.'

'I think he's just tired today,' Mother said. 'He had that operation last year, you remember.' I nodded. 'The specialist assured us that it was non-malignant. I think it's just that he's tired and upset.'

'I should think so,' I said, but I didn't think so at all. 'Tell me, has there got to be an inquest?'

She nodded. 'Dr Bateman, he's the coroner. He's coming out tomorrow morning, with the police. Dr Stanley was here again this afternoon. I think there's got to be a post mortem.'

'Why did she do it, Mum?' I asked. 'Was she depressed?'

'I don't think so,' she said. 'She was just as usual, I think. She was a very reserved girl, Alan. She never talked about herself or her own affairs, like most women do. It was rather difficult to know what she thought of anything. She was always just about the same.'

'Was she attractive, Mother? Attractive to men?'

She shook her head. 'I don't think so. She was rather plain. I'm sure it wasn't anything like that.'

It was puzzling; we seemed to have come to a dead end. 'Have you got any idea why she did it?'

My mother said, 'I think it was an accident, Alan. I think it must have been. There was this bottle of sleeping tablets by her bedside, quite a big bottle, with only two left in it. Dr Stanley said he thought she must have taken at least twenty.' She paused. '*I* think she took one, perhaps, when she went to bed and then had a nightmare or something, and got up, sort of sleep-walking, and took tablet after tablet. I'm *sure* it was an accident.'

It was a possibility. 'There were two tablets left in the bottle?'

'Yes.'

'If she was going to commit suicide,' I said, 'she'd have taken the lot. She'd want to make sure of it. You don't think she had any motive for wanting to make away with herself, Mother?'

'I'm sure she hadn't, Alan. She seemed just the same as ever.'

I thought for a moment. 'Did she get any letters yesterday?'

'She never had any.'

'Never had any letters?'

My father came back with the tea strainer and the hot-water jug and put them on the trolley. 'I was telling Alan about Jessie,' she said, and now there was a suspicion of moisture about her eyes, and a break in her voice. 'He was asking if she got a letter yesterday.'

'She never got any mail at all, according to Annie,' my

father said. 'She never got a letter all the time that she'd been here. I never saw one addressed to her, and nor did Annie.'

'I never did,' said my mother.

I stared at them. 'That's very unusual, surely. Did she write any?'

'I don't think so,' said my father. 'I usually take the mail in when I go, but she never gave me one to take. I don't even know her handwriting. Annie says she never wrote a letter, and she never got one.'

'Could she write?' I asked. Sometimes a domestic servant can't.

'Oh yes. She was a well-educated girl,' my mother said. 'Very well educated. *I* knew her handwriting. She used to take down messages on the pad in the hall, when someone telephoned. You've seen them, Richard. You *do* know her handwriting.'

My father said, 'Oh, yes, of course I do. But that's the only place I've ever seen it.'

My mother leaned from her bed and poured out the tea.

'Do you know anything about her relations?' I asked. 'You've sent a telegram?'

My father said, 'We haven't, Alan. There's not a scrap of anything in her room to tell us who she was.'

My mind, of course, was still concerned with the details of travel. 'There must be something,' I said. 'Vaccination and inoculation certificates. She must have had a passport, too.'

My father said, 'There isn't anything at all, Alan. There's no document of any sort in her room. There's only her clothes and a few novels. Practically all of those are from the house, too.'

'That's all right,' my mother said, and again there was a tremor in her voice. 'I told her she could read any of the books she wanted to, at any time.'

She passed me my tea, and I sat with it in my hand in silence for a minute. I did not want to say what I was thinking, that here was clear evidence of suicide, because my mother wanted to believe it was an accident and maybe it was better that she should. But if the girl before her death had taken pains to destroy evidence of her identity it meant that her death was planned beforehand. It must mean that.

I glanced at my father. 'So we've got nobody to telegraph to, to tell them that she's dead? We don't know who she was, or where she came from?'

'That's right, Alan,' said my father. 'We don't know who she was, or where she came from. She came to us from the Post Office Hotel,' and he went on to tell me what I knew already.

My mother said, 'Annie says that she had worked in Sydney. She thinks she came from England several years ago. But I don't think that's right. She said once that she only landed in Australia a few weeks before she came to us from the hotel.'

'She never told anyone what she'd been doing before she came to Forfar, to the hotel?' I asked.

My mother shook her head. 'She never talked about herself at all.'

'She was probably married,' I suggested.

My parents stared at me in astonishment; the thought was quite a new one to them. I said slowly, 'An unsatisfactory marriage, here in Australia, that she wanted to forget about. That would explain why she didn't talk about her past life. If all her documents were in her married name, it would explain why she destroyed them. She would have wanted to make a completely fresh start.'

My father said, 'Well, that's a new idea entirely.' He paused. 'It certainly seems to fit the facts.'

I pursued my line of thought. 'Proctor is almost certainly her maiden name. We'll have to try and find the husband, or the police will. I suppose it's their job. He'll have to be found and told about her death. They'll have to start looking for a man who married an English girl called Jessie Proctor, probably in Sydney, probably two or three years ago, and who probably left him fifteen or sixteen months ago a little time before she fetched up in Forfar and came to you. It'll mean a bit of work for them, but it won't take them very long.'

My father sighed with relief. 'I think you've got it, Alan,' he said. 'It's far the most likely idea so far. And it accounts for everything.' He turned to me. 'I don't mind telling you,

I've been worried over this. The inquest is tomorrow, and it's going to make a lot of trouble if we don't know who she is.'

'Don't worry about it, Dad,' I said. It seemed to me that he was in no state to get worked up about anything, and I had come home to unload him. 'I'll go to the inquest.'

'I'll have to come with you,' he said. 'It would certainly be a help if you came too, Alan. I suppose living here in the country one gets rather out of touch with the world. It certainly never occurred to me that she might be a married woman.'

My mother said nothing, and it seemed to me that we had talked about this rather unsavoury business long enough. I began to ask them questions about the property. Rabbits, it seemed, were now reduced to manageable proportions thanks to myxomatosis and my father's energy. The result had been a progressive increase in the stock upon the property, partly due to pasture improvement but mostly, I think, due to the reduction of rabbits. Old Jim Plowden who had been a boundary rider when I went away had fallen from his horse and broken his thigh some years ago; as he was over sixty my father had put him in charge of the rabbit pack, a miscellaneous assortment of about thirty mongrel dogs kept in a kennel and run as a disciplined force in the war against the rabbit. This war went on continuously with tractor-drawn rippers to destroy the warrens, with smoke bombs and ferrets, and above all with the rabbit pack to chase and destroy the vermin as they were flushed from their burrows. Seven rabbits will eat as much feed as a sheep, and on Coombargana after the neglect of the war years there must have been a hundred thousand rabbits, or more.

My father had been experimenting with spreading superphosphate from the air on paddocks that were too rough and stony to make spreading it from trucks a possibility, and this again had increased the carrying capacity of the land. Two Tiger Moths had done the work efficiently and well, and he was going to have more paddocks treated in this way in the coming summer. He had built new shearers' quarters soon after I had left which I had never seen, of course, and in the last year he had remodelled the shearing shed and had installed new machinery throughout. He had built four new weatherboard houses for the station hands to replace the last of the older, two-roomed shacks of my grandfather's time, and a couple of years ago he had put up a considerable power station with a diesel engine of no less than sixty horsepower to provide electricity not only for our house but for each of the eleven houses on the property.

My father was only able to give me the bare outline of all these activities during tea, and my mother, of course, wanted to know all about my life in London, so that we had much to talk about. My mother seemed much brighter when she had had her tea, and announced her intention of getting up for dinner, which I thought was a good thing and better for her than lying in bed thinking about the dead parlourmaid upstairs. It was arranged that my father would drive me round the property for a couple of hours in the Land Rover before dinner while my mother got up and dressed and organized the dinner with Annie our old cook and Mrs Plowden, who was usually brought in to help with the washing-up in times of domestic crisis.

We finished tea and put the cups and plates back on the tea trolley, which my father proceeded to wheel out through the big, galleried central hall to the pantry. I stayed for a moment with my mother before going out to carry my suitcases up to my bedroom on the upper floor.

My mother said, 'I think you're wrong about Jessie, Alan.'

'In what way?' I asked. 'Wrong about what?'

'About her being married,' said my mother quietly, 'I'm sure she wasn't.'

I was silent, because it's a difficult subject for a bachelor to dispute with a woman of my mother's age. 'Did she ever say she wasn't?' I asked at last.

My mother shook her head. 'She never said anything at all about her own affairs. But I'm quite sure she wasn't married.'

CHAPTER TWO

As OLD age had crept upon my father and mother they had reduced the scale of their expenditure upon themselves to quite a small proportion of their net income. They never had kept racehorses as many of our neighbours do, and they had outgrown the pleasures of spending money. They got a book each month through the Book Society and they bought a few gramophone records when they were in Melbourne, but with increasing years and infirmity they got more pleasure out of old things than new, out of old books that they had read fifteen or twenty years before and turned back to now with pleasure, out of old gramophone records, out of furniture that they had bought thirty years ago when they took over Coombargana.

Helen's allowance and my own had absorbed a good slice of their net income after taxation, which in recent years had fluctuated between twenty and thirty thousand pounds a year. Much of the rest had been saved and invested prudently to provide for death duties on an estate which might well be assessed at a quarter of a million pounds upon my father's death, but this cash reserve was now adequate for any calls that were likely to be made on it. In other countries and in other circles a prosperity such as ours might be accompanied by wild parties in the city, with a nude girl in a bath of champagne in the middle of the dinner table and a dozen crashed motor-cars next morning. In the Western District things had never been like that; perhaps an agricultural prosperity doesn't go that way. Certainly Australian wool producers, those who survived the hard times of the thirties when wool was down to a shilling a pound, got such an economic fright as would keep them in the straight-and-narrow path for the rest of their lives. I can vouch for it that at Coombargana and all the other stations that I know the money made seems to be spent prudently and well.

My father's great interest was in the property, and all his spare money was now going into improvements. Wherever I looked as we drove round in the Land Rover there was something new, new stockyards, new spray sheep dips, new vehicles, new pumps, new generators, new houses, new fences, new windmills, and new dams. In the hard times before the Second War, when I was a boy at Coombargana, much of this expenditure would have been classed as rank extravagance, but times had changed and my father had had the wit to change with them. Labour costs had trebled since the thirties and the output of the property had doubled, so that any machine that would save an hour of a man's time was now a good machine.

We went in to the long shearing shed, now empty and swept clean, of course, for the shearing was over and the shed would remain unused till next year. He showed me how he had rearranged the stands and the tables and the bins, and the new machinery. He had made a job of it all right; I could visualize the production line, so to speak, when this place was going full blast and sheep were passing through at the rate of three hundred an hour. I was keenly interested in all that he had done, for this was my job from now on, but the dead parlourmaid was still the background of my mind.

We rested for a few minutes in the long, cool aisle of the shed, leaning against a table, looking round. 'Mother doesn't seem to think much of my idea that the girl was married,' I said.

'She doesn't?'

I shook my head.

'I'd never thought of her as a married woman, myself,' my father remarked. 'She might have been, of course.'

'How old was she?'

'Twenty-eight or thirty, I should say. It's difficult to judge.'

'Harry said she never took a holiday.'

'I don't think she did. I think she went into Ballarat once or twice for shopping, but apart from that I don't think she left the place the whole time she was here.'

I wrinkled my brows. 'What did she do on her days off?'

He thought for a minute. 'I think she was interested in the property,' he said. 'She used to go out with Jim Plowden and the rabbit pack. I think she liked the dogs. She liked shooting, too. I never had much to do with her outside; she kept her place, you know. The men say that she was a very fine shot at rabbits, either with a gun or a rifle. They say she never seemed to miss.' He paused. 'I've been wondering if she was a farmer's daughter perhaps, back at home.'

I nodded. 'You don't know what part of England she came from?'

'I don't,' he said. 'Annie thinks she came from London, but I don't think she really knows.'

'That doesn't line up with her being a farmer's daughter.'

'I know.'

We sat silent for a minute. Then I glanced at him, and said, 'The coroner's coming here tomorrow morning, with the police?'

He nodded. 'They've got to give a certificate for burial. There'll have to be an inquest, of course.'

'Bit awkward, if we don't know who she was.'

He bit his lip. 'I know,' he said. I glanced at him, and there was an old man's tremor moving his head, the first time I had seen it. 'It makes us look – well, careless.'

'I wouldn't worry about that, Dad,' I said. 'It's not as if she was a young girl that you were responsible for. She was a grown woman.'

His hand moved to his chin, as if to stop the tremor. 'I know,' he replied. 'But it looks bad all the same. As if we didn't care.'

He turned to me. 'It's a very good thing for your mother that you've come home, Alan. It's going to take her mind off it. Be with her as much as you can till the funeral is over. Tell her about England – anything.'

'She's going to miss her, is she?'

He nodded. 'She's going to miss her a great deal. When a woman's getting on in years and not very well, it's a great comfort to have a girl about the place who's sensible and responsible. She's a great loss to your mother, Alan.'

I nodded slowly. 'Mother was fond of her?'

'I think so. Yes, I think she was,' my father said. 'The girl

27

kept her place, but she used to think ahead and do things for your mother before she thought of asking for them, if you understand what I mean. She was very thoughtful for your mother in that way.'

If she had been thoughtful for my mother it seemed to indicate that she had liked being at Coombargana; indeed, everything that I had heard seemed to point that way. She had never even bothered to take the holidays that were due to her. Then why had she taken her own life? I glanced at my father. 'What do you think about this theory of Mother's, that it was an accident?' I asked. 'I didn't want to say too much in front of Mother. Would you say she was a suicidal type?'

He said, 'I simply don't know, Alan. I don't know what a suicidal type looks like. To me she was just an ordinary, decent girl, not very good looking. I wouldn't have expected her to commit suicide – I'd have said she was too level-headed. But who's to say?'

'Do you think it was an accident, Dad?' I asked. 'I've never heard of anyone taking an overdose of sleeping tablets by mistake. I mean, you've got to eat such a lot, and gulp down such a lot of water. How many does the doctor say she took?'

'More than twenty.'

'Well, surely to God, that couldn't have been a mistake. You can't go on taking tablet after tablet till you've taken twenty, by mistake. If it had been one, or even two, it might be possible. But not twenty.'

'If it was deliberate,' my father said, 'she wouldn't have left two tablets in the bottle, would she? She'd have taken the lot, to make sure.'

There was a pause. 'I can't think it was an accident,' I said at last. 'I'm sorry, Dad, but I should say it was deliberate.'

He stood up, and I was deeply sorry for him, for he looked so old. 'Well, don't tell your mother that,' he said. 'It's better if she thinks it was an accident. I'm hoping that we'll get the coroner to see it that way in the morning. If it *was* deliberate we'll probably never know the reason, and there's no sense in stirring up trouble.'

We left the shed and got back into the Land Rover and

went on with our tour around the property. In the evening light we came to his trout hatchery by the river, a series of little pools with water running through controlled by little sluices from the river, overhung by weeping willow trees. When I had written to tell them that I would be coming home next spring my father had had this disused hatchery put in order and commenced to breed up about a thousand little fish with which to re-stock the river against my return; he intended to keep them a few months longer and then discharge them into the main stream. Next year the fishing should be very good indeed.

We paused by the pools, in the rippling sound of running water, and he began to ask me questions about my time in England. I had taken my degree in Law at Oxford, but I hadn't enjoyed it much. 'It was a bit like Rip van Winkle, Dad,' I said. 'I was so much older than the others, and things had changed so. It would have been different if I'd gone back straight after the war, in 1945 or '46, when there were other Service people up. There was no one there like me in 1948, or hardly anybody, and nobody at all when I went down in 1950. They were all boys straight from school on Government grants. The people I got along with best were the young dons.' I paused. 'I want to get one or two of them out here on a visit, but it's difficult because they're all so hard up.'

He nodded. 'That's always a difficulty. But you never can get people to come out from England on a visit. It's not only the money.'

I went on to tell him about my time in chambers, in Lincoln's Inn. 'I don't know that I haven't wasted my time,' I said quietly at last. 'I don't know that being called to the Bar is going to help me much in running Coombargana.'

He smiled. 'Do you think you'll want to go back and live in England?' he asked.

'I don't think so,' I said. 'I think I've got that out of my system. I'd like to go back again some day for fun, say in about ten years' time, and see how it's all getting on. But I won't want to live there again. I don't think so.'

'Not like Helen?'

'No.'

29

'What's Laurence really like?' my father asked. He had never met him, for with their increasing age my mother and father had not felt equal to leaving Coombargana to travel to England. It was one of my secret irritations with my sister that she had not thought fit to bring her husband out to Australia on a visit to let Dad and Mum meet him, though perhaps it was better so.

'He's all right,' I said. 'I've not got a lot in common with him, Dad, and I don't think you would have.' My father had served all through the First War in Gallipoli and France, and had spent three years of the Second War organizing truck transport in the heat and sweat of the Northern Territory when he was over sixty years of age, while Laurence had had trouble with his health and had served his war with the BBC. 'There's nothing wrong with him. He's getting very well known as a dramatic critic – people think a lot of him.' I glanced at my father. 'I'm not sure that he's not a bit of a passenger in this world, but he probably thinks that of us.'

'He's making her a good husband, is he? Not a lot of other women, or not more than a reasonable number?' My father grinned.

I laughed with him. 'I don't think there's any trouble of that sort.' There wasn't likely to be, either, because Helen has quite a lot of character and she kept control of her own money. Laurence wasn't the type to sacrifice all for love.

'What about you, Alan?' my father asked. 'Did you ever think of getting married?'

I shook my head.

'You ought to think about it,' he said. 'You're getting on, you know. Thirty-nine, isn't it?'

I nodded. 'It's never happened to come my way.'

'You ought to think about it,' he repeated. 'It's going to be mighty lonely if you try and carry on this place alone after our time.'

'It's not so easy when you're a cripple,' I said. 'It needs special qualities in a girl to settle down married to a chap that's got no feet.'

'Well, think it over,' he said irresolutely. And then he said, 'You never thought of flying again, I suppose?'

'As a matter of fact, I did,' I told him. 'Not in Typhoons,

of course. I did quite a lot of flying at the London Aeroplane Club, at Panshanger, on Tiger Moths and Austers. I didn't tell you in the letters because I was afraid it might worry Mother.'

'Are you going on with it here?'

'I doubt it,' I said. 'I just wanted to show myself that I wasn't afraid of it and that I could do it still, even with dummy feet. I did about a hundred hours in all. But I don't want to carry on with it, unless there was some object. Which there isn't now.'

He smiled. 'What was it like when you got into the machine for the first time?' he asked with interest. 'Were you scared?'

'A bit,' I said. 'About as much as on my first solo. But of course, one knew it was dead safe in a pipsqueak thing like that.'

We left the pools of the trout hatchery and walked slowly back to the Land Rover. 'Your mother's been concocting an exceptional dinner for you all day,' my father said. 'Do you want to change?'

'She'd like it, wouldn't she?' I asked. 'What do you usually do?'

'I generally put on a dinner jacket in the winter, when it's dark,' my father said. 'In summer when one may want to go out afterwards I usually change into a suit.'

'I've got a dinner jacket in my bag,' I said. 'The shirt's probably a bit tatty after travelling round the world. Let's change. Mother 'd like it.'

At the house we found my mother in the drawing-room seated before the log fire, wearing a long black evening dress with a shawl round her shoulders. We stood warming ourselves, for the evening was turning chilly, and drinking a pink gin while we chatted about London and about Helen; then I went up to my room to change. In my bedroom somebody had lit a fire and left a huge basket of gum-tree logs, scenting the air with the fragrance of the burning eucalypt. Somebody, perhaps old Annie, had unpacked one suitcase and had laid out my evening clothes upon the bed.

It struck me as I unpacked my other suitcase in my old, familiar room, savouring all my old belongings, that I would be the only person sleeping on the upper floor of the main house that night. My father and mother, who had had the bedroom, dressing-room, and bathroom next to mine, now slept on the ground floor and their bedroom was now the billiard room. On the other side of the corridor to their room was the corner room that had been Helen's and was now a spare room, and next to that and separated by the second bathroom was the guest bedroom, empty tonight, of course. Beside my room there was another bathroom, and opening from that was Bill's room, very seldom used now. Bill had been killed in Normandy in the spring of 1944; by the time I got back to Coombargana my father and mother had taken all Bill's possessions and pictures out and had refurnished and redecorated the room as a second guest room, thinking perhaps that too intimate a reminder of Bill and the war in Europe would have been bad for me. Nothing of Bill remained there now, but they had forgotten the bathroom. Since 1946 I had never sat in that bath without glancing at the door into Bill's room with the thought that it would open and he would come striding in, seventeen or eighteen years old, with little or no clothes on.

That happened to me again that evening as I bathed before dressing for dinner. Bill was still a very real person in my life, though ten years had gone by since I had met him last, at Lymington in Hampshire, and sixteen years since we had shared that bathroom. One does not easily forget one's only brother.

As I sat in the bath thinking of these things and enjoying the benison of hot water after days spent in the aeroplane and in the Sydney hotel, I felt a little lonely up there on the first floor by myself. I was not quite alone, of course. Beyond the stairs and the gallery that overlooked the big central hall of the house lay the servants' wing over the kitchen quarters, their bedrooms separated from those of the main house by a swing door. There were four servants' bedrooms there, relic of the days of more plentiful domestic service, and in one of these Annie, our old cook, would be sleeping that night. In another, the house parlourmaid would be sleeping now.

I had not drawn the curtains, and there was still a little

light outside as I dressed before the fire. I stood for a few minutes looking out in the last of the light before turning to the mirror to tie my tie. Below me the wide lawns ran down to the river, with the formal flower gardens upon the right and the screen of oaks, gums, wattles, and pines upon the left that hid the station buildings. Beyond the river our pastures stretched over and beyond the rise a couple of miles away, and far on the horizon the long ridge of the Grampians stood black against the last of the sunset light. There was contentment here, with no war and no threat of war, no aircraft, no tanks, and no soldiers. This was a place to which a man might come when he had had the great world and its alarms, to do a good job in peace. Some day a war might come again and I would have to leave my peace and go and do my stuff as my father had before me, but for the moment I was glad to be out of it all and back at Coombargana as a grazier.

I finished dressing and went down to the drawing-room. My father and mother were both there waiting for me and wanting to know if everything in my room had been all right. 'Fine,' I said. 'I might have walked out yesterday instead of five years ago,' and I laughed. Actually, in five years one changes and there were things in that room that I would alter as soon as I could. There were things there that I now had no need of, like the stick from my crashed Typhoon, or the compass from the first Me 109 I got, over Wittering. These things had solaced me in 1946, but that was eight years ago; I did not need them now, and they were better out of the way.

I had another pink gin with my father, and then dinner was announced. Mrs Plowden put her head in at the door. She was untidy as ever with a wisp of grey hair falling down over her face; her sleeves were rolled to the elbow and she wore a coarse apron of hessian. She said brightly, 'It's all in, on the table, Mrs Duncan.' My mother thanked her, and she withdrew.

I saw my mother glance at my father, and caught his glance in return. Things must have been different in the days of the parlourmaid, and they had to adjust themselves to new ways and new manners.

33

We went into the dining-room. To me the bare, polished table with the lace mats and the silver was well laid, but to my mother everything was in the wrong place and she hobbled about, rearranging salt cellars and wine glasses, moving dishes from the table to the sideboard, till the arrangement was as she was used to having it. 'I'm afraid everything's a bit higgledy-piggledy tonight, Alan,' she said. 'We'll get things organized in a few days.'

I said, 'It looks all right to me, Mum.'

She said quietly, 'I suppose the fact of the matter is that we've been spoiled for the last year or so. I'd almost forgotten what it was to have to train somebody to do things nicely.'

'She was good, was she?'

My mother said, 'She was an educated girl, so one only had to show her how to do a thing once. I think she must have come from a good home, where they lived nicely.'

My father said, 'She used to work the radiogram.'

'The radiogram?'

My mother said, 'Whenever your father and I had a little celebration here, on my birthday, or when we heard about the wool sale, we used to have a bottle of champagne with dinner, and music. Your father would put on a long-playing record in the drawing-room, *Oklahoma* or *South Pacific* or something nice like that, and we'd leave the doors open so that we had music during dinner. And then we found that Jessie knew how to change the record, and she knew most of the records that we liked, so after that we didn't have to bother.'

'She got to know our ways,' my father said. He turned to my mother. 'Remember when we heard Alan was coming home? She finished handing the entrée and asked if she should put on a record.'

My mother nodded. 'It will be a very long time before we find another girl like Jessie.'

We seemed to have drifted back on to the difficult subject. I cast about hurriedly for something fresh to tell my mother that would take her mind off the dead parlourmaid, but I seemed to have told her most of the things already. The thought of Bill came into my mind and the new details I had learned about his death, but I rejected this hurriedly as a subject that had better wait for another time. My journey home was something that I had not told her of, that might amuse and interest her and take her mind off the more sombre topic. 'I stayed four or five days in New York,' I said. 'It's a stimulating place, but I don't know that I'd like to work there.'

My father played up, sensing the move. 'What's it really like?' he asked. 'Is it like you'd think it was from the movies?'

'I suppose it is, physically,' I said. 'You know more or less what it's going to look like before you get there. But as regards the people, I've never yet met an American that was much like the people that you see upon the movies, and I didn't this time. I suppose there *are* Americans like that.'

My mother said, 'They probably exaggerate their own types, Alan, when they put them on the stage or on the screen. We do that, too. All countries do it. You don't often meet people who behave like people on the stage.'

My father carried on the steering of the conversation. 'I suppose they have to make them larger than life on the screen, in all their characteristics. Did you go to Los Angeles?'

'No,' I said. 'I spent a few days with a chap in San Francisco.' I carried on talking about the United States, and the topic lasted us all through dinner. My parents eat little at their age, but what little they do eat they like to be good, and I think Annie our old cook had made a special effort, though I can only remember the fresh asparagus from the garden and the jugged hare. I pleased my mother by appreciating the dinner, and promised her that I would speak to Annie about it. They had put a good deal of thought into getting together the dishes that I would like best. My father opened a particularly good bottle of Burgundy from somewhere on the Hunter River, and a glass of vintage port from South Australia served with the dessert was really very like the real thing.

We went through to the drawing-room after dinner. My parents had always gone early to bed; one does so in the country where it is usual to be up and about the property at seven in the morning to keep the men from getting slack. Since his operation my father had been ordered to bed at nine o'clock by his doctor, and with the increasing infirmity of my mother they had both got into the habit of retiring about that time, though I think they usually read in bed for an hour or so before sleep. When I had lived at home before, after the war, I had frequently played a game of chess with my mother after dinner; I had not played since then and I had all but forgotten the moves, but now to take her mind off our troubles I suggested we might have a game to celebrate my return. She was pleased at the idea though she had played very little in my absence, so I brought up the inlaid chess table that they had bought in Paris before the war and that had once stood in some château or other in Touraine, and now stood in somewhat similar surroundings in the Western District, and found the box that contained the eighteenth-century carved ivory chessmen, and set them up by my mother's chair before the fire. We played two games and then it was half past nine and time for them to be in bed.

I put the things away and helped my mother up out of her chair. 'It seems terribly early to be going to bed on your first evening,' she said. 'I feel rather badly about it, Alan, but it's what Dr Stanley says we've got to do, especially because your father gets up so early.'

My father said, 'Help yourself to a whisky, Alan. And there's the paper here.'

I smiled. 'Don't worry about me. I'll probably take to going off early myself in a few days, and getting up early. It's the best way in the country.'

I walked with my mother as she hobbled slowly to the door and opened it for her. In the hall as we walked together to her room she said, 'It *is* good to have you home again, Alan. You don't know how we've been looking forward to you coming.' She paused, and then she said, 'It's really getting too much for your father now. And then this trouble . . .'

'Don't worry about that, Mum,' I said. 'It'll all be over in a few days now.'

'Yes, I suppose so,' she said quietly. She hobbled on a step or two, and then she said, 'She must have been so terribly unhappy, to take her own life, and I had no idea of it. If she was unhappy, I should have known about it, and I didn't. I feel that I must be very much to blame, as if I've failed in some way, or made her unhappy without any idea that I was doing it. And I just can't imagine what it was I did . . .'

'Don't worry about it, Mother,' I repeated. 'It's nothing to do with you. We all think it was an accident.'

'Perhaps it was. But I wish I could really think so.'

We reached her door. 'Goodnight, Mother,' and I kissed her.

She held me for a moment. 'Goodnight, son. I am so very, very glad you're home.'

When my father and mother had gone to bed I went back to the drawing-room and stood for a moment before the fire, deep in thought. This matter of the parlourmaid was evidently worrying my mother very much indeed, and the more I thought about it the more inexplicable it seemed. I could not accept the idea that my mother had made the girl unhappy. Invalids, of course, are frequently bad-tempered and querulous. I had been away for five years and I felt able to regard my mother objectively; she had never seemed to me to be bad-tempered and she did not seem so now. Whatever the reasons had been that had made the girl take her own life, I was quite sure it was not that. Yet it had been deliberate, or she would not have destroyed her documents and letters. I wondered what she had done with them.

The thought of murder crossed my mind, of course, and I put it out of my head. We read too many detective stories, which set one off upon the most unlikely trains of thought. Nothing suggested any conceivable motive for murder in this instance, nor any possibility of it in Coombargana House.

Annie might know something that she had not told my parents, and it was time that I saw Annie anyway. Annie had been at Coombargana before I was born. She came from some village near Peterhead in Scotland, and as a young girl she had worked in the fisheries, gutting and packing herrings on the quays. I think my grandfather knew her father, old

37

McConchie, as a boy, or perhaps he met him when he went home in 1895. In any case, Annie came out with her brother James to work for my grandfather in 1908 or 1910, when she was probably about twenty years of age. James was still working as a stockman with us when I was a child and Annie was the kitchen maid, but James left us in 1920 and took up a property near Mortlake, helped by a bank guarantee from my grandfather. He and Annie, being Scots, lived frugally and saved every penny that came into their hands, with the result that in the Depression of the thirties, when everyone was going broke and all the properties were coming under the hammer at a knockdown price, the McConchies were prudently buying land. Jim McConchie has a property of two thousand acres over by Mortlake now where he runs Merinoes and a stud of Angus cattle; he makes a trip back home every two or three years to buy stud beasts and last year he paid three thousand five hundred pounds for an Angus bull at the Royal Agricultural Show. Annie still works for us in Coombargana House; she never married and would scorn to live on James, though she is very proud of his success.

I wondered if Annie was still up. I left the drawing-room and went through the dining-room; the light was still on in the kitchen. I opened the swing door and there she was, standing by the table.

'Evening, Annie,' I said. 'How are you today?' She was not much changed, a little smaller perhaps, and the grey hair a little thinner.

'I'm fine,' she said. 'How have you been keeping? It's good to see you home again, Mr Alan.'

'I'm very well,' I said. 'Very glad to be home.'

'Aye,' she said. 'There's no doubt about it, your own place is the best. How do you find your father and mother, Mr Alan?'

'Not too good,' I said. 'It's time I came home. I didn't realize that they were getting so old.'

'Ah well,' she said, 'we none of us get any younger.'

'You haven't changed a lot,' I said.

'I keep pretty fair,' she said. 'I get the rheumatism now and then, but I keep pretty fair.'

'I think this trouble today may have upset my mother,' I remarked.

'Aye,' she said. 'It's a great shock to the lady when a thing like that happens in the house.'

I leaned back against the bright steel sink. 'I don't understand why she did it,' I remarked. 'Was she unhappy, do you think?'

'I would not say so,' she replied. 'Very quiet she was, these last two or three days. But then, she was always quiet.'

I cast about for some clue. 'Was she sulky?'

She shook her head. 'She was not. She was very even-tempered, very easy to get on with, but she never talked about herself. We got on fine, because maybe I'm a bit that way. I never sought to pry into her business, nor she into mine.'

'Do you know if she was in the habit of taking things to make her sleep?' I asked. 'Was she a girl who took a lot of medicines?'

She shook her head. 'There's a bottle of Eno's Fruit Salts on her washstand, and a tube of Veganin. Then there was the bottle by her bedside, that the doctor took away.'

'You don't know what those sleeping tablets were?'

'I do not, Mr Alan.'

'And there were no letters or papers in her room?'

'Not a scrap. There was nothing written at all, saving one or two books from the house.'

I glanced at her. 'That's very extraordinary, because she must have had some papers. She must have had a passport to come from England. What's happened to that?'

She shrugged her shoulders. 'Maybe she got rid of everything when she decided to make an end to herself.'

'You think she did decide to do it, Annie? You don't think it was an accident?'

'It's not for me to say, Mr Alan. But if it was an accident there would be some papers or letters of some kind, I would think.'

I thought for a minute. 'Where could she have burnt things?'

'In the coke boiler, out behind,' she said. She meant the central-heating boiler. 'She could have burned them there.'

'Without anybody knowing?'

'Oh, aye. It gets made up in the morning, and at midday, and at night, but in between times nobody goes there.'

I glanced at the slow-burning cooking stove. 'Not here?'

She shook her head. 'I tend this myself, and I would soon have known if there was any paper. I would not think that she burned anything here.'

I stood in silence for a time, thinking over this conundrum. Then I looked at her. 'Is there really nothing, nothing at all amongst her things, to tell us who she was? No ornaments, or lockets . . . anything?'

She shook her head. 'Would you like to have a look inside her room, Mr Alan?'

I hesitated, reluctant. It seemed an invasion of the dead girl's privacy to go into her room to try to find out things she evidently preferred to keep from us. Yet other people had already done so; my father had certainly been there, and perhaps my mother. The police had been there, turning over with unaccustomed hands the underclothing and the dresses. It was doubtful if I could add anything to what had already been done and I didn't want to go, yet to refuse had something of an element of cowardice attached to it.

'She's up there, is she?' I asked.

'Aye, she's lying there,' she said. 'Covered over with the sheet.' She glanced at me, remembering perhaps the little boy that had been running about Coombargana House when she was a young woman. 'There's nothing to be feared of, Mr Alan.'

'I know,' I said. 'It's a bad thing to intrude unless you've got some very good reason. But I think perhaps I ought to have a look.'

'I'll come up with you,' she said.

She motioned me to go before her, but I told her to lead the way and we went out to the back lobby and up the bare, scrubbed back stairs to the servants' bedrooms. There was a short corridor ending in the swing door to the main house near my own bedroom, and there were two rooms on each side of this short corridor. I was not very familiar with this part of the house, though I had been in it as a child.

Annie led the way to the second door on the left. I

40

checked her before she opened the door. 'This is her room?'

She nodded.

'Which room do you sleep in?' I asked.

'In there, Mr Alan.' She indicated the next room on the same side. 'The mistress, she said to use these rooms because they have the better light and view. The others are a wee bit dark.' I nodded; the two rooms they occupied looked out in the same direction as my own, and shared the same view over the property towards the Grampians. In the house Bill's room and the bathroom lay between my own room and that of the dead girl.

I asked, 'Did you hear anything unusual last night, Annie?'

She shook her head. 'Nothing at all.'

She paused for a moment, and then opened the door and switched the light on, and we went into the bedroom. It was a bare room, with white paint on the woodwork and cream water paint upon the walls. It was furnished adequately but simply with a cheap bedroom suite of Australian hardwood, consisting of a bed, a chest-of-drawers with a mirror on it, and a wardrobe. In addition there was a table and a chair. On the bed a sheet was stretched over the dead girl.

On the table was a small, folding, travelling alarm clock of an American make, and a bottle of fountain-pen ink. With letters and documents in the forefront of my mind I unscrewed the top of this bottle; the top came off readily, the bottle was half full. I turned to Annie. 'Had she got a pen?' Instinctively I spoke in a low tone, as if in a church.

'Aye,' she said. 'I saw a pen in her bag.' She opened the left-hand small drawer of the chest-of-drawers and took out rather a worn, fairly large bag of dark-blue leather. She opened it, and picked out the pen. It was a Parker 51, dark blue in colour, in good condition; the ink was still fresh in the nib. It had been used for writing very recently.

I put it back in the bag and examined the remainder of the contents. There was a compact, a purse with a little money in it but no papers, and the usual things that a woman carries round with her, a comb, a lipstick, three keys on a ring, a clean handkerchief that had evidently been there for some time. There was nothing to be learned from these. I glanced at the contents of the drawer, mostly handkerchiefs and stockings; they conveyed nothing to me. I came back to the purse and opened it again. 'What did she do with her money?' I asked in the same low tone. 'This isn't all she had?'

'She had a savings-bank account in the post office, Mr Alan. She'd go to Forfar once in a while and pay her money in.'

'Where's the book for that?' I asked. 'Is that here?'

She shook her head. 'I would say no. I have not seen it, Mr Alan, and I was here when the police made the search.'

'Do you know how much money she had in the bank?'

She shook her head. 'I do not.'

There were three books on the chest-of-drawers, but they told me nothing except that her tastes were catholic; *The Last Days of Hitler* was sandwiched between *Anne of Green Gables* and *Hocus Pocus*. I looked for a Bible or a prayer book, and found neither. Annie asked, 'Do you want to see the clothes, Mr Alan?' and put her hand on the first drawer.

I shrank instinctively from the intrusion. 'There's nothing there, is there? You've turned them over?'

'Aye,' she said. 'The police, they went through everything very carefully.'

'Leave them be,' I said. I turned from the chest-of-drawers and looked around the room. Two suitcases lay one on top of the other in a corner. I moved over and examined them. Both were old and one was in an unfamiliar style, probably foreign, but both were empty and without labels. 'Is this all the luggage she had?' I asked.

Annie hesitated. 'I *think* it is,' she said. 'I've been wondering, perhaps there should have been another. I mind she had to make several journeys when she came here first, carrying her luggage from the outside door up to this room. She wouldn't want to carry more than one of these up the stairs, one at a time. Maybe she went up and down twice only. It's a while ago since she came, and I was cooking at the time and didn't notice her particularly.'

'You didn't come in here much?'

She shook her head. 'I never went into her room, Mr Alan, nor she into mine. The mistress, she comes round once in a while and looks in at the rooms, to see that everything is tidy and kept nice.'

I stood looking round the room; there was little more to examine. The room was fitted with a wash basin with running water, and here the soap and the toothpaste were of normal brands. The Eno's and the Veganin were on a shelf nearby, but there were no medicines in evidence, and practically no cosmetics or lotions, which seemed to me unusual for a woman's room.

There was nothing to stay for, nothing to be learned. I moved towards the door. Annie paused by the bed, and said in a low tone, 'Would you want to look at her?' Her hand moved towards the sheet.

I shook my head; there was nothing to be gained by that, and we had done enough intruding. 'Leave her be. There wasn't any locket, or anything under the pillow?'

She shook her head. 'Nothing of that, Mr Alan. We looked carefully, when the police were here.'

I went out into the corridor and she followed me. 'Well, thanks, Annie,' I said. 'It'll be a good thing when all this is over and we can get back to having things normal.'

She nodded. 'Aye. It's been upsetting for everybody. Your parents must be very glad to see you home again.'

I nodded. 'I'm glad I came in time to help them out with this.' I paused. 'Well, goodnight, Annie. Thank you for showing me.'

'Oh, that's nothing,' she said. 'Goodnight, Mr Alan.'

I went through the swing door to the main house and my own bedroom. The fire was low; I threw on two or three logs and went downstairs at my slow pace, to get a whisky and to look around the house a little before going up to bed.

I poured myself a drink and went and stood in front of the dying embers of the drawing-room fire, in the silence of the house. I was still glad to be home again, glad to be taking up the work that was my proper job, that I had spurned five years ago, but my pleasure was swamped and tempered by this matter of the dead parlourmaid, so that I could think of nothing else. In this comfortable, homely atmosphere there had been a deep and secret trouble that nobody had known anything about, so deep that it had led a girl who seemed to have been normal and balanced in her mind to take her own life. It was incongruous at Coombargana. In a great city such things happen now and then, where people are too strained and hurried to pay much attention to the griefs of others, but in a small rural community like ours, led by wise and tolerant people such as my father and mother, staffed by good types culled and weeded out over the years, such secret, catastrophic griefs do not occur. Troubles at Coombargana had always been small troubles in my lifetime. Nothing like this had ever happened there before, and it was disturbing that it should have happened now. Was something very wrong in all these easy, comfortable surroundings, something that nobody suspected, something that we none of us knew anything about? I felt that I would very much like to know the answer to that one. In fact, it was my duty to find out.

I could not put my mind to the affairs of the property; I could think of nothing but this trouble. What curious impulse had it been that had led this girl to burn every scrap of evidence of her identity, to burn even her bank book? Perhaps there was no money in her savings bank, of course; perhaps she had withdrawn all that she had and used it in some way. That would have to be checked by the police. By all accounts she had lived very quietly, spending practically no money. I knew approximately what wage she would have been getting; in fifteen months she might have saved two or three hundred pounds. What had happened to that? Perhaps the savings bank had made a transfer of her balance which would provide us with a clue. Was it a possibility that some solicitor, perhaps in Ballarat, might have a will? It was conceivable, though hardly likely, that she had made a will.

How carefully planned, how deliberate it had all been; how certain she had been in all the movements leading to her death! Practically nothing that was personal to her was left behind. The passport – that could go into the fire; she would not need that again. Letters and papers – they could go, for she would be reading nothing more after tomorrow.

44

Photographs and souvenirs – she would not need them now for she would have emotions no more to be stirred; into the furnace with them. The bank book – she would have no need of money for the journey she was setting out on; let it burn. She had cleaned out her life as one might clean out a house or a bed-sitting-room before leaving it, and having done so she had lain down to die. In any normal person some enormous emotional upset would have accompanied the sum of all these sacrifices, and yet apparently there had been nothing of the sort. By all accounts, if she had planned her death she had gone to it cheerfully, with a quiet and an easy mind. She had appeared unmoved to my mother and to Annie, though both had remarked that she seemed rather quieter than usual.

The bizarre thought crossed my mind that if the sleeping tablets hadn't worked she'd have been in a bit of a spot, having destroyed her passport and her bank book and everything else. If by some chance she had been discovered before the drugs that she had taken had proved fatal, if she had been rushed into a hospital and her life had been saved, she would have plumped straight from the sublime to the ridiculous and she might have had a lot of bureaucratic difficulties in getting hold of her money and in getting another passport. I smiled cynically and checked the smile, for after all the girl had been in deep and secret trouble and it was no laughing matter. But how certain she had been of death!

How could she have been certain of her death? There are ways of committing suicide that really are certain, but taking sleeping tablets isn't one of them. When you take sleeping tablets you go to sleep, and death, if it occurs, occurs several hours later. Even then, only a doctor experienced in the particular drug and in its effect upon a wide variety of patients could say with certainty that the dose she took would really prove lethal at all, or would prove lethal before she was found in the morning. Nothing I had heard indicated that this girl had any close or intimate knowledge of medical practice; she might conceivably have been a nurse at one time, but if so she had never betrayed the fact to my mother, who was an invalid.

Everything that I had heard indicated that this girl was an educated, intelligent, and rational person. How could she possibly have been so sure of death as to get rid of everything by burning in the furnace? Surely it must have crossed her mind that suicide in the way that she proposed, though easy and pleasant, was by no means certain. She must have had some special knowledge of the drug, or she would not have destroyed her things.

The whisky may have been responsible though I had not had very much, because the sentence came into my mind inverted. She would not have destroyed her things unless she had some special knowledge of the drug. She would have hidden them.

She would have hidden them, so that she could regain them if, in fact, she survived the sleeping tablets. I had assumed after talking to Annie that she had burned everything in the central-heating furnace, but there was not a scrap of evidence that she had done anything of the sort. With Annie in my mind, the question of the suitcase came forward again. Annie had been vaguely puzzled that there were only two suitcases in her room. Perhaps, in fact, there had been a third. Perhaps she had packed into that third suitcase all that she valued of her personal possessions and deposited it somewhere where she could get it if she did survive – in the baggage room of a railway station, for example.

That wouldn't work, because at Coombargana it would be impossible for her to get a suitcase off the place in privacy. No bus or other public transport comes to Coombargana or within five miles of us. She would have had to take it in to town in one of our cars or trucks. She could not possibly have taken a suitcase out of the house without someone noticing and commenting upon it, and no one had suggested anything of the sort. If she had hidden her belongings in a suitcase it would probably still be in Coombargana House; she would have had difficulty even in getting it down the stairs and out into the grounds without Annie noticing. It was at least a possibility that all the evidence that we were looking for was in the house with us.

I poured myself another drink, a small one, and sat down in my father's chair beside the dying fire. I never believe in dashing at things, and this needed thinking about. Suppose the girl had wanted to hide a suitcase in the house, where would she put it? It had to be where nobody would think of looking, somewhere accessible to her, where nobody would see her as she went to hide it.

That seemed to mean the whole of the top floor. When Annie was in the kitchen or away the whole top floor of the house was hers to do what she liked with, for my parents seldom went up there now. Her case could be in any of the cupboards or closets, in any of the bedrooms. Downstairs would be far more difficult with Annie and my parents about. It would be difficult for her to take it out to one of the outbuildings, for the gardeners were frequently around or else the station hands; she could not count on being unobserved. But upstairs, on the bedroom floor of Coombargana House, she could definitely count on being unobserved at almost any time of day.

If one were to take a look through the top floor of the house, where would one start? Where would she be most likely to hide a suitcase if she wanted to do so? There were the two empty servants' bedrooms opposite her room and Annie's; those, I knew, were used as lumber rooms or box-rooms now. A suitcase in amongst a pile of our own ancient, disused cases would lie there for years covered in dust, till in the future someone clearing out the room to send the contents to some jumble sale might find this one and puzzle over what was in it, when the very name of Jessie Proctor had been long forgotten.

The more I thought of it, the more convinced I became that her belongings might be just across the corridor from her room. It was the rational and reasonable place for them to be.

I left the drawing-room and made my way upstairs through the silent house. I looked in at my own room and put another log upon the fire, hesitated, and fetched a small electric torch from the dressing-table; I never travel without one of those. Then I went into the corridor and passed through the swing door into the servants' quarters, paused for a moment opposite the dead girl's room to make quite sure that I was right, and opened the door on the opposite

47

side of the corridor. My torch showed me the light switch, and I turned it on.

It was a bedroom, a room with two beds, furnished sparsely as a servant's room. This must be where they slept the married couple, when they had one. Except for the furniture it was completely empty; there were mattresses but no bed-clothes on the beds. I opened the wardrobe door and all the drawers in turn and looked round for a cupboard, which wasn't there. There was nothing in that room, at any rate.

There was another bedroom, the one opposite Annie's room. I went along the corridor and opened the door of that one. This was the room I remembered, the one used as a boxroom. There were beds dismantled and stacked by the wall, trunks, suitcases, garden furniture, deck and steamer chairs, beach umbrellas, curtain poles of an antique design, an old commode, spears, boomerangs, and woomeras, and all the junk that a country house accumulates throughout the years. I stood in the doorway looking at all this stuff, wondering where to begin my search.

There was movement in the room behind me, Annie's room, and a light switched on and showed under the door. I stood cursing and embarrassed in the door of the boxroom, till Annie came out of her room, dressed in a faded blue dressing-gown, with wisps of thin grey hair hanging to her shoulders. 'It's all right, Annie,' I said a little testily. 'I was just taking a look in here.'

She said, 'Oh – I'm sorry, Mr Alan. I heard a noise and wondered what it was.' She made a movement to withdraw into her room, and then she paused, and said, 'Were you looking for anything in particular?'

I hesitated. 'It just crossed my mind that the girl might have had another suitcase, and that it might be in here.'

'I do not think so, Mr Alan,' she replied. 'I looked in there this afternoon.'

I stared at her; we had evidently been thinking along the same lines. 'You did?'

'Aye,' she said. 'After the police went away it came into my mind she could have packed some of her things away and put them in this room. I had a good turn-out in here this afternoon.'

'You didn't find anything?'

She shook her head.

I glanced around the piles of junk. 'Not amongst those suitcases?'

She shook her head. 'I opened every one.'

'Nothing in that cupboard?'

'Only the candlesticks and lamps we used before the electricity.'

'Did you look in those two trunks?'

She nodded. 'There's only curtains in that one, and the other's full of the Colonel's uniforms and tropical clothes. I took a good look through everything, Mr Alan.'

There was nothing, then, for me to do in there. I turned and closed the door behind me. 'Very thoughtful of you, Annie,' I said. 'It was just an idea I had.'

'Aye,' she said. 'I was thinking the same thing, that she might have left some of her stuff in there. I think she must have burnt it all, Mr Alan.'

'Maybe she did,' I said. I turned up the corridor. 'Well, goodnight, Annie. Sorry I disturbed you.'

'Goodnight, Mr Alan.'

I went back through the swing door to my room, disappointed, for I had expected to find something in the boxroom. It seemed to me to be by far the best hiding place for a suitcase on the top floor of Coombargana. I sat down in the long easy chair before the fire in my bedroom and lit a cigarette, and loosened one of the straps below my left knee which had been chafing me a little. I sat there smoking and wondering about places where a suitcase could be hidden, and then it seemed to me that possibly the boxroom wasn't such a good place, after all. It was too obvious. Both Annie and I had thought of looking there after a very few hours. Perhaps she had been cleverer than that.

It was conceivable that she had simply put her suitcase in one of the empty bedrooms, or even in my own room, working on the principle that a thing that is in practically full view is frequently overlooked. It did not seem a very likely one, but I got up and took my torch and made a tour of the top floor of the house, going into all the rooms and opening all the drawers and cupboards. It did not take me very long and it yielded nothing.

There was only one other place, and that was in the roof. The possums used to get in to the roof of Coombargana House to nest when I was a boy, though the measures that my father had taken seemed to have defeated them and I don't think we had had them in the house for a number of years. I had been up into the roof once or twice on possum hunts twenty-five years ago. It was reached by a trap in the ceiling of the corridor outside Helen's rooms, ten or eleven feet above the floor, inaccessible without a ladder.

Where had I seen a ladder? I had seen one somewhere, very recently, a ladder of light alloy, painted red. It was a fire ladder. I remembered it. It hung on hooks along the wall of the servants' corridor above three fire extinguishers. It was to put out of the window of the corridor to reach down to the flat roof of the scullery in case fire isolated people on the top floor of the building.

It was worth having a look up in the roof, and I could probably manage to get up and down the ladder if I was careful and took my time. I opened the swing door wide and went into the servants' quarters, hoping that Annie wouldn't come out again, and took the ladder down from the wall, and carried it into the main house, shutting the swing door behind me. I set it up in the corridor and poked the trapdoor upwards with the top end of it; it stood at a convenient angle, firm and adequate.

It would be very dirty in the roof and I was in my evening clothes. Moreover, for a man with my disability to get up into a roof would be something of a gymnastic feat entailing much use of the arms; I had developed a good deal of muscular strength in my arms and chest in compensation over the years. I went back into my room and put on an old pair of trousers and a pullover, and then, with the torch in my pocket, I went up into the roof.

Getting up into the roof wasn't too difficult, but when I was up there there were only a few planks laid loosely on the rafters above the plaster ceiling, with nothing to hold on to if I stood up. I looked around and there was nothing unusual to be seen: various tanks and water pipes, and brick chimneys, and electrical conduits. I hesitated to stand up and walk upon the planks, and crawled on hands and knees away from the trapdoor and the ladder, till in the end I found what I was looking for.

It stood upon the rafters behind one of the tanks and in an angle formed by the brickwork of a chimney, a little shadowed place where it might have rested for fifty years and never come to light. It was a small suitcase, fairly new and free from dust or dirt. It had the initials J.P. embossed on the lid, and it was locked.

There was a bit of rope up there lying on the rafters, perhaps some relic of our possum hunts, and with this I lowered the case down through the trapdoor into the corridor. I replaced the trap and eased myself carefully down the ladder to the floor, and took the case into my room. I was very dirty, and I washed my hands before doing anything else. Then I replaced the ladder on the wall of the servants' corridor, and went back to my room and put the suitcase on a table by the fire.

I knew where the key was, of course. There had been three keys on a ring in her bag, but I was reluctant to go back into her room to take them from her. I had a bunch of keys of my own for my own suitcases and for the trunks that were on their way to me by sea, and I tried these all in turn to see if I had one which would unlock her suitcase.

I failed; none of them would fit. There was nothing for it; with a heavy heart I went back through the swing door, and opened the door into her room. It seemed a despicable thing that I was doing. The girl had been in trouble and she was dead, lying there beneath the sheet in the room with me. She had gone to great pains to maintain some privacy in her affairs. Now she was dead and could no longer defend herself; I had all but breached her privacy and now I was robbing her bag, to find out things about her that she wanted to keep from us.

Standing by the chest-of-drawers opening her bag I imagined I could feel the horror and the protest from the girl beneath the sheet upon the bed behind me. I whispered, 'My dear, I'm sorry to be doing this to you,' and took the keys, and thrust the bag back into the drawer, and got out of her room and through the swing door and back to my own place as quickly as I could.

I was in no hurry to open her case, now that I could do so. I was a little shaken and upset, and not at all sure that I was doing the right thing. I left the keys lying on the suitcase and went slowly downstairs to the drawing-room. There were still red embers in the grate and warmth in the room, and I poured myself another whisky and soda to steady my nerves. The clock struck eleven while I was doing so.

I stood in front of the fire, glass in hand, recovering my self-possession. I was intensely reluctant to open that case. To do so would clearly be an act in opposition to the dead girl's earnest wish, and one should respect the wishes of the dead. The Law might require me to do so, but I had the power to tell the Law to go jump in the lake, for nobody but I knew that the case existed. There was no evidence that the slightest harm would come to anybody if I took that suit-case now and thrust it deep into the central-heating furnace, and if I did that I should certainly be carrying out the dead girl's wish.

On the other hand, I was responsible for the happiness and well-being of everybody in our little community so far as lay within my power. Amongst our little party there had been enormous catastrophic grief that had made this girl take her life. Unless I knew what it was, that grief might come again. It might be something that did not affect Jessie Proctor alone. It might be something to be rooted out of Coombargana, some evil that had grown up with the ageing of my father and relaxation of the firmness of control. We might have got a sadist or a pervert of some kind on the property. If I left this uninvestigated the grief might come again, upon some other person. Some other person might now be suffering as this girl perhaps had suffered.

It was my job to open up that case and see if I could find out what the trouble had been. A brief inspection by the coroner might have to follow, but after that it could all go into the fire and the sooner the better. But opened it would have to be.

I went up to my room again presently, with a quiet mind. There was nothing now to wait for; I shut the door carefully behind me and turned the key in the lock. Then I went over to the fireside and opened the case upon the table with one of her keys.

It was full of papers of all sorts, neatly arranged. There were letters and bank books, and about a dozen quarto manuscript books at the bottom. I shuffled through the things on top, and her passport caught my eye. I pulled it out, and stood dumbfounded by the name upon the cover. I opened it and had a little difficulty in turning the pages, for my fingers were all thumbs. I stared at the photograph that stared back from the page at me, the broad, square, kindly face that I remembered so well, the bushy dark eyebrows.

This wasn't Jessie Proctor. It was Janet Prentice.

Leading Wren Janet Prentice, that I had met with Bill in April 1944, at Lymington in Hampshire, before the invasion of Normandy.

CHAPTER THREE

THERE WERE little, practical jobs to be done mechanically, that saved me the necessity of thinking for a minute or two. I started to unpack her papers on to the table and arrange them into little heaps in order that I might examine them methodically, and very soon I came upon the photograph frame. It was a little leather thing that opened like a wallet to stand upon a table, that held two photographs beneath a cellophane glaze. I stood for a long time with it open in my hand. I knew one of them; it was the one that Bill had had taken by an indifferent professional photographer in Portsmouth, when he had been in training with the Royal Marines at Eastney. It showed him in the uniform of a private before he had attained a rank, rather a stiff, hack portrait. My mother has a print of it that stands upon the table in her room, with one of Helen and one of me. I wondered what she would have thought if she had known that her house parlourmaid had a copy of it, too.

Opposite this one, in the other glazed frame, was a more living picture. It was a snapshot of Bill taken shortly before his death, in the battledress uniform of a sergeant in the Marines, taken in the open air upon the roadway of some camp. Janet Prentice was beside him in the uniform of a Leading Wren; he had his arm around her shoulders and they were laughing together.

I knew that one existed, though I had never seen it; my mother did not know of it at all. Bill had told me about it when I met him in the spring of 1944. I was at Fighter Command in those days, after two hours of operations, first on Hurricanes and then on Spitfires. It was so long since we had met that when a job cropped up that was to take me to a conference at Beaulieu aerodrome I had shamelessly extended it and snatched an extra twenty-four hours from my office on Sunday in order that I might see Bill before 'Overlord', before the balloon went up. I flew down in a Spit from Northolt late one Saturday evening and landed in the dusk. Tony Patterson was there and he had laid a car on for me to take me in to Lymington, where I had booked a room at the Roebuck Hotel, and Bill had met me there for dinner.

In the first exchanges over a couple of drinks before we ate, Bill told me that he knew Beaulieu aerodrome. It was nearly two years since we had met; I had been in Egypt and the Western Desert before my office job, and when I was drafted back to England he had been up at some Commando training place on the west coast of Scotland. So much had happened to us both, so differently had we developed, that it took us a few minutes to establish contact again and to reach the point when we could talk about the matters we both wanted to discuss. The gin helped, of course.

'What were you doing at the aerodrome?' I asked. 'You don't go arsing about up in the air?'

He shook his head. 'There's a flight-sergeant there in charge of the PR unit,' he said. I nodded; Beaulieu aerodrome was now a mass of fighters, Thunderbolts and Typhoons in readiness for close support of the invasion landings on the other side, but previously there had been a photographic reconnaissance flight of Lightnings there and the photographers with their equipment for developing and printing were still in one of the buildings. 'He's a good type,' said Bill. 'Nobody's allowed to have a camera down here, of course.' I did not know that, but with the intense security precautions necessary before the invasion it was obviously so. 'He'll take anybody's picture for a dollar and let you have the prints. Good pictures, too. I went up there with Janet this afternoon and he took one of us. I'm going to pick them up on Wednesday.'

This was getting near the subject we both wanted to discuss. 'Where's Janet now?' I asked. 'Is she here?' I had never met her then, of course.

He shook his head. 'She only got a three-hour pass. She caught the ferry back to *Mastodon* from just outside the aerodrome.' He meant the naval truck that plied between Exbury Hall upon the Beaulieu River that was now HMS

Mastodon, and Lymington. 'She's got a full day off tomorrow.'

'Got anything laid on?'

'She's got a boat,' he said. 'When have you got to go back?'

'Be all right if I get off at dawn on Monday,' I replied. 'I've got a natter on with the Americans tomorrow evening – I've got to be up at the aerodrome at six o'clock. And I'll have to slip out to the aerodrome in the morning to ring up the office. That won't take more than half an hour. After that I've got all day, till six o'clock.'

'You could make the call from here.'

I shook my head. 'It's got to be a scrambled line. It won't take long. I've got transport laid on to collect me here at half past eight.'

He looked me up and down, and grinned. 'All these bloody rings and gongs,' he said. 'I suppose they give you transport any time you want it.'

I ordered two more gins. 'Mum was asking in the last letter if you were ever going to get a commission.'

'Not much,' he said. 'I get more fun this way. If I'd been an officer I wouldn't have met Janet.'

'Don't you believe it,' I replied. 'Most of the officers' popsies that you see are in the ranks. They don't give commissions to the best popsies. Reserve them for a higher destiny than being a wing officer.'

'Reserve some of them for a job of work,' he observed.

I glanced at him. 'What does she do?'

'O A,' he told me. 'Ordnance Artificer at *Mastodon*. Leading Wren. She looks after the guns on the LCTs and the LCIs. *Force J* mostly, in the Beaulieu River.'

I glanced around, for this was careless talk and there might be some security snooper listening to us. But there was no one within hearing. 'Services the guns?'

He nodded. 'If a ship reports defects in its Oerlikon or twin Lewis she goes on board and checks it over, and if it's crook she takes it on shore to the armoury and swaps it for another.'

I raised my eyebrows a little. Most of the popsies that had come my way were ornamental young women from the ops room, or in radar.

Bill grinned. 'She knows her stuff.'

'Are you engaged to her?'

'No,' he said thoughtfully. 'Nothing like that.' He stood fingering his glass upon the bar. 'Not till after the balloon's gone up. Time enough to think about that then.'

I said, 'You'd like to be?'

He nodded. 'She's a beaut girl.'

'How would she go down with Dad and Mum?' At Lymington in Hampshire, in the British Forces, we were a long way both in distance and in thought from Coombargana in the Western District.

'She'd be all right.'

'Does she know anything about Australia?'

He grinned. 'Not a thing. They none of them do. It's no good trying to explain, either. I told her we were farmers. They understand that.'

I nodded. I had had some of this myself. When I was new to England I tried once or twice to explain to people how we lived, and found that they thought I was shooting a line. I had soon learned to shut up and to identify myself as a farmer's son – which, of course, was true.

'Got any idea what you're going to do when this is over?' I asked him.

'When what's over? "Overlord"?' He dropped his voice for the last word, as one which ordinary people did not speak aloud.

'No. The war.'

'When's that going to be?'

'Maybe this autumn. It probably won't go another year.'

'Is that what they are saying at your place?'

I nodded. It was difficult for either of us to credit such a thing, after five years. 'Think you'll go back to Cirencester?' Bill had come to England in July 1939, when he was nineteen years old, to go to an agricultural college. He had stayed there, unwilling, for a few months in the period of the phoney war before enlisting in the Marines.

He shook his head. 'I'd never go back to school now. What about you?'

I had done two years of Law at Oxford, at the House, on

my Rhodes scholarship. 'I wouldn't mind going back for a bit, finish off what I started.'

'Go home and see the parents first of all?'

'Oh, I think so. Go home for a month or two, and then come back to finish off at Oxford.'

Bill put his glass down thoughtfully upon the bar. 'I don't want to do that,' he said. 'I'd like to marry Janet and go back to Coombargana, and stay there looking at the sheep for a long, long time.'

I glanced at him quickly. 'Like that, is it?'

'A bit.' He was a frogman at that time, of course. I did not know the full scope of his work then, though I knew that he went repeatedly to the beaches of Northern France in the dark night, to go ashore and to survey the tetrahedrons and the Elements C with landmines tied to them with which the Germans were fortifying the landing beaches. I had seen the air photographs that the Lightning pilots had returned with, taken as they flew along through flak at fifty feet, and I knew that one of Bill's jobs was to go by night in MTB or submarine, to swim ashore or paddle in a folboat in the darkness under the noses of the Germans at the head of the beach, to examine these things and report on them. It seemed to me that he was starting to feel the strain, but there was absolutely nothing I could do about it. I had been through periods of strain myself.

I said, 'One of us ought to get back there as soon as possible. Helen says the rabbits are just terrible.' With my father on service in the Northern Territory Mother was running the station, with Helen nominally helping her but spending most of her time in Melbourne doing something with the Red Cross. Mother was putting up a marvellous show, but with half the men away at the war the property was obviously going downhill.

He glanced at me. 'You won't be going back yourself?'

I shook my head. 'You go. Marry the girl and make an honest woman of her' – he grinned – 'and go back and help Dad work it up again. If I go back to live at all, it won't be for years.' I knew what he was thinking: that I was the elder son. 'If ever I come back, it's big enough to split up into two.'

He nodded. 'If we don't do that, somebody'll do it for us. It's too much land to hold as one property in these days.'

'Maybe,' I said. 'Anyway, you go back and run it, soon as you like. Take Janet with you, and give her a shock.'

He laughed. 'She'll get that all right. A farm here means about a hundred acres.'

'Who is she, Bill?' I asked him curiously. 'What's her background?'

'Good middle class,' he said. 'Nothing social, or upstage. You may know her father. He's a professor or a don or something, at Oxford.'

'Professor Prentice?' Or was it Dr Prentice? The name was somehow familiar.

'I suppose so. Do you know him?'

I shook my head. 'There's such a lot of them. Do you know what college he's in?'

'Is there one called Wyckham, or some name like that?'

I nodded. 'He's at Wyckham?'

'I think so.'

'Do you know what he teaches?'

Bill grinned. 'Semantics,' he said. 'I learned that word.'

'Christ. Do you know what it means?'

'Well, it's not Jews,' said Bill. 'Janet won't have that. It's words or something.'

I nodded. I didn't think there was a chair of semantics in the university; it was probably a research subject. He might be a professor of modern languages or English literature if, indeed, he was a professor of anything. In any case, it was a decent background for the girl to have; she would be able to hold her own in feminine society in the Western District.

Bill asked, 'Do you know him?'

'I don't think so. What's he like to look at?'

'I don't know,' he said. 'I've never met the family. I'll probably get round to doing that when the balloon's gone up.'

Our lives hinged upon the date for 'Overlord', still all unknown. It was not very close, for there must be great concentrations of troops and landing craft in the last week or two, and they were not there yet. It was not very far away, because the ground was drying hard after the winter rains, and tanks could operate across country now, or would be able to very shortly. Up at Fighter Command we none of us knew the date; from the internal evidence that passed across my desk I guessed it to be about six weeks off. I could not make that known to anybody, even to Bill.

A picture came into my mind of a broad-shouldered, broad-faced man of fifty-five or sixty, a man with a square, rugged face and very bushy eyebrows, iron grey like his hair. I thought that was Dr Prentice but I was not sure, nor could I remember where I had met him. In any case, it didn't matter now.

We went up to the dining-room for dinner, a poor meal in those days of tight rationing, and we drank watery beer. It was no fault of the hotel that they served us a poor meal, with all their staff called up and put into the Services to cook for us, but when the sweet that was not sweet came to the table I said to Bill, 'I hope your Janet can cook.'

'I shouldn't think so,' he replied. 'I don't think she's ever had to do it.'

'How old is she?'

'She joined the Wrens straight from school in 1941,' he said. 'I suppose she was eighteen and a half then – I think she was. She'd be twenty-one now.' He paused. 'Somehow, she seems older than that – the way she goes on with the ratings. They're scared stiff of her on the LCTs.'

I smiled. 'Scared stiff of her?'

'My word,' he said, 'you ought to see her carry on if she goes on board a ship and finds the gun rusty. They're more frightened of her than they would be of a CPO.'

'She must have quite a reputation.'

He nodded. 'She has that. She's probably the only Leading Wren in the Navy who's ever been congratulated personally by the First Sea Lord.'

I stirred, and came back to my room in Coombargana, to the present. A wood fire does not burn for very long; I laid the little photograph frame down upon the table and crossed mechanically to the fire, and put on two or three more logs. I did not go back to investigate the suitcase further; there was time enough for that. So many memories of Bill and Janet Prentice ...

May Spikins, Viola Dawson, and Petty Officer Waters had all told me about Janet Prentice and her life in the Wrens, when I found them one by one in the post-war years, in 1950 and 1951. She had not kept in touch with any of them and they were little help to me in finding her, but they filled out the picture of the girl that I had met with Bill on that fine April Sunday before 'Overlord', when we had gone down the river in the small grey naval motor boat into the Solent and had picnicked on the sand spit near Hurst Castle.

She was born in Crick Road in North Oxford; I went and found the big old house in 1948 when I went back to finish my Law course. Her old house and most of the neighbouring houses had been cut up into flats and only one old lady in the road remembered the Prentices. She had a sister some years older than herself, who in 1948 was married and probably in Singapore, but I never succeeded in discovering her married name. She had no brothers. She had lived all her early life in the pleasant, easy, academic atmosphere of Oxford. It had all been laburnum and magnolia and almond blossom in her childhood, and talk of the Sitwells and Debussy and Handel. That was her life till 1939, when she took School Certificate and the war began.

'It all came to an end then,' she told Viola Dawson once. 'I was going up to Lady Margaret Hall in 1941, but the war put paid to that. I was jolly lucky to get into the Wrens; I wouldn't have liked it in the Army or a factory. If it couldn't be Oxford, I'm glad it was the Wrens.'

I think that her last year at school was probably spoilt for her by the war. Academic life had died in Oxford as the phoney war was succeeded by the real war. Her father joined the Observer Corps and spent long hours of most nights at a watch point on Boars Hill, a telephone headset strapped across his beret, watching, reporting the movements of aircraft in the skies to the central plotting room fifty miles away. After a night of that a man of sixty has little energy next day for any but routine work, and her father laid aside research and confined himself to his lectures to small groups of undergraduates and large groups of officers from various Services who were brushing up their languages.

In that last year of school her home was crowded with evacuees, irritating strangers who were always there when you wanted them away, always talking when you wanted privacy. Her education suffered, for school work in the evenings was unthinkable at the time of the Battle of Britain, and she spent much of her leisure time at a depot that made up and dispatched Red Cross parcels. There was no fun in Oxford in those days.

It was a relief when her time came to join the Wrens. She was a big, broad-shouldered girl at eighteen and a half, still awkward with the gaucheness of a puppy. It was a relief and an unpleasantness at the same time; her first few days of readjustment at the Training and Drafting depot were not happy ones. She was to prove herself a good mixer when the Service had formed her character, but at the time of her entry she had never mixed. She had never shared her bedroom with anybody since childhood days; now she had to sleep on the top bunk of a double-decker in a hut with thirty other girls of every social grade. She had to undergo the most intimate medical examinations, the least offensive of which was a close examination of her head and underclothes for lice. She had to learn the language. Going out of the depot gate to visit the local cinema was 'going on shore'. She got sternly rebuked by a Wren petty officer on her third day for incautiously referring to the galley as 'the kitchen', and it was weeks before she could remember what time was indicated by four bells in the forenoon watch. She very soon learned, however, that if you put the counterpane on your bunk with the anchor upside down the ship would sink.

At the end of her fortnight of basic training she had begun to take it easy; the crudities of Service life were gradually ceasing to offend. At that point she had to volunteer for her particular category of work.

She had no ambition to become a cook or a steward; she was good at Virgil, which nobody seemed to want, but ignorant of shorthand, typewriting or book-keeping. She would have liked to be a boat's crew Wren but the competition was terrific and she had little knowledge – at that time – of boats. She had a vague, unexpressed sympathy with things mechanical; she liked oiling her bicycle or tinkering with the mowing machine; she could replace the worn flex of a reading lamp. She elected on these qualifications to go to the Fleet Air Arm, and because she had once or twice fired a shotgun and was not afraid of it she became a qualified Ordnance Wren.

She was sent to an Ordnance depot where she was taught to dismantle, clean, and check a Browning .300 and to load the belts into an aircraft; she mastered that without difficulty and graduated on to the 20-mm Hispano cannon. Her education was complete then, and with a batch of other Ordnance Wrens she was sent down to Ford near Littlehampton on the south coast of England, where she settled down to ply her trade from December 1941 to June 1943.

At Ford aerodrome she passed the most formative eighteen months of her life. She went there as a callow, undeveloped schoolgirl, unsure of herself, awkward and hesitant. She left it as a Leading Wren with no great ambition for any higher rank, reliable, efficient, and very well able to look after herself; a mature young woman.

She became a pleasant young woman, too, and a popular one. She never aspired to any film-star type of beauty, but she was an open, cheerful, healthy girl with a well-developed sense of humour. She was better in overalls and bell-bottoms than in a backless evening frock, more usually seen with a smear of grease upon her forehead where she had brushed back a wisp of hair than with anything upon her face from Elizabeth Arden. The pilots of the flight she worked with grew to like her and to have confidence in guns that she had serviced; from time to time they used to take her up in Swordfish or in Barracudas to fire a gun from the rear cockpit. She was quite a good shot with a stripped Lewis. Physically she had always been broad-shouldered and athletic, and lugging loaded drums and belts and canisters of ammunition about all day made her as strong as a horse.

She was all things to all men and spent most of her life being so, because the men outnumbered the girls at Ford by four to one. Every evening there was a dance or Ensa show, or a party to the movies in Littlehampton. She learned to talk in terms that they could understand to the shy young sub-lieutenant fresh from school or to the uncouth rating fresh from a Liverpool slum; on occasion she could express herself on matters of sex in good old English words that would have shocked her father and puzzled her mother. She learned to suit her language to the company that she was in.

War moulded her and made her what she was. When first she went to Ford the German bombers used to come frequently to bomb the aerodrome, during the night; she spent long, weary nights down in the shelters. She learned quite soon what a dead man looked like, and a dead girl. She learned what a crashed aircraft looks like, and what a frail and messy thing the human body is when taken from the crash. The first time she saw this she wanted to be sick, and then she wanted to cry and was afraid of being laughed at. After the fifth or sixth such incident she wanted to do neither, and was content to do what she could to help in cleaning up the mess.

She got home to Oxford now and then on leave, and gradually she became distressed for her parents. War was hitting them much harder than it was hitting her. She was merry and well fed and confident, serene in the knowledge that she was doing a worthwhile job; she could put on her Number Ones and doll herself up smartly to go home and cut a dash. At home she found her mother tired and worn with the work of cooking and catering for a large household with little or no help at a time of increasing shortages, and harassed by six strange children from the East End of London living in the house. Her father seemed smaller and greyer than she had remembered him; he was no longer the jovial don who took life easily with good conversation and good port in the Senior Common Room. There was no port in Oxford in those days and little time for conversation; her father seemed to be able to talk of nothing but the Observer Corps, its administration, its efficiency, and its discipline. Before she had been a year at Ford Janet came to look forward to her next pass with something close to apprehension; it was pitiful to see her mother ageing and be unable to help her, to see her father turning into just another poor old man.

In the early summer of 1943 she got an opportunity to change her job. CPO Waters told me about it when I talked to him in his tobacconist's shop in Fratton Road, in Portsmouth, in 1951. He remembered Leading Wren Prentice very well indeed, for she was the subject of one of his best and most frequently told stories. 'It was in 1943, in the summer,' he told me. 'Gawd, that was a lark!' He savoured the memory, grinning. 'They wanted Ordnance Wrens to look after the guns on the invasion fleet. Combined Operations. They sent a chit all round the Ordnance depots asking for Wren volunteers. These girls, they didn't know what the job was on account of it being secret; they thought it was to work on MTBs, but really it was the tank landing craft and that. Every LCT Mark 4, she had two Oerlikons, and every LCS – and there were thousands of them. No wonder they had to rob the other branches of the Service for Ordnance Wrens! I dunno how many Oerlikons there were in the Normandy party – thousands and thousands of 'em.'

The 20-mm Oerlikon was not unlike the 20-mm Hispano that Janet was used to servicing, so the work would present no difficulty to her. She felt that she would like to make a change and to see another side of the Navy; it seemed absurd that she had been in the Wrens for nearly two years and she had never been near a ship. With half a dozen other Wrens from Ford she volunteered for the new Service, and was sent on a short course to Whale Island to convert to Oerlikons.

Whale Island lies in Portsmouth Harbour and it is the site of HMS *Excellent*, the naval gunnery training and experimental establishment. Whale Island is a very serious place, full of ambitious regular Naval officers with black gaiters on their legs and a stern frown on their foreheads, all intent on advancing themselves in their career by developing a new system of fire control or improving an old one. Janet Prentice was ten days at Whale Island and to her delight the curriculum of her course included two afternoons of firing the Oerlikon at a sleeve target towed by an aeroplane; this practice was carried out upon the grid at Eastney firing out over the sea. It was considered necessary that the girls should be able to test the guns that they had overhauled with a short burst of fire, and to make the matter interesting for them they were given a brief, elementary course of eye-shooting at a towed target, using the simple ring sight.

On the first afternoon of their shoot, when it came to Janet's turn to fire, the target sleeve mysteriously began to disintegrate into ribbons. She went on firing for about twenty rounds, and it parted from the towing wire altogether and fluttered down into the sea. 'The rest of 'em all missed astern,' the Chief Petty Officer told me, years later, leaning across the counter of his little shop. 'You get them sometimes like that – natural good shots, but this was the first time I ever knew it in a girl. I give her a coconut out of the ready-use locker, there on the grid. Gunnery officers on ships from West Africa or India, they used to bring me back a sack or two of coconuts, 'n I'd always have one ready if that happened. Makes a bit of fun for the class, you see. Makes 'em take an interest.'

Two days later they were taken to the range again for their final shoot. Their visit coincided with a demonstration to the Naval Staff of a new sort of towed target designed to replace the sleeve, a little winged glider that looked just like a real aeroplane and which seemed to tow much faster than the linen sleeve.

At that time the Naval Staff were divided into two schools of thought regarding the best method of fire control against low-flying aircraft. The Director of Naval Ordnance held that all guns should be predictor-controlled. The Director of the Gunnery Division held that all guns should be radar-controlled. This battle was raging at the time more fiercely than the one against the Germans. The one point that both agreed upon was that eye-shooting was no use at all for bringing down an aeroplane.

The Fifth Sea Lord wanted to see a shoot against the winged target, the First Sea Lord wanted to see if radar was really any good against an aircraft at close range, and both wanted a day down by the sea. With their attendant brass they drove down in style from the Admiralty, had lunch with the Captain of HMS *Excellent*, and went out full of good food and Plymouth gin for their afternoon's entertainment at Eastney.

The range officer at that time was a certain Lt-Cdr Cart-wright, RN, whose ship had been torpedoed in the North Atlantic by two German submarines simultaneously while he was busy depth-charging a third. His subsequent immersion for two hours in the North Atlantic in midwinter followed by thirty-six hours in an open boat had done him no good. After his convalescence he had been relegated to shore duties for six months, to his immense disgust, and had been sent down to take charge of firing operations on the grid at Eastney.

Commander Cartwright was a general duties officer, a salt horse, whose profession was commanding a ship; he had little use for gunnery specialists and their toys. To him a simple weapon was a good weapon and a complex weapon was a bad one; it was as straightforward as that. His administration of the range included both the experimental and the training shoots; in his own mind he gave strong preference to training and had little patience with experimental work, especially when it interfered with any of the courses. To him the visit of the Board of Admiralty that afternoon was a sheer waste of the time of busy people. It meant that he would have to stop his training shoots when the brass arrived and he would have a hundred ratings and a dozen Wrens standing idle for an hour or so, waiting till this damned experimental nonsense was over.

He let off at his RNVR assistant in hearing of the CPO. 'Half of them won't get a shoot at all unless we stick our heels in,' he said irritably. 'Well, I'm not going to have it. I won't pass them out until each one of them has had a proper shoot. These muggers from the Admiralty seem to think that training doesn't matter.'

When all the admirals and captains came to the grid he was stiffly correct in his black gaiters, inwardly furious. The towing aircraft appeared dead on time, and far behind it a small winged object streaked across the sky. It was the first time that any of the brass had seen it and nobody knew how large it was or how fast it was going. The technical officers examined its flight with some concern. The predictor boys spoke in low tones to the Director of Naval Ordnance protesting that some knowledge of the size was necessary to their fire control. The radar boys spoke in low tones to the Director of the Gunnery Division explaining that the thing was giving an uncommonly poor response upon the cathode ray screen, and voicing their suspicion that it was made of wood, which clearly wasn't fair.

The two Directors hesitantly preferred these objections to one or two of the lesser admirals. The First Sea Lord, overhearing, remarked that they would listen to the technicians after tea. In the meantime, he was there to see that thing shot down.

They fired at it for an hour, in ten runs past the grid at varying angles of approach and altitudes. They fired at it with the quadruple Vickers, with the multiple pom-pom, with a predictor-controlled twin Bofors, with a radar-controlled triple Oerlikon, and with a comic thing that fired a salvo of sixteen rockets all at once. At the end of the hour the target was still flying merrily about the sky, and half the officers were laughing cynically and half were speechless with frustration.

Commander Cartwright was a very angry man. His training classes were standing idle and laughing at each failure; clearly their morale was suffering. They would have little confidence after a show like this that they could hit an aeroplane, if all the experts couldn't. It was intolerable that they should have to witness an exhibition of this sort that brought his training effort into ridicule.

His instructor, CPO Waters, who had had ten years of experience upon the grid, sidled up to him. 'I got a Wren down there that could hit that thing,' he said out of the corner of his mouth. 'That one what hit the sleeve on Monday. She's a natural, she is. She could hit that, sir.'

The officer's eyes gleamed. 'Think she could?'

'I think so, sir. What's it doing? Hundred and eighty knots?'

'About that, I should say.'

'She could hit it, sir. Ask if some of the training class can't have a go, and leave the rest to me.'

Commander Cartwright went up to the observation tower, caught the eyes of the Captain of HMS *Excellent*, and saluted smartly. 'We have three courses waiting down on the grid, sir, each for their final day of eye-shooting. Could we save time in getting out another aircraft by letting them shoot at this?'

The Captain said, 'I think that's quite a good idea. It would be interesting to see the comparison, too.' The Director of the Gunnery Division said, 'I don't think you can expect much from that.' The First Sea Lord said, 'I have no objection. What time is it now? I must be off by half past four.'

Down on the grid the Chief said, 'Here you, Leading Wren Prentice. On the Oerlikon.' She stepped forward, bursting with importance, and slipped her shoulders into the half rings. The Chief pulled the strap behind her shoulders and made it fast for her. 'Take it easy,' he said quietly. 'Try it first about a hundred and eighty knots, 'n if that don't work, feel it up towards two hundred, like you been taught. Now wait till I tell you to fire.'

Janet grinned at him. 'Okay, Chief.'

Up on the observation tower where the high brass were congregated the Vice-Admiral who was ACNS (W) looked down to the Oerlikon. 'What's that – a Wren?'

By his side Commander Cartwright said, 'It's the eye-shooting class for Qualified Ordnance Wrens, sir. Ladies first.'

Down on the grid Janet moved up on the circumferential steps behind her as she depressed the Oerlikon to the approaching target. A hundred and eighty knots, fairly near the outer ring but two-thirds in from that because it was diagonal, flying a little below the centre because of the range. She had never had the slightest difficulty with this; it all seemed common-sense to her. By her side the old Chief said quietly, 'Wait for it. Remember, don't look at the tracer, just keep looking at the sight, and mind what I told you. Wait for it.'

She had it fair and square between the rings at about four o'clock, exactly as she wanted it. The little target glider grew quickly larger.

'Now – fire!'

She pressed the grip and the gun started shaking rhythmically, and the noise was great, and the smoke of cordite

69

was all around her. She had the little glider held fixed in her sight exactly as she wanted it; she swung her body across and down to keep it there and the gun swung slowly with her. Deliberately she felt the target back towards the outer ring, moving it very slowly, anticipating the violent throbbing of the gun, bracing herself to master this wild thing that she had started with her grip.

She was exultant. This was really living; it was *fun*!

And suddenly there were two flashes on the little glider, one on the wing and one on the body. It rolled over on its back and one of the wings came off and began to flutter down. The Chief roared in her ear, 'Cease Fire!'

She released her grip and the clamour of the gun stopped, and she stood watching with the smoke all around her. The glider was plunging violently and wildly in the air at the end of its mile-length of cable, in fantastically irregular flight. Then the cable suddenly went slack as the observer in the towing aircraft cut it free, and the target fell in spinning confusion into the sea with a small splash.

On the grid the class were cheering wildly. The Chief released Janet from the back strap; reaction was upon her and she was trembling as if she still fired the gun. From the ready-use ammunition locker the Chief produced another coconut; she took it from him, laughing.

Up on the observation tower the range officer said dryly to his captain, 'There's something to be said for the old methods, after all.'

His captain said, 'Oh, certainly. But it's exceptional. She's probably a Senior Wrangler in civil life, and teaches trigonometry.'

The higher admirals were perfectly delighted, especially the Fifth Sea Lord. 'There, DNO – and you, DGD. What about it? Beaten by a girl with five bob's worth of sights upon the gun! I haven't had an afternoon like this for years!'

Somebody said resentfully, 'She's probably a crack shot in civil life, sir.'

The First Sea Lord said, 'Well, I should like to know about that. Let's have her up here for a minute.'

An RNVR officer was dispatched down to the grid at the

double to fetch CPO Waters and Leading Wren Prentice to the Presence; Janet fumbled with her coconut and gave it to May Spikins to look after for her, put her hat on straight, and went with the warrant officer up to the tower. Here she was passed quickly to Commander Cartwright, by him to the Captain of HMS *Excellent*, and by him to the First Sea Lord. She looked at him nervously, a red-faced old gentleman with heavy gold braid rings upon his cuff that seemed to go right up to the elbow, and a fruit salad of medal ribbons on his chest. She was still trembling from the clamour of the gun, from reaction, and from fright.

He said kindly, 'That was very good shooting, young lady. I congratulate you. Had you done much shooting before you joined the Service?'

She said, 'I had fired a shotgun, sir. Only twice.'

'Have you done much shooting since you joined?'

She hesitated, because at Ford it was against the regulations for Wrens to fly. Then she decided it was better to tell the truth. 'I was in the Fleet Air Arm before coming here,' she said. 'They used to take us up sometimes to test the observer's Lewis or Browning by firing it.'

'What did you fire at? Something in the sea?'

'Yes, sir. A bit of wood or seaweed – anything.'

All the officers were studying her. The First Sea Lord asked, 'What are you in civil life?'

She said awkwardly, 'Well, sir – I wasn't anything. I mean, I was at school.'

The Captain of *Excellent* asked, 'What were you best at, at school?'

She hesitated. 'Well, I liked Latin best, I think.' It seemed a pretty crackpot sort of question to her, and it must have been, because one or two of them laughed.

The First Sea Lord asked, 'Did you have any difficulty in learning eye-shooting?'

'No, sir.' She had a natural flair for it. All the rest of her class had been much puzzled by it, and she had spent an hour trying to make May Spikins see what seemed so obvious to her. 'I just did what the Chief taught us.'

That brought in Chief Petty Officer Waters. The Admiral asked him, 'Is this Wren exceptional, Chief?'

He answered stiffly, 'She's better than the general run, sir. I'd say that she's a natural good shot.'

'That's why you put her on to shoot?'

'Yes, sir.'

Somebody else asked, 'What are the Ordnance Wrens like, in general, compared with the ratings?'

He said, 'They're better, sir – no doubt of that. Of course, they're better educated, mostly, than the called-up classes that we're getting in now.'

The First Sea Lord said, 'Well, I congratulate you on this young lady, Chief. It was very good shooting.' The Petty Officer beamed with pleasure, storing up each word in a retentive memory, to retail to me in the end eight years later.

He withdrew with Janet and they left the tower together and went down to the class on the grid. He sent her back in to the ranks, and called the squad to attention. 'Now look here, you Wrens,' he said in measured tones. 'I just been congratulated by the First Sea Lord himself, on account of what Leading Wren Prentice, No 3 in the front rank, just did. Now you see what can be done with eye-shooting if you troubles to learn how to do it. What Leading Wren Prentice did any one of you can do, if you takes the trouble. Otherwise you better change your category and go for a cook. Now, stand easy.'

They all bent towards Janet. 'Did you see the First Sea Lord? What did he say?'

'I saw him,' she told them. 'He asked me what I did before I joined up, and I said I didn't do anything. And then the Captain of *Excellent* asked what I was best at, at school, and I said, Latin. I think they're all crackers, if you ask me. Mad as March hares. No wonder they can't hit the bloody aeroplane.'

I know she said that, because May Spikins told me all about that day when we talked in her council house up on the new estate at Harlow. May Cunningham she was by that time, with a little boy two years old and a baby of six months; her husband was a clerk in the municipal offices at Enfield and he was away at work when I called to see her, in 1950. Warrant Officer Finch had told me about her when I went to see him about Bill, and I motored down to see May Spikins because I thought that she might be in touch with Janet Prentice, or at least know what had happened to her. But she knew nothing; they had not met or corresponded since Janet left the Service. She had known Bill slightly as Janet's boyfriend, and when I told her that I was his brother from Australia she loosened up and invited me into the parlour, and made a pot of tea, and we talked for a long time of those far-off weeks and day at Beaulieu, before 'Overlord', before the balloon went up.

I know she said that, because she was a very outspoken girl in those days, and when May Spikins told me that I knew that it was true, because the words were exactly the words that Leading Wren Prentice would have used. It was probably this quality of character and ability to express herself in a masculine way that made the ratings in the invasion fleet afraid of her displeasure; to be ticked off by a Wren who used all the vigour and language of a petty officer was intimidating, and there was a certain feminine ruthlessness about her that made them feel she would not hesitate to implement her threats.

I felt something of the same quality in her when I spent the Sunday with her and Bill, at Lymington, in April 1944. There was a forthrightness about her, a directness of speech and community of experience that was infinitely restful to men strained to the limit in those weeks before the invasion. She was obviously very good for Bill. He didn't have to put on an act for her. She would have laughed and been embarrassed if he had given her flowers, and by then he was too tired and preoccupied with his trips over to the other side to think of giving anything to anybody. It was she who produced the motor boat that day for our run down the river to the Solent. It was a little grey painted Naval boat fifteen or sixteen feet long, a fishing boat that had been taken over by the Navy, I should think. She had it at the quay by the Ship Inn when I got back from Beaulieu aerodrome at about half past ten. The WAAF driver took me to the quay and there was Bill in battledress and gumboots with his dog, and Janet Prentice in rather dirty blue serge slacks, and gumboots, and a blue jersey, and a greasy duffle coat. I dismissed my car and went down to the boat.

Bill introduced me, and I shook hands with the girl. She looked me up and down smiling. 'Bill's got an oily for you,' she said, 'but I don't know about your clothes. I'm afraid this boat's in a bit of a muck.' There was a pad of dirty cotton waste upon the engine casing by her side, and she wiped the thwart with it.

The uniform that I was wearing was my oldest, threadbare with much cleaning and still marked with oil stains that would not come out. 'I'll be right,' I said. 'Don't bother about me.'

'I'm afraid you'll get that lovely uniform all dirty,' she said. 'Put on the oily anyway; it may be a bit wet outside, if we go round to Keyhaven.'

'Tide's flooding and there's not much wind,' Bill said. 'It won't be bad.'

She turned to crank the engine. I offered to do it for her, but she refused, making me feel that I had done the wrong thing. 'She kicks back if you're not careful,' she said. 'One of the ratings broke his arm on her the other day, but she's all right when you know her. I'll do her myself.' She tickled the old carburettor, bent to the handle, and gave the heavy flywheel a vigorous heave over; she was evidently a very powerful girl. The engine began thumping away beneath the box, and she moved to the stern and cast the stern rope off and drew it in, dripping with sea water, and coiled it expertly. Bill cast off from the bow and the girl took the tiller, kicked the lever forward with her foot, and we moved off down the river.

There were no civilian boats or yachts afloat upon the South Coast at that time, but the river was full of landing craft, box-like grey, painted things of steel with ramps to let down at the bow, with diesel engines thumping away inside them to charge batteries as they lay moored bow and stern to the buoys, with soiled white ensigns drooping at the stern, with bored ratings fishing over the side and staring at us as we threaded our way past. I did not know the function or the name of any of these ships, but Janet and Bill knew them all and told me shortly what they were, and what they were

74

to do, as we chugged past. This, was the LCT Mark 4, the standard tank landing craft, British built and the most common of the lot. This, was the Mark 5, American designed and built and shipped to England on the decks of ships, an unpleasant and relatively unseaworthy little craft that would go in first in the assault, bearing the Sherman tanks that were to swim ashore, and the work tanks, the armoured vehicles RE that were to clear the beach of obstacles so that the landing craft could come in safely, and detonate the mines, and bridge the trenches in the sandhills on the other side. This, was an obsolete mark of LCT converted as a rocket ship to fire a salvo of nine hundred rounds at one push of the button to blast the shore defences. This, bristling with Bofors guns and Oerlikons, was a gunnery support craft, manned and commanded by Marines. This fast powerful open landing craft coming up the river towards us at speed, manned by American sailors in white, upturned caps, and with the name *Dirtie Girtie* proudly painted on her bow, was an LCVP, an American infantry landing craft so powerful and well designed that ratings with a minimum of training could handle her. All these were known to Janet and Bill, but there were other things afloat upon the Solent that they knew nothing of, great box-like things of concrete bigger than a cross-Channel steamer floating moored or building on the shore, things like a monstrous reel of cotton fifty or sixty feet in diameter floating on the water, flat rafts with grotesque girders sticking up into the air.

Once Janet said in a low tone, 'I wonder what the hell they're going to do with that?' but neither of us answered her. Bill may have known; if so, he kept his mouth shut, as was right. Each of us had our own secrets at that time, our own part in the affair, dominating our minds. I asked once casually, 'Do you get many German aircraft over here, having a look?' It was always possible that something might have slipped in my office, some information that we might have missed, something the locals might know about that we did not.

The girl grinned and said, 'We've not had a Jerry over here for weeks – two months, I should think. I can't think

75

what he's up to. You'd think that he'd be over every day, photographing all this.'

'You'd think so,' I replied idly. It was all right. The fighter patrols organized from my office were on top of the Germans on the other side of the Channel; nothing had slipped past us. Our combat losses might be averaging three machines a day on these security patrols alone, but nothing had got past us save one Messerschmitt 110 ten days before, and that one we had got on his way home. The Germans probably knew very little still of what was massing up against them in the Solent.

We reached the end of the river and the West Solent lay before us, blue and shimmering in the April sun. Bill had moved to the stern beside the girl. I turned to say something to them, but they were both looking over to the shore of the Isle of Wight, four miles across the sea. Bill said, 'That Sherman's still on the beach.'

'They're not bothering about it,' she said. 'They can't tow it up the cliff.'

I asked, 'What's that?'

They pointed to the beach on the far side of the channel. 'That tank up at the head of the beach, see it? Under the cliff. They were doing practice landings from an LCT on that bit of beach. That Sherman was wading ashore but it went down in a hole.'

The girl turned to me. 'It went right under water,' she explained. 'A chap got drowned in it – the driver.'

It was a simple statement of fact, unemotional.

Bill said, 'They could salve it if they took a bit of trouble. They could bring in an LCT and tow it back on board and take it somewhere.'

'It's no good,' the girl said. 'Viola heard about it from a Pongo. When it went under, the water got into the engine and wrecked it – blew off all the cylinder heads. It's not worth bothering about. They took the gun off it.'

'When did this happen?' I asked.

'About five weeks ago,' said Bill. He grinned at the girl, and said nonchalantly, 'That's how I met Janet.'

I learned a good bit about what had happened on that day

76

when I met Viola Dawson six years later, and Warrant Officer Finch told me a little more when I was talking to him about Bill. It was in March, perhaps about the twentieth of the month. Janet had been in *Mastodon* for about nine months. When she went there she had thought that she was going to a base of Coastal Forces to service guns on motor torpedo boats; security had masked the fact that she was destined for the build-up to the invasion of Normandy.

She found that HMS *Mastodon* was a stone frigate. It was Exbury Hall, about three miles up the Beaulieu River from the Solent. The river runs in to the New Forest through country that is wholly rural. For the first three miles it is a fair-sized tidal river capable of accommodating landing craft up to two hundred feet in length if they don't object to going on the mud now and then, but after Bucklers Hard it becomes very shallow at low water. At the entrance there are leading marks in from the Solent, and a row of disused coastguard cottages, and Lepe House, a timbered mansion overlooking the entrance to the river. From Lepe the river runs up westwards for a mile in a long reach between sea marshes, and then turns northwards inland till it comes to woods on either side that shroud fine houses of the wealthy. One of these was HMS *Mastodon*, and it came as a surprise to Janet Prentice and May Spikins when the truck deposited them there in June 1943.

They reported to the duty officer and were handed over to a Wren petty officer who took them to their quarters in a hut that was built on a tennis lawn. That evening the two girls wandered round with mixed feelings, bemoaning the fate that had landed them into a place where there was nothing operational going on and which was ten miles from the nearest movie. At the same time, they were forced to realize that the Navy had sent them to one of the most lovely country houses in England. It was a stone-built, fairly modern country house in the grand style, with a flagstaff flying a white ensign on the lawn in front of it. All afternoon the two girls wandered up and down woodland paths between thickets of rhododendrons in bloom, each with a label, with water piped underneath each woodland path projecting in stopcocks here and there for watering the specimens. They found streams and pools, with ferns and water lilies carefully preserved and tended. They found a rock garden half as large as Trafalgar Square that was a mass of bloom; they found cedars and smooth, grassy lawns. They found long ranges of greenhouses, and they learned with awe that the staff of gardeners had been reduced from fifty to a mere eighteen old men. And finally, wandering entranced through the carefully tended woods, they found the Beaulieu River running up between the trees, still tidal. The path ended at a private pier with a hut and a small dwelling house at the shore end. They walked out to the end of the pier and stood looking up and down the broad river at the running water. It was a quiet, sunny evening, very beautiful. Doves were calling in the woods, and seagulls drifted by upon the tide. A Naval motor cutter manned by two Wrens in jerseys and bell-bottomed trousers surged up the river from some errand and landed two RNVR officers at the pier.

'It's not a bit like the Fleet Air Arm,' said Janet thoughtfully. 'But it really is a lovely place.'

'All right if you never want to see a movie,' said May Spikins practically. 'And what about the ships? I thought we'd come to service Oerlikons, but I haven't seen a sign of one here.'

They soon discovered that there were only one or two LCTs in the river though more were expected before long; the Admiralty had been ahead of the game in providing Wrens to look after the guns. The Ordnance officer was busy with the erection of a new hut down by the pier which was to serve as their workshop. He was an earnest, competent young RNVR officer who had been wounded in the raid upon Dieppe a year before; he had a petty officer that he could use on the construction of the workshop, but the two Wrens were frankly an embarrassment to him at that time, and he told them so. 'Look, you girls,' he said. 'I haven't got a job for you, and I shan't have for the next six weeks. I've fixed things to attach you to the boat's crews for the time being, so that you can go about with them and learn the river and the layout of the moorings so that if you hear that a ship's down at No 16 buoy you'll know where to find her.'

That's a good mike for you, but you'll have plenty to do later on. If you give any trouble I shall send you back to store and indent for two more when the work comes along. If you don't behave yourselves you'll lose a darn good job.'

The next months were a sheer joy to Janet. She had hardly realized it, but her eighteen months with the Fleet Air Arm at Ford had been hard work; she was more tired than she knew. Here in this lovely place upon the Beaulieu River there was no war, and at first practically no work; if she had chosen to do so she could have spent most of that summer sitting in the sun in the rose garden reading poetry. Instead, she followed her directions and attached herself to Leading Wren Viola Dawson in the Naval cutter, with Sheila Cox and Doris Smith, and spent most of each day with them. When a new tank landing craft or LCS came in and moored in the river Viola Dawson would take the cutter alongside and put Janet on board, and leave her there for a couple of hours. She would report to the petty officer of the ship or to the No 1 and ask if there were any gun defects or ordnance stores deficiencies. There usually were, and she would spend an hour with one or two ratings dismantling the Oerlikon or recharging the drums, her hands in a wet slough of coopers' grease. She had a mechanical sense, and rust upon a gun was a physical hurt to her. 'Just look at that!' she would say severely to an abashed rating. 'If I find it like that again I'll bring the Ordnance officer to see your captain. No, I'm not kidding. I will. I've never seen a gun in such a bloody muck in all my life.' To the young captain of the ship she would say, 'I see you've only got stowage for two drums in the RU lockers, sir – all the other Mark 4s seem to have stowage for six. I'll report on that for you to Mr Parkes. I think we might be able to find you four more drums, but the stowage is a dockyard job. Oh, and I've been over the port gun with Jones – it's getting a bit rusty.' Invariably she would stay for a cup of tea either in the wardroom with the officers or in the mess deck with the men. Then the cutter would come alongside for her and she would get back to the pier and tell her officer that LCT 2306 was short of four drums and the stowage for them, and worry around the naval system till she found somebody who would do something about it.

Throughout the autumn and the winter activity increased in the Beaulieu area, and with it came mysteries. Lepe House, the mansion at the entrance to the river, was taken over by the Navy and became full of very secretive Naval officers; it became known that this was part of a mysterious Navel entity called *Force J*. Near Lepe House and at the very mouth of the river a construction gang began work in full strength to make a hard, sloping concrete platform running down into the water where the flat-bottomed landing craft could beach to refuel and let their ramps down to embark the vehicles or tanks. This place was about two miles from *Mastodon*. A mile or so along the coast a country house was occupied by a secret Naval party who did strange things with tugs and wires and winches, and with what looked like a gigantic reel of cotton floating in the sea; this was 'Pluto', Pipe Line Under The Ocean, which was to lay pipes from England to France to carry petrol to supply the armies which were due to land in Normandy. On a bare beach nearby a thousand navvies were camped making huge con-crete structures known as 'Phoenix', one of many such sites all along the coast. It was not till after the invasion that it became known that these were a part of the artificial har-bour 'Mulberry' on the north coast of France.

Inland it was the same. Every wood was littered with dumps of shells and ammunition in little corrugated iron shelters, thousands and thousands of them spaced at regular intervals. There were radar stations upon Beaulieu Common and Bofors guns at Bucklers Hard; there was radio every-where, the slim antennae pointing up from hedges, from haystacks, and from trucks. Over the whole countryside as winter merged into spring there was continuously the roar of aircraft, symbol of modern military power.

About the middle of March Janet was waiting on the pier one morning for a boat to take her down the river to an LCS for a routine visit. Sheila Cox and Doris Smith were there with her, but Viola Dawson, the coxswain, was still up at the office at *Mastodon* getting her instructions for the day's work. The girls sat in a row on the edge of the pier dangling their legs over the water, talking about Cary Grant and next week's dance.

Viola Dawson came running down the path through to the pier, most unusually; the girls got to their feet in surprise. The Coxswain panted, 'We're taking the LCP – there's been an accident and it's a beaching job. Get her started up quick. We've got to pick a party up at Needs Oar Point.'

They were away at full speed down the river in a couple of minutes, Janet with them to be dropped on her LCS as they passed. As they went Viola, seated at the wheel and recovering her breath, told them what she knew. While she had been in the office several small radio transmitters in the area had burst into life, and in half a minute everyone concerned was in action. There had been an accident to a tank upon a beach near Newtown in the Isle of Wight, and the tank was under water. Some of the crew were trapped in it, and probably drowned. The party that they were to pick up at Needs Oar Point was some sort of a salvage crew of Royal Marines.

There were points of mystery about this story. Doris Smith asked, 'How did a tank get under water?'

'I don't know.'

Sheila asked, 'What sort of a salvage party is it? There's nothing down at Needs Oar Point, is there?'

'I don't know that either. The orders were to get down there as quick as possible and embark this party, and take orders from them.'

Needs Oar Point marks a bend in the Beaulieu River a mile from the entrance, a windy, barren place of flat pastures and sea marshes. When they got there they saw a Naval truck at the end of a track leading to the river and three young Marines waiting for them, a captain and two sergeants. Their arms were full of strange equipment, waterproof suits and queer packs holding metal cylinders. The landing was difficult; Viola ran the sloping prow of the LCP gingerly up over the sea marsh and the young men scrambled muddily on board over the bow. She backed off with some difficulty. The officer said, 'You know where to go?'

'No, sir.'

'You know Newtown? Well, half a mile east of the entrance. Open all the taps you've got. If we're quick enough there's just a chance we might get some of them out.' He swung round to his sergeants. 'Get that walkie-talkie going and let's know the form.'

Viola said, 'Can I go alongside the LCS to drop this Wren, sir? She's Ordnance. She's got a job to do on board it.'

'No, go flat out for Newtown. Drop her on your way back.' He went aft past the canopy to his men in the stern behind the engine. Presently he took the walkie-talkie from the sergeants and began talking and listening in turn. The two sergeants started to undress. The officer diverted his attention for a moment. 'You girls, keep your eyes forward,' he said.

When after a quarter of an hour they looked aft again the two sergeants were standing dressed in tight-fitting light rubber suits with rubber helmets tight around their faces, with goggles pushed up on their foreheads. Janet had heard incautious talk about frogmen but she had never seen one before, and she had no idea that there were any in her district. The officer came forward to the wheel, where Viola was steering. 'This is the form, Coxswain,' he said. 'An LCT was landing a Sherman tank upon the beach. You know how they do it? The ship goes in and grounds with the bow in about four feet of water and lets down her ramp; the tank goes down the ramp and wades through the water to the beach. Well, there's a hole in the beach or something, and the tank went right under. They say its turret is just awash. Everyone got out of it except the driver, and he's in it still. They've been trying to tow the tank out with another tank, but it's in gear and they can't shift it. They've been trying to get down inside to get the driver out, but his body is across the gear lever and caught up in some way. He's in there still.'

Viola asked, 'When did this happen, sir?'

'Ten-fifty.'

She glanced at her wrist watch; it was then eleven twenty-five, and they were still about two miles off, though behind her the engine was roaring at full throttle and they were doing about fifteen knots. 'He'll be dead, won't he?'

'Not necessarily. Now look, I want you to do this. The tide will be running to the westward. Go to the tank and land these two chaps on its turret. Approach it from the lee side, that's from the west, and go right up to it. Make fast to the turret if you can, but if there's nothing you can get a rope on to, hold your position with the turret just under your bow. Got that clear?'

'Aye, aye, sir.'

He went aft to his men. Janet came to Viola. 'What do you want me to do?'

The Coxswain said, 'Give the Marines a hand if they want it. I'll need Sheila and Doris for the boat.'

They were close now to the shore. The LCT, relieved of the weight of the tank, had floated off the beach and backed away, and was now lying a little way out anchored by the stern. Halfway between the ship and the sand they saw a small disturbance in the surface of the water which was the turret of the tank awash, its thin wireless aerial sticking up on high. There was another tank standing on the beach, and a number of soldiers, some in battledress and some stripped naked and wet. Viola turned the LCP and went straight for the tank, and throttled back, and felt her way to it gently in the last few yards with the turret on her port hand till the open hatch was right beside her wheel and the bow of the LCP had grounded on the gun barrel; she held the craft there with a little engine. It was a delicate and skilful bit of sea-manship.

The two frogmen were over the side in an instant, masks and goggles covering their faces and air bottles on their chests. One of them wormed his way down through the hatch, twisting his body to right and left to clear the apparatus on his chest and helped by his comrade, who stayed waist-deep upon the flooded tank peering down into the turret. Presently he reached right down, head under water, and then the overalled body of the corporal driver appeared, pulled by the man on top and pushed up from below by the man inside the tank under the water. The Marine captain in his battledress got over the side on to the tank, and working waist-deep in the water with the top frogman manoeuvred the body of the driver to the LCP. Janet and Sheila Cox took him as the men passed him up to them and pulled him up on to the flat foredeck of the landing craft, and Janet rolled him over on to his face and began the motions she had learned at school for artificial respiration. He was a young man with a small moustache, in overalls, his face blueish white in colour, dead cold to the touch.

The three Marines climbed on board again, helped by the other girls. The one who had gone down inside the tank said, 'I put her in neutral, sir'. He seemed to Janet to speak with a slight accent, possibly cockney, but she paid little attention to that at the time.

They stood dripping on the side deck holding on to the canopy rail, watching Janet as she worked rhythmically on the body. One of them said presently, 'Dead, isn't he?'

She looked up. 'I think he must be. Does anybody know how to do this? Am I doing it right?'

The officer said, 'I think so. Go on as you're doing. Coxswain, take us in to the beach and we'll get him ashore.'

Viola Dawson said, 'I may not be able to get off again if I go in there, sir. The tide's falling pretty fast.' She meant that if she stayed on the sand more than a minute or two the LCP would be stranded and must wait for the next tide to float her off again.

'Go on in,' he said. 'I'll make that right for you. They've got transport there, and there's just a chance a doctor may be able to do something for this chap.'

They went in, and the landing craft grounded some distance from the water's edge. An Army lieutenant in battledress waded out to them and they pulled him in over the bow. Janet said, 'Somebody else take a turn at this. I'm not doing any good.'

The Lieutenant hesitated and then knelt down and took over the attempt at artificial respiration; a couple more men climbed up over the bow. Janet got up, only anxious to get away from the dead man she had been handling. She went aft to the stern, where she came upon the two Marine sergeants naked to the waist, scrambling awkwardly out of their rubber suits.

She said, 'Oh, sorry'. And then she said, 'Have either of you got a cigarette?' She was very glad to be free of the chill deadness of the body on the foredeck, and to be with live young men.

One of the sergeants, the fair-haired boy with the slight

accent, said, 'I've got some here'. He turned over his clothes and searched the pockets of his battledress, and passed up a packet and a box of matches to her as she sat upon the canopy.

She took them from him. 'Thanks awfully. Go ahead – I won't look.' She lit a cigarette from the packet with fingers that trembled a little, and blew a long cloud, and relaxed.

From the stern below her, where the men were dressing, the fair-haired young man said, 'Dead, isn't he?'

'I should think so,' she replied, without looking down at the speaker. 'There wasn't a sign of anything.'

The young man said, 'Well, he was under water the best part of fifty minutes. There's no future in that.'

She sat in the warm sun smoking, looking out over the blue sea of the Solent; on the flat bow of the LCP men in khaki were still labouring over the body of the driver. It was a warm day for March with all the promise of summer, the sort of day when the beach should have been associated with bathers, and small boats, and children making sand-castles and paddling, instead of with waterlogged Sherman tanks, soaked uniforms, and dead men. An LST, the first she had seen, came in by the Needles passage and made its way up towards Southampton; she watched it with interest as it passed. A flight of Spitfires passed overhead on their way to France. Three MLs in line ahead went by, and a couple of motor minesweepers.

The fair-haired sergeant stood up by her in shirt and trousers and helped himself to one of his own cigarettes. He seemed to her a clean, good-looking boy – which, of course, Bill was. He glanced towards the bow. 'Not doing any good, are they?'

'I don't think so.' She hesitated, and looked down at him. 'Was I doing it right? I've never had to do it in earnest before.'

Bill said, 'You were doing it all right. He was under water for the thick end of an hour. Ten minutes – well, you might have got him back. But an hour's different. You did all that anyone could do.'

He looked over to the LCT; she was weighing anchor to get away before the falling tide left her stranded, too. She still had three tanks on board; apparently the exercise was cancelled. 'They ought to survey the beach before these practices,' he said. 'It only needs a chap to wade ashore ahead of the tanks, that's all. If he has to swim for it the beach is crook.'

She wondered a little at the word, but each Service at that time had its own slang; to her the Army were all Pongoes. 'Couldn't do that operationally,' the other sergeant said. 'Not with Jerry on the beach.'

The Marine officer came aft to them. 'Well, we're here till six o'clock, the Coxswain says.' Already the LCP was high out of the water on the beach; in another quarter of an hour they would be able to get off her dryshod. He picked up the walkie-talkie and got communication with some station on the other side of the Solent, and told them to telephone a message to *Mastodon*.

Presently they were able to climb down from the deck of the LCP on to the wet sand. They stood talking with the soldiers about the accident while the tide went down still further till the tank lay half submerged in a long pool of sea water on the beach. 'There's been another LCT there,' said the officer. 'That's where she used her engines, getting off. That's the wash from her propellers did that, scoured away the sand and left that hole . . .'

Dinner was arranged for the Marines and Wrens by the Army at a gun station on the cliff half a mile away; Janet and Bill walked up together and had dinner in a mess tent after the Bofors crews had finished. 'Where are you stationed?' she inquired. 'I didn't know about your party.'

'We're at Cliffe Farm,' he said. 'About two miles west-wards down the coast from where you picked us up today. I was over at your place the week before last, but I didn't see you.'

She said, 'I was probably down the river.'

They lunched sitting side by side in the mess tent, a heavy, badly served meal of stew and jam roll. After lunch they all strolled down again to the beach. The LCP lay high and dry, far from the sea. An ambulance stood at the cliff top and medical orderlies were loading a stretcher covered with a blanket into it. 'What's your name?' asked the sergeant.

She told him. 'What's yours?'

'Bill Duncan,' he said. He indicated the other sergeant. 'He's Bert Finch.'

She asked, 'Do you live in London?'

'He does, but I don't. I'm Australian. Did you think I was a Londoner?'

She was confused, not wanting to be rude. 'I don't know why I thought that.'

'It's the way I talk,' he said. 'Back at home people would say I hadn't got any Australian accent, but they know it all right here.'

She was intrigued. 'Have you been in England long?'

'I came over just before the war,' he said, 'after I left school. I was at Geelong Grammar.' The Eton of Australia meant nothing to her. 'I was doing a course of agriculture when the war broke out. We've got a farm at home.'

'What made you go into the Marines?' she asked.

'More fun than just the ordinary Army,' he replied. 'More special jobs, like this sort of thing.'

She knew too much about the Service to ask specifically what he did when he wasn't pulling drowned men out of tanks. Instead, she said, 'You volunteered for this?'

He grinned at her. 'I always did like swimming.'

They walked across the beach together to inspect the tank; it lay in the middle of a long pool in the sand with the tops of the tracks just showing. Presently there was a clatter of tank tracks on the cliff and a 'priest' appeared, a Sherman chassis mounting a gun-howitzer. It nosed delicately down a very steep slope to the beach, loaded with men and steel ropes. The soldiers coupled the wires to the towing eyes on the sunk tank; the 'priest' went ahead and towed the Sherman from the pool above high-water mark. It made an attempt to tow the Sherman up the cliff but the incline defeated it; the men uncoupled the wires and the 'priest' struggled up the cliff alone and made off.

Bill stayed with Janet all the afternoon and she was glad to have him; she found him an unassuming young man, easy for her to talk to. She admired him a little, too, for the instant courage that had sent him down into the interior of the flooded tank. He told her that he had never been inside a tank of any sort before, and it had been rather dark, but he had managed to find his way around all right. She had once been inside a tank, stationary, in broad daylight on dry land, and she knew a little bit about the contortions that you had to make to move about in them. She felt that his effort for the drowned man had been a good show, and she told him so.

They strolled up to the AA site again and got the cooks to give them cups of tea; then they went down and sat smoking and chatting in the LCP while the tide rose around them. Soon after six she floated off, and Viola turned the boat and headed her for the Beaulieu River.

They turned in to the long entrance reach between the sea marshes in the cold dusk of the March night. At Needs Oar Point the truck was waiting for the Marines; as they approached the mud flats Janet said, 'We've got a dance on Saturday. Why don't you two come over?'

That's how it all began.

FOUR

I SAT there by the fire in my room at Coombargana fingering the photographs, lost in memories. I sat there in the still night thinking how different everything would have been if Bill hadn't been killed. He would have come back to Coombargana directly the war was over, and almost certainly he would have brought Janet Prentice with him. They would have made a good pair to run the property after my parents' time. Bill was never very keen on going to England; I think he only went to Cirencester for his course of agriculture because it was the thing to do, because it is fashionable for young people in my country to reach out for wider experience than they can get at home. He would have been happy to return and make his life at Coombargana, and I think he would have made a better grazier than I.

Janet would have come to Coombargana as its mistress-to-be, not as its house parlourmaid. Presently I would have to violate her privacy further to find out why she had come at all. The answer to that one lay almost certainly within the case upon the table by my side, amongst her private papers that I was reluctant to explore. I could stall a little longer, sit a little longer by the fire thinking of the girl that I already knew so much about.

It was probably true that I knew more about her than I would ever have learned if she had come to live at Coombargana as Bill's wife, living with him in my parents' old room just along the corridor from mine. If it had turned out that way I might have gone back to England in 1948 to take my degree at Oxford, as in fact I did, but I wouldn't have gone back to look for Janet Prentice. I would never have met or talked with Warrant Officer Finch at Eastney Barracks or with CPO Waters in the Fratton Road, and I would never have met May Cunningham or Viola Dawson.

I knew so much about her, most of it from hearsay, and I

had packed all that knowledge away for good, as I thought, only a few days before, sitting in my bedroom in the St Francis Hotel. I had packed all that knowledge away as in a trunk, and put it in a lumber room out of my life, and now the trunk had burst open before me when I least expected it, spilling all that knowledge and those memories into my life again. The memories, of course, concerned the one day only, the day that we had spent together in the boat before the balloon went up. That day remained etched sharp in my memory; ten years later I still knew exactly how she moved and spoke and thought about things, so that it gave life to all the knowledge I had gleaned about her from these other people.

Bill had got rather English in the five years he had been away from home, I think, or perhaps he had been lonely. At home I don't think he would have made a pet of a mongrel dog like Dev, short for de Valera. Dev was an Irish terrier by courtesy that had strayed into their camp one day, probably about two years old, probably a part of some military or naval unit that had moved away. He had adopted Bill and Bill had adopted him and made a pet of him, and now he was adopting Janet, too. At home Dev might have been a candidate for the rabbit pack; he would certainly never have been allowed inside the house. I doubt if he'd have made the grade for the rabbit pack, though. He wasn't fierce enough; he was one of those bumbling, good-humoured, rather incompetent dogs, good for a lonely man or girl to look after.

They had Dev in the boat with them that day when we went round from Lymington to Keyhaven, sitting up in the bow looking out forward, ears pricked, obviously enjoying his trip. 'I think he's a love child from an unsatisfactory family,' Janet said, explaining him to me. 'He's such a fool you can't help liking him.'

When we reached the entrance to the Lymington River she turned the boat to the west and we began to skirt the marshes on the north shore of the Solent. The sea was rough outside, but moving along close inshore we were in calm water. 'We'll keep fairly close in because of your uniform,' she said. 'Keep a look-out for snags or stumps or anything sticking up out of the mud. I'll get in a fearful row if I knock a hole in this boat on a trip like this. It's not as if I were a boat's crew Wren, even.'

Bill and I stood up and watched the water ahead. I asked, 'How did you manage to get hold of a boat at all?'

She grinned. 'I've been here long enough to know the ropes. As a matter of fact, they're not very fussy on Sundays when the boats aren't being used.'

We had great luck with the weather, for it was a warm, sunny day. We skirted along the mud flats for the best part of an hour under the lee of the long spit that terminates in Hurst Castle, and then turned in to the next river to the west of Lymington, which led to Keyhaven. We went up between the mud flats till we came to a tumbledown jetty at the end of a track across a meadow; Janet brought the boat along-side this and we made her fast, and went ashore. We had brought lunch with us from the hotel and three bottles of beer, and on shore we settled down to lunch and talk and smoke, lazing upon the short grass in the sun not far from the boat, looking out over the Solent. It was so seldom in the war that I had had the chance of a day like that.

As we ate she said curiously, 'Bill told me you were at Oxford before the war.'

I nodded. 'I was at the House.'

'Were you really? What were you reading?'

'Law,' I said. 'You live in Oxford, don't you?'

She nodded. 'My father's a don at Wyckham. We live in Crick Road.'

'I know Crick Road,' I said. 'It's a nice part.'

'I've lived there all my life,' she said. 'What made you come to Oxford? Can't you do Law in Australia?'

'I did a little Law at Melbourne University,' I told her. 'I'm an old, old man. I don't know why I came to Oxford, except that I wanted to. I got a Rhodes scholarship, and it seemed a waste not to use it.'

She opened her eyes, for this meant something to her. 'You're a Rhodes scholar?'

'Yes,' I said. 'It was a bad year for the selectors.'

'Did you go into the Air Force when the war broke out?'

'I was in it before, in a way,' I said. 'I was in the University Air Squadron.'

'Bill said you were in the Battle of Britain.'

'I suppose you'd call it that,' I said. 'I did two operational tours on fighters, the first at Thorney Island and the second in the Western Desert. I did a bit of instructing in between. After the second one they sent me up to Fighter Command.'

'Do you like it there?'

I shook my head. 'I want to be operational again. My present job comes to an end when the balloon goes up. I'll put in for an operational posting then.'

She said, 'Will they give you a wing?'

I laughed. 'A wing commander doesn't get a wing, and I'm only acting, anyway. I'll have to drop a rank. Lucky if I get a flight to command.'

She said in wonder, 'It's a bit hard to have to come down in rank. Does it make a lot of difference in the pay?'

'A bit,' I said. 'But I've had the office.'

'Are you going back to Oxford after the war?'

'I don't know. I think I'd like to go back for a bit and take a degree. They had a sort of shortened course for Service people after the First War.'

'Wouldn't you find it awfully slow, going back to school, after all this?'

'I'd like to finish off what I began,' I said. 'One doesn't like to leave a loose end hanging out.' I glanced at her. 'What will you do?'

'I was going to try and go to Lady Margaret Hall,' she said. 'I don't know if I'd have got in. I can't see myself getting in there now. I don't know what I'll do. I haven't thought about it.'

Bill laughed. 'We'll all get bumped off when the balloon goes up,' he said. 'Then it'll be decided for us.'

A new sort of landing craft came down the Solent. I forget what it was; it wouldn't have meant much to me anyway, but it was of great interest to Janet and to Bill. They began to talk about it, and about other sorts of ship that were novel to the invasion, and I had leisure to lie quietly on the grass in the warm sun and study her. I wanted to do that because it was pretty clear to me that this girl was to be my sister-in-law. True, they didn't appear to be engaged and she wore no ring, but from the way she talked to him and the way he looked at her it was clear that they were very much in love. When the balloon had gone up and they had more time for personal affairs they would almost certainly become engaged, and they might marry before the war was over. I thought of that one and approved the idea. Bill was tired and strained with the exacting work he had been doing, and a long engagement could only mean an added strain. I had seen some of that in the RAF and I had become fanatically opposed to long engagements in wartime. If they were going to marry, let them marry and have done with it.

When they became engaged or married my mother would want to know what the girl was like. She could not come twelve thousand miles from Australia in time of war to meet Bill's girl, nor could she leave the property even if travel had been possible. She would want my assurance that this girl would make Bill a good wife, and studying her quietly as she talked to Bill I felt that I could make my mother happy on that score. She wasn't a good-looker. Her face was too square and homely, her shoulders too broad; her short, dark hair had little wave though there were pretty dark-brown lights in it. I could assure my mother, anyway, that Bill hadn't fallen for a glamour girl.

I tried to visualize her as the mistress of Coombargana in the future, to speculate on how she would be able to adapt herself to the Western District. She had strength of character and a directness of speech that would make her good with the men; she would be able to control the station hands all right when Bill was away. She was a good shot with a gun, which would help her prestige a little. She probably couldn't ride a horse, but she was young and quite capable of learning to ride. In any case, that wasn't so important as it used to be in the old days. She was very practical; which was the important thing, and she was fond of dogs. She might well become really interested in the cattle and the sheep, and in the conduct of the work on our big property.

On the social side, she was probably adequate. She would never be much interested in any social functions, perhaps never dress very well, never take much pleasure in the organization of charity balls or Red Cross garden parties. Her interests would probably lie more in the home; she might become a typical homestead wife. She would always be a pleasant hostess to visitors to Coombargana but she would never want to give great entertainments there, unless she changed very much. She was much more likely to develop an interest in Australia itself, and to want to travel widely over our vast country. She might want to keep a seagoing motor yacht or something of that sort, and if so Coombargana could afford it.

My report on Janet Prentice to my mother would be wholly good. She was not the sort of girl my mother would have visualized or expected as a daughter-in-law, but I was confident that she would grow to like her and to appreciate her very solid virtues. She would make a good mistress of Coombargana in the future, and a good wife to Bill, and lying there upon the grass at Keyhaven that day I thought he was a very lucky man.

I listened unashamedly while she talked to Bill, half oblivious of my presence. The dog, Dev, had laid his head upon her knee as she sat upon the grass, in sentimental affection, and she was fondling his ears. 'You're very lucky to be able to keep a dog,' she said to Bill. 'I wish we could.'

'Can't you?'

'I don't know. I don't think anyone has tried. I don't believe the Captain would allow a dog in *Mastodon*. Everyone would want to have one if he did.'

Bill nodded. 'We wouldn't be allowed dogs if we weren't in such a lonely place. I don't know what'll happen to him when we get moved on.'

'Are you likely to be shifted soon?'

'I don't think so,' he said. 'We seem to be able to do everything by going off on a party from here. We'll get moved on some day, of course.' There was no permanency in the Services. He looked down thoughtfully at Dev. 'I don't know that it's really a good idea letting us have dogs,' he said thoughtfully. 'You get too fond of a dog, and then you're in trouble when you get moved to a place where you can't have one.'

'You can't send him home, of course,' she said. 'Not to Australia. Haven't you got any relations in England you could send him to?'

He shook his head. 'No one like that.'

She said, comforting, 'If you're stuck I might be able to get Mummy to have him.'

'Difficult, with the rationing,' he replied.

'I know. If Daddy's home I think he might quite like to have him, though. It's worth trying, if you get in a real jam.'

'I thought your father was in Oxford all the time,' he remarked.

She turned to him, fresh and animated. 'Oh, I forgot – I haven't told you. There was a letter waiting when I got back on board last night. Daddy's probably going on the party.'

He stared at her. 'Not this party?'

'This party,' she told him, laughing. 'He's gatecrashed it. When the balloon goes up, Daddy goes too.'

'Over to the other side?' he asked incredulously.

'Over to the other side,' she said. 'At least, he's put in to go. He doesn't know yet if they'll have him.'

'But what's he going as?'

'Aircraft identifier in a merchant ship,' she told him. 'They're putting one or two people from the Observer Corps in every merchant ship to stop the DEMS gunners firing on our own aircraft. They've asked for volunteers and Daddy's put in for it.'

'But how old is he?'

'About sixty-three, I think,' she said. 'He seems to think that doesn't matter. I think it's the funniest thing ever.'

Bill turned to me. 'Have you heard anything about this, Alan?'

As a matter of fact, I knew quite a lot about it, for some of the papers concerning it had passed across my desk. So many cases of our fighters being fired upon by friendly ships had occurred that we had stuck our heels in, and demanded better aircraft identification before we laid on close support over the beaches by our fighters flying low over a thousand ships. I rather think that the suggestion to put members of the Royal Observer Corps into the merchant ships had come from us. 'I did hear something vaguely,' I admitted.

'It's a good show,' said Bill. 'A good show for a man of sixty-three.'

'I think it's the limit,' the girl laughed. 'Here I've been in the Wrens three years but no one ever asked me if I'd like to go to the party. Daddy comes along at the last minute and walks right in.'

'Are any Wrens going?' I asked.

She shook her head. 'I haven't heard of any. They won't let us do anything operational, or anything that means living in a ship. We're all shore-based.'

I asked her what she did in the Navy and she told me, answering my questions with the candour born of competence in her job. 'It's quite good fun, and closer to operations than most of the jobs we get,' she said. 'Not so good as being a boat's crew Wren, but better than being a steward or a cook. It's a bit of a mike at times, but when you get a dud gun changed in a ship you feel you've done a bit to help.'

Bill asked, 'Do you get a lot of trouble with the Oerlikons?'

She shook her head. 'Not much, and then it's mostly through bad maintenance. Last week an LCT came in and the captain said his port gun jammed its breech block solid after twenty rounds and they had to wait half an hour till it cooled down before they could free it. It did, too. I cleaned it down and went out to the Needles in the ship and fired it myself, and it was just like they said. The tolerances were wrong or something. It was one of the first ones they made in England. They'd put in several reports about it and nobody believed it wasn't just that they'd let it get rusty. They've got a new one now.'

We went on chatting about Service matters most of the afternoon, sitting there upon the grass at Keyhaven. I had arranged with the WAAF driver of the car to pick me up at the hotel in Lymington at six o'clock for I was dining at the aerodrome that night with a couple of group captains and a colonel in the USAAF and going through the papers in my briefcase with them after dinner. By four o'clock we had to make a move. We rounded up Dev from some rabbit holes among the gorse bushes, mud all over his nose, and got him into the boat, and cast off from the little jetty, and made our way down to open water and along the mud flats to the Lymington River and so back to the quay.

I said goodbye to Janet Prentice then, because she had to take the boat back up the river before meeting Bill again to spend the evening with him. I shook hands with her in the boat before getting out. 'It's been a grand day,' I said. 'The best I've had for years. Thanks so much for the boat, and everything.'

'Boats are meant to be used,' she laughed. 'Especially on Sundays. Goodbye, sir. Don't go and prang yourself on the way back to London.'

'I take that as an insult,' I said laughing. The 'sir' to my uniform hurt a little, but after all she was Bill's girl, not mine. 'Goodbye, Janet.'

She sheered off from the quay and went away up river through the bridge, with Dev still with her in the boat, standing up in the bow and looking forwards. Bill and I watched till she was out of sight, and then turned up the long hill of the main street to the hotel. 'Well,' he asked presently. 'What do you think?'

'I think you're bloody lucky,' I told him.

'So do I,' he said. 'It's not in the bag yet, though.'

'You've not said anything to her?'

'She knows, all right,' he said. 'We've fixed to go on leave together after the balloon goes up, and sort things out then. We've both got too much on our plates just now to think about the future.' He grinned. 'Maybe there won't be a future. If there is, we're going off on leave together somewhere. That's the way it stands.'

'Sounds all right to me,' I said.

He glanced at me. 'Think there'll be an uproar at home?'

I shook my head. 'There'll be no uproar,' I told him. 'She'll go down all right.'

He nodded. 'I think so, too.' He hesitated. 'You won't say anything about this in your letters? I haven't said a word about it yet, and I shan't, not till it's all buttoned up.'

'I won't say anything,' I told him. 'Let me know when you put out a communiqué, and then I'll write to Mum and say she's okay.'

'That's good of you,' he said gratefully. 'That 'ld help a lot. I want her to start off on the right foot with Mum.'

My RAF car was waiting outside the hotel when we got there, with the WAAF driver sitting in it. I said goodbye to Bill on the pavement. 'I don't know when we'll meet again,' I said. 'I shan't be able to take another day off till the balloon's gone up. Some time after that, I should say.'

He grinned. 'Some time after that I'm going on leave.'

'All right,' I laughed. 'I won't come and peep through the keyhole.'

On that note we ended, and he went off down the hill to meet his Janet at the boatyard and to spend the evening with her. I stood watching him till he was out of sight, while my WAAF driver waited for me.

I can see him now.

I think it was only a few days after that that the Ju 188 came over Beaulieu. Viola Dawson told me a good bit about that when we met in 1950, and May Cunningham, then May Spikins, told me about it, too, when I had tea with her at Harlow. After that I got in touch with Tom Ballantyne, who had been with me in Fighter Command, and who in 1951 was a group captain doing a term at the Air Ministry. He was very helpful and put someone on to dig into the records, and found the accident report, and showed it to me in his office.

What happened was this. On a Saturday morning at the very end of April the Ordnance officer at *Mastodon* sent Janet down the river with four Sten guns and four boxes of ammunition for the LCTs. It had been suggested that after the first landing in Normandy the Germans might counter-attack and re-take a beach while the tank landing craft were stranded, and it was thought that the ships ought to have some more adequate weapons on board for close-range fighting than revolvers. Sten guns were in good supply, and these were being issued for the first time to the officers of the ships.

Each ship was to get one gun and one case of ammunition. The LCTs were lying in pairs all down the river, moored bow and stern to buoys, and half their crews had gone off on weekend leave. Viola Dawson took Janet down the river in the LCP to where the ships were lying near Needs Oar Point surrounded by the open marshes of the estuary and went alongside LCT 968. The captain came to the rail; he was an RNVR lieutenant called Craigie. From the boat Janet said, 'Good morning, sir. I've got a Sten gun here for you, and one for each of 538, 946, and 702.'

'Morning, Janet,' he said. '702 is lying alongside us here. Pass up a couple of them. Wait, I'll get a chap to help you.' A rating came down into the boat and they passed the guns and the heavy ammunition boxes up into the tank landing craft. Janet swung herself on board after them. They passed one gun and one box of ammunition across on to the next ship, whose captain was on leave. A sub-lieutenant met Janet at the rail. She knew how to deal with hesitant and incompetent-looking young officers. 'I've got to get a signature for these,' she said. She pulled a pink form from a trouser pocket. 'Just sign it there. It only means that you've received them in good condition. Put the number of your ship there, and the date *there*, sir, and sign it at the bottom, *there*.' The sub took the form from her and went off to the wardroom to find his pen.

Janet turned to Lieutenant Craigie beside her. 'I'm sorry we could only let you have one, sir.'

'Every little helps,' he said. 'You might let me know if there's a chance of getting another.'

'I will indeed,' she said. The sense of impending battle was very heavy on her; it would be intolerable if any serviceable weapons should remain in her store when the balloon went up. 'We should be getting a lot more in a few days.'

There was a sound of firing from the Isle of Wight, between Newtown and Yarmouth. Craigie turned to look, and Janet turned with him. There was an aircraft there, quite low down, flying more or less towards them, at eleven o'clock in the morning of a bright spring day. And there were little puffs of smoke in the blue sky all round it.

For a moment they stood staring, unable to believe the evidence of their eyes. It was many months since the Germans had done anything like that. Then Craigie shouted, 'Enemy aircraft over! Anti-aircraft stations!' and men came tumbling out on deck.

On the LCT beside them the sub and several ratings came out and looked with interest at the coming aeroplane; it was not more than a thousand feet up. Janet, furious at their slowness, said, 'That's a German. Better man those Oerlikons.'

The sub looked at her helplessly. 'Can't. Both gunners are on leave.'

The girl said, 'My bloody Christ!' and slipped over the rail on to the other ship. Behind her Craigie roared, 'Okay Janet – you take the port gun and I'll take the starboard!' The inner guns of both ships were practically useless, their field of fire blanked off by the other ship. 'You – Jamieson! Get the RU lockers open and pass out the drums! What the hell are you standing there for – don't you know the drill? And where are your tin hats?'

At the gun Janet pulled the cocking lever and slipped the heavy drum in place with quick, experienced hands; she released the securing catch and put her shoulders in the hoops. Behind her someone strained the strap across her back. She swung the gun at the approaching aircraft but it was turning away. It was two thousand yards from her and broadside on now, a hopeless shot. She stood watching it in disappointment, and called across to Craigie, 'Everything all right on your side, sir?'

He called back to her, 'All okay here, but I'm afraid we've lost him'. The aircraft was flying westwards over the middle of the Solent now, a heavy, black, twin-engined thing; they could see the white cross upon the fuselage. One or two ships were firing at it at long range, and a Bofors from a cliff top to the east of Yarmouth, but it was momentarily out of range of most guns in the district.

She called across, 'What sort is it?'

Craigie replied, 'A Junkers 188'.

'What's he up to?'

'Making a survey, I suppose. Photographing everything he can. He's got a bloody nerve.'

The aircraft began turning towards the north. It went on turning, and now it was flying more or less towards them from the south-west. From behind her Craigie called, 'I shall be blanked out by monkey's island in a minute. It's all yours, Janet.'

The Junkers was not more than a thousand feet up now and coming straight towards them, a beautiful, copybook example of a sitting shot. She had it fixed below the centre of her sight exactly as she wanted it; she swung her body slowly, waiting for it, savouring the moment. It was impossible that she could miss; she felt too confident. She pressed the grip and opened fire, and the gun started beating rhythmically, and the smoke of cordite and burnt grease was all around her. She swung her body down slowly till she was crouching almost on her knees, holding it exactly as it should be in the sight.

As she fired the wheels came down; she knew that something had happened but it meant nothing to her. She went on firing and the glass and perspex nose of the cabin shattered, and three bright stars appeared inside the cabin quickly in succession. It reared up suddenly and passed right over the LCTs in a steep climb towards *Mastodon*; she scrambled round with the gun to get it on a reverse bearing, but now her own ship blanked her fire. She swung her body to the side to look round the obstruction and saw it again. A Bofors from the shore opened up on it as it passed from the river marshes over land, it stalled with full power on and fell into a dive, and as it fell the Bofors blew its fin off. It plunged steeply into a field near the marshes and crashed with a great thud, and a whoof, and a towering pillar of flame, and a huge cloud of black smoke. Janet stood trembling in the harness of the Oerlikon, appalled at the sight.

Around her men were clamouring and shouting; she stood bewildered while they unfastened the back strap for her. It was incredible that this had happened because of what she did. By her side Craigie cried, 'Good show, Janet! I bet you're the only Wren who's ever done that!' A rating said, 'That's bloody right, sir.'

She said stupidly, 'Did I do it? Wasn't it anybody else firing?'

'Of course you did. My gun was blanked off by the bridge. You got three direct hits in the pilot's cockpit. It was marvellous shooting.'

'Four hits, sir,' said the rating. 'She hit it four times. I saw 'um. Eh, ba goom, I never seen shooting to touch it.'

She became concerned about the cleaning of the gun that she had fired, both gunners being on leave; she told Craigie that she must get down to work at once and clean the gun. I think psychologists would call that a defence mechanism or something; her mind turned to the routine job rather than face the implications of what she had done. The officer called a gunner from his own ship and set him to work upon the Oerlikon; she left it reluctantly and went back on board his ship with him. Viola Dawson and Doris Smith were on deck to congratulate her; for a few minutes she moved about the deck amongst the men in a welter of praise. Craigie stood looking over to the fields in front of *Mastodon* where a little black smoke was still eddying up. 'I'm going on shore to have a look at it,' he said. 'Like to come, Janet?'

An awful fascination seized her; she would have to go. She said, 'Yes, please'.

He hesitated for a moment. 'You know what it's going to look like? Think you'd better come?'

'I'm all right, sir. I was in the Fleet Air Arm before I got drafted here. I know what a crash looks like.'

He was relieved. 'Oh well then – come along.'

They got down into the LCP. The tide was flowing, and Viola nosed the boat gingerly through a small channel in the marshes to a little disused jetty; from there they walked across the fields to the crash.

The Junkers had been pulling out of the dive when she hit the ground; she had not plunged straight in. She had hit first on a little mound covered in low bushes, and here one of her engines was lying. She had then cut a swathe through a hedge, across a lane, and through the other hedge. The wings had been torn from the fuselage here and had taken fire from the fuel in the tanks; what was left of the aircraft had spread itself all over the field in scraps of torn duralumin sheet. It bore no resemblance to an aeroplane at all.

A number of soldiers were already there; under the directions of an officer they were gathering up the bodies and laying them in a row under the hedge. All were dead, all very badly mutilated, and there seemed to be a great many of them. The subaltern had found two parachute packs relatively undamaged in the wreckage and he was fumbling with the unfamiliar fastenings to open them to get the silk out to lay over the bodies; evidently he had done this job before.

Craigie went up to him. 'Do you mind if we have a look? This Wren shot it down.'

'I wish to God she'd done it somewhere else,' the young man said testily. 'Look all you like, so far as I'm concerned. It's nothing whatever to do with me, but one can't just leave them lying in the field.'

Craigie asked, 'How many of them were there in it?'

'Seven.'

'Seven? I thought the Ju 188 had a crew of four.'

'So did I. Go and count them, if you like. They must have been jammed in, sitting on each other's knees. We've telephoned the RAF, but I don't suppose they'll be here for a bit yet.'

Craigie hesitated, and then, impelled by morbid curiosity, he walked over to the hedge to look at the bodies. Janet followed him. The bodies were poor, battered hulks of things that had once been men; all were either corporals or sergeants, dressed in the blue uniform of the Luftwaffe.

Janet had seen a good bit of this sort of thing before, and she was not particularly upset at the sight though a couple of glances were enough for her; she turned away. It was difficult for her to associate these grotesque, battered things with living men. It was sobering to think that she had killed them, but she had seen her own friends and acquaintances killed at Ford by Germans in air raids and reduced to bodies that looked just like that. She would rather that she had not had to fire the Oerlikon, rather that somebody else had had the job of doing this and not her, but she felt no particular sense of guilt.

She went back to the LCP with Craigie, and Viola Dawson took them back to the tank landing craft. Craigie drafted a long signal to be sent by Aldis lamp to the signal station at Lepe House and then to his commanding officer, with a copy for the Captain of *Mastodon* since Janet was involved. Janet went on with her job and finished distributing her Sten guns and then went back to *Mastodon* for dinner.

She was working in the Ordnance store after dinner when Third Officer Collins, her Wren officer, telephoned down to tell her to go back to her hut and put on her No 1s and then come to the office; the Captain wanted to see her. Twenty minutes later she was shown in to the Captain's office and stood to attention before his desk. There was an RAF officer, a flight-lieutenant, sitting beside him.

'Leading Wren Prentice,' said the RN officer. 'I understand that you shot down a German aeroplane this morning.'

'I shot at it and hit it, sir,' she said. 'Other people hit it too. I don't know if I was the one to shoot it down.'

'Lieutenant Craigie tells me that you hit it first,' he said. 'Tell me, why did you fire at it at all? It's not your job to fire at enemy aircraft. You're not part of an operational unit.'

She was taken aback. 'There were no gunners on 702, sir, and the sub wasn't doing anything about it. It seemed the right thing to do, that somebody should man the guns. I think I asked Lieutenant Craigie – I'm not sure.' She hesitated. 'It all happened so quickly.'

'I know.' He paused, and then he said, 'You can stand easy, Prentice. Sit down.' She did so. 'Lieutenant Craigie says that you were acting under his orders. Actually, he had no business to give you any orders at all. You're not a part of his command and you haven't been trained for operations. You understand that?'

She said quietly, 'Yes, sir'.

The naval officer turned to the Flight-Lieutenant, who leaned forward. He was an Intelligence officer from Beaulieu aerodrome. 'The Army say that at about the time you started firing the machine put its wheels down,' he said. 'Did you see that?'

She hesitated. 'Yes, I think I did.'

'You're not sure?'

'I remember noticing the wheels were down after it passed over and was going towards the shore,' she said. 'I think I shot them down.'

'Shot the wheels down?'

'Yes, sir. I know the wheels came down while I was shooting. I'd say that I'd hit the machine once at least before that happened, but I couldn't be quite sure.'

'Did you go on firing after you saw the wheels come down?'

She said, 'Yes, I think I did.'

'Do you know what it means when an enemy aeroplane puts its wheels down?'

She had a vague idea. 'Does it mean that he wants to surrender?'

'That's generally the meaning. In a case like this it's difficult to judge. I'm not blaming you, Miss Prentice. I've just got to establish the facts, whether the Junkers was making a motion for surrender or not.'

She said unhappily, 'A lot of other people were firing at it after the wheels went down, after it passed over us.'

'I know. We don't know for certain that you were responsible for its destruction. The trouble is that we now think that the machine was trying to find an aerodrome and make a peaceful landing.'

She stared at the Intelligence officer. 'How could that be, sir?'

He shrugged his shoulders. 'There were seven men in a machine with seats for four, they were all NCOs, and their paybooks show they were all Poles or Czechs. They may have stolen the Junkers to fly it over here and surrender.'

The Captain said, 'If so, they picked the hottest spot on the South Coast to try and land.'

'Maybe,' the Air Force officer remarked. 'But they wouldn't have known that. They couldn't have been briefed at all for this flight, or they'd never have come over in the way they did. We think that they were probably escaping from the Germans to join our side.' He turned to the Naval captain. 'That's all I wanted to establish for the report, sir, whether the wheels came down before this Wren began firing, or afterwards. As regards the aircraft, there's no need for anybody to lose sleep over it. I think it possibly *was* trying to land, but who's to say?'

'No more questions for this young lady?'

'No, sir.'

The Captain turned to Janet. 'Well, I'm not going to take any disciplinary action, Leading Wren Prentice. I don't blame you for acting as you did. But remember this in future. You've not been trained for operations and you don't know operations. You have absolutely no right to fire any gun against the enemy, because in doing so you may make very serious mistakes. Remember that. That's all. You may go now.'

She went back to her hut to change back in to working clothes, dazed and unhappy. Normally she would have seen Bill next day, which was a Sunday; I think that must have been the weekend following our trip to Keyhaven. In the normal course of things neither of them worked on Sundays, and they were in the habit of meeting then and spending most of the day together. But Bill was not available. He had told her that he had a job to do over the weekend, and he would meet her one evening in the following week, as soon as he got back. Piecing together what he had been doing in the weeks before 'Overlord' from information that I could collect about him six years later, I think this must have been the time that he was taken in a submarine to St Malo by night, to paddle ashore in a folboat to make a survey of obstacles upon the beach at Dinard.

Janet had the weekend alone to brood over what she had done. 'She took it badly,' May Cunningham told me, years afterwards. 'I mean, after all, it's what any one of us might have done, and nobody knew really what the aeroplane was up to. But she got it fixed firm in her mind that they were on our side, and that she'd killed them. I tried to tell her – we all tried – that the Bofors hit them too – I mean, if she hadn't fired at all they'd have been dead anyway, whoever they were and whatever they were up to. But she couldn't see it like that. She didn't cry or anything. Might have been better if she had. She just carried on, but she got very quiet – hardly talked at all. It's a pity her boyfriend – your brother

– it's a pity he wasn't around so she could talk it over with him.'

Looking through her documents at Coombargana ten years later, I found two letters, each dated April 29th, 1944. I think that date was the same Saturday on which she shot down the Junkers, and so she would have got these letters on the Monday morning after her weekend of troubled thought about the crash. One of them was from her mother and one from her father. The one from her mother read,

My darling girl,

Daddy went off yesterday with Mr Grimston; they were to report at the headquarters of the Observer Corps in London but they didn't know where they would go after that except that it would be to a place on the South Coast somewhere for a week in training and after that they would be sent to join a ship. It seems very lonely in the house without him, but I have plenty to do of course. I think he is going to write to you when he knows where he is going to be. Poor dear, he was getting terribly disappointed because he volunteered nearly three weeks ago and Mr Grimston heard on Saturday, but then he's two years younger than your father, only sixty-two, and Daddy thought they might have decided that he was too old to go. But then the letter came on Wednesday and he was to go in the same party as Mr Grimston. It *is* nice they'll be together, isn't it? I try not to think of what may happen. I do wish he was safe in England like you are but, of course, all the fighting will be over by the time the merchant ships get there, he says, and he's afraid they won't have anything to do at all. I *am* glad they took him in the end, because he did want to go so badly.

I must stop now because I have seven pounds of gooseberries from the garden and just enough sugar to make jam.

Your loving,
Mother

Sitting in my quiet room at Coombargana, far from all

wars and rumours of wars, I have wondered why she should have kept that letter. There were not many letters in that case of hers; she did not hoard letters that were not important to her. I think perhaps she read it very humbly on that Monday morning; I think it must have made a deep impression on her. One must remember that her success in shooting down the aeroplane had brought her no peace of mind; she was deflated, conscious that she might have made a ghastly mistake. And now this news had come to her; Daddy had pulled it off. Daddy, who could not read a thing without his spectacles, whose straggling grey hair did little to conceal his bald head, the tired old man who through the war had given everything that was in him to the Royal Observer Corps. Daddy was still as young in heart as any of the captains of the LCTs she serviced; he had gatecrashed the party and was to go in 'Overlord'.

I think perhaps that letter made her feel very humble; I think that is probably the reason why she kept it. The second one was from her father and I think she kept that for another reason.

Dear Janet,

Mother will have written to you by this time to tell you I have volunteered for two months' service in the Merchant Navy as an aircraft identifier. We are at the Royal Bath Hotel in Bournemouth not very far from you and I shall be here till Friday evening. I cannot leave here because we have talks and lectures and identification practice from early in the morning till six-thirty at night, but could you get over to see me one night and have dinner with me in the mess here? I will arrange for a car to drive you back to *Mastodon* after dinner; it can't be more than thirty miles. Come if you can possibly get away, my dear.

I am terribly glad to have got this job because I missed the last war, you know. I was afraid I would be too old, but there are several older than me in this course. The medical officer has his surgery on the top floor of a seven-storey building near here and there is no lift. If you can get up the stairs to see him he passes you as fit.

After this week I go to some port, to join a ship; there won't be any leave. We are so close; do come over if they will let you.

Daddy

She went over to Bournemouth to see her father one evening that week, perhaps on the Tuesday or Wednesday. The visit made a deep impression on her and probably took her mind off her own troubles, for she talked a lot about what was going on in the Royal Bath Hotel to Viola Dawson and to May Spikins, and they told me six years later what they could remember. I found Mr Grimston when I was in Oxford after the war and trying to find Janet Prentice. He runs a chain-store grocery in Cowley and he remembered her visit to the hotel to see her father; he had spent a quarter of an hour or so with them. He told me a good bit about what went on in the hotel that week. I looked in once when I was travelling the south coast of England in 1952 and had a meal there, but it was then a very different place and I found nothing that would put me in mind of Janet Prentice.

She got to the Royal Bath Hotel at about six o'clock. She found it to be a large, fashionable place with well-tended gardens overlooking the sea, situated on a cliff above the broken pier in the middle of the town. The old ladies and the wealthy residents had disappeared and most of the furniture had been removed; it was full of swarms of ageing men and schoolboys in the light blue RAF battledress of the Observer Corps.

Her father was in the lobby, and he came forwards to meet her with the enthusiasm of a boy. She kissed him, and stepped back to look at him. He seemed to have dropped off twenty years since she had seen him last; he looked hardly more than forty. He wore the blue battledress she knew, but on his shoulder was a letter flash SEABORNE, and sewn upon his arm was a lettered brassard that said simply, RN. He was no longer the father she had known, the poor old man in Oxford, harassed by overwork. He was a clear-eyed, confident leader.

She said, 'Daddy, you look fine! Are you enjoying it?'

He laughed. 'It's pretty hard work. We've only got a week here, and there's a lot to learn.'

She asked in wonder, 'Why did they pick this place?'

'It's handy for the invasion. It's our permanent head-quarters, this. If our ship gets sunk we have to get on board one of the landing craft and find our way back here and report, to get re-equipped and sent off again. We have to have a base, you see, and it's convenient to have it on the South Coast. Well, this is it.'

He was rated, she found, as a petty officer in the Navy. She went rather shyly and dined with him in his mess, sitting at long tables with a couple of hundred men; she was the only girl. Most of these men were over fifty and some of them were very old indeed; she saw one upright, white-moustached old man that she would have said was seventy-five. She asked her father about him. 'He says he's sixty-three,' he told her. 'If you don't walk with a stick they don't ask too many questions.'

Beside her at the mess table sat the bald-headed proprietor of a summer hotel in Scotland. 'There was the fower of us, ye understand,' he said, 'all in the Obsairver Corps, myself, the cook, the waiter, and the boots. When this notice came roond I said that I was going, and were they wi' me? But they couldn't see it, said it was too risky. So I told the wife, "Jeannie, my love," I said, "I must away to this", and I closed down the hotel and sacked all three of them and came down here. So that's what they got for running out on the Obsairver Corps. Still, we don't want fellows like that in this pairty.'

She had wanted to talk to her father about the Junkers, to unload on to him some of the trouble she was in. She had debated in her mind whether there would be a security breach in telling her father what had happened, and she had privately decided that security could go to hell. As the evening went on, however, she got less and less opportunity. Her father was glowing with the glamour of his approach to war; his mind was set entirely upon aircraft identification. 'I got ninety-six per cent in this morning's test,' he told her with pride. 'The only one I got wrong was the Me 110; it was a dead stern view. I said it was a Mitchell. Only two people got that one right. I got all the others.'

She said, 'How splendid! Do you do that all day, Daddy?'

'Oh no. We do seamanship in the morning.' There was an RNR lieutenant-commander who had spent his whole life in the Merchant Navy; he took them in a class and made them practise slinging and stowing a hammock, and practise climbing a rope ladder up the side of a house to simulate the side of a ship. He had a sense of humour and punctuated his lessons with gruesome stories of bad food and unpleasant heads in merchant ships, indoctrinating them skilfully into the seamy side of seafaring amid roars of laughter. He taught them the parts of a ship and the points of bearing till they could shout, 'Enemy aircraft on the starboard bow!' so that it was heard over half Bournemouth.

Her father's mind was set entirely on these things; he had sloughed off all the petty cares of home and work, all the responsibilities of normal life. He had set all that aside and he was going to the war with joy in his heart, and two hundred other old men with him. In all her naval life Janet had met no such morale as she found that night in the Royal Bath Hotel. It was the Dunkirk spirit over again, that turned aside from every personal affection and from all material ties, and thought only of the prosecution of the war. That spirit flowered in England for a few months in the year 1940. It flowered again in the early summer of 1944 in the Royal Bath Hotel.

'I'm trying to get a motor transport ship,' her father told her. 'They go over very early, I know. I believe they get there on the evening of D-day, or D plus one at the latest.'

He listened absently when she told him of her work, for he was absorbed in his own. They sat in the lounge after dinner on hard wooden chairs, and a sergeant of the local Home Guard arrived on the lawn outside the window carrying a Lewis gun. A wide circle of old men formed around him, seated or kneeling on the grass, as he proceeded to dismantle it and lecture to them on the gun. Her father said to Janet, 'I really ought to be there, but I don't suppose it matters.'

'Would you like to, Daddy? I don't mind. I know the

stripped Lewis, of course, but not the one with all that stove-pipe on the barrel. I'll come with you if you'd like to go and listen. Or wouldn't they like that?'

He said eagerly, 'Oh, that won't matter. They all know you're an Ordnance Wren; if you aren't careful you'll find yourself telling us about the Oerlikon.' So they went together and sat on the grass till dark, listening to the ser-geant as he showed them the Lewis, fingering the bits of it as they were passed around the circle.

She had not got the heart to spoil his pleasure with her own troubles. There was nothing he could do to help her, nothing to be gained by telling him about it now. It would only distress him and spoil the glamour he was living in. He had put off all personal cares and left them with his wife in his home at Oxford. Mentally he was stripped now for the fight; he would not see her mother again till he had done his stuff and 'Overlord' was over. She could not break in now and load him up with her troubles. It wouldn't be fair.

'We've got a course in first-aid tomorrow,' he told her. 'None of these merchant ships carry doctors; the captain usually knows a bit but he'll be terribly busy all the time, of course. So they're going to cram some of that into us. There's such an awful lot to learn, and no time to learn it . . .'

At ten o'clock her car was at the door, and he came to the steps of the hotel to see her off. 'If you're writing to Mummy, tell her I'm all right, won't you?' he said. 'I've been a bit worried – that I ought not to have left her. But I simply couldn't miss this one.'

She laughed. 'Of course not, Daddy. Mummy 'll be quite all right. I'll write to her tomorrow and tell her that you're as fit as a flea and having the time of your life.'

'You know,' he said in wonder, 'really – I believe I am. It's having to do with things, I suppose, after spending one's whole life dealing with ideas. It's having something really solid to bite on. Something definite to do.'

'You won't want to go back to Oxford,' she told him.

'Oh yes, I shall,' he replied. 'Oxford is where the long-term, valuable work gets done. If I can just have this, I'll be quite happy to go back to Oxford. If I can take this back with me, and think about it now and then.'

'Look at it, like a pressed flower in a book,' she said.

He nodded. 'Just like that. Just like a pressed flower in a book.'

She kissed him goodbye and got into the car, and was driven off to Lymington. She had to dismiss the car there because petrol shortages restricted the radius of hired cars to eight miles, but at Lymington she picked up the late ferry to *Mastodon* and got home in the truck. She was glad that she had not told her father of the Junkers, and said so to Viola Dawson as they went to bed. I think she must have been looking forward very much to talking it all over with Bill.

As a matter of fact, I doubt if she did so. I am not quite sure of this, but I don't think she ever met Bill again. He came back from his Dinard survey and was at Cliffe Farm for about two days; it is just possible she might have met him then though it was in the middle of a working week. Then he went off to join a party setting out from Gosport in an MTB. He was drowned on the night of May 5th at Le Tirage in Normandy, exactly a month before 'Overlord'.

CHAPTER FIVE

It was not until I got back to England that I was able to get any very satisfactory account of what had happened to Bill. I got a telegram commencing 'The Admiralty regrets . . .' three days after his death, at Fighter Command, for I was Bill's next of kin in England. I tried, as anybody would, to find out what had happened to him, but immediately I came up against a blank wall of security. At the Second Sea Lord's office in Queen Anne's Mansions they told me politely but quite firmly that no details of his death could be released until the war was over, and I already knew sufficient of his work to realize that this was not unreasonable. I don't think the news came as a surprise to me, for he was strained and tired when we met at Lymington. He should have been relieved and put on other duties, but in the weeks immediately preceding 'Overlord' perhaps that wasn't possible.

He was my only brother, and I still miss him a great deal.

When the war ended I was still in hospital, and I left England for Australia in 1946 before I could get about very much on my own. I had written guarded and unsatisfactory letters about Bill's death to my father and mother at Coombargana, because the little that I did know of his work was classed *Most Secret* at that time, and the war still had to be won. I said nothing to them about Janet Prentice in those letters because I was pretty sure that Bill hadn't told them about her; my mother didn't know her and could do nothing to help her, and I thought that letters from my mother in Australia could only embarrass and distress the girl. When these things happen, I think one must accept the fact that a clean break is the best way to take it.

I meant to get in touch myself with Janet Prentice directly 'Overlord' was over and go down to see her, but it was

August before I got another day off from my job and I had been to France three times since the invasion. I wrote to her then suggesting a meeting, but I got no answer to my letter; I now know that by that time she was out of the Wrens. Soon after that I got a posting to command my Typhoon squadron, and with that she slipped into the background of my mind.

In 1948 I met Warrant Officer Finch in Eastney Barracks in Southsea and he told me what had happened to Bill. His account is obviously right because he was with Bill in the water at Le Tirage up till a few minutes before his death. He told me that they usually worked together; apparently it helps in operations of that sort to know your mate well, so that when a pair of men team up they may go on together for some time.

What happened was this. Le Tirage is a little seaside town on the north coast of Normandy between Le Havre and Cherbourg. It was to be the scene of one of the landings of the British and Canadian forces in 'Overlord' a month later, but at that time, the Warrant Officer told me, security was so good that neither he nor Bill appreciated the very great importance of the job they had been sent to do.

A small river runs out into the sea at Le Tirage, flowing through flat, marshy land behind the town. This river is furnished with lock gates to hold the water back when the tide falls and make it navigable by barges which carry agricultural produce from the inland districts to the sea in time of peace.

It was an operational requirement that when we invaded Normandy these lock gates should be captured intact, in order that the lock and the navigable river might be used to supply our army after landing. A large number of Thames lighters, shallow-draft steel vessels capable of carrying a hundred tons of cargo or more, had been fitted hastily with engines and a steering gear making them capable of crossing to France under their own power, and these were to be used in the build-up of the army after landing, penetrating inland by the navigable rivers and canals as the army advanced. This had been foreseen by the Germans. The French Resistance had informed us that the lock gates at Le Tirage had been mined with explosive charges under water near the bottom of each gate, which could be detonated by electricity from a small building nearby which housed the operating mechanism of the lock gates. At the first alarm that indicated a landing, the Germans had only to throw a switch in this small building, the gates would be destroyed, and all the water would run out of the canal making it impossible for our lighters to use it.

Something, therefore, had to be done about these mines on the lock gates. The gates were about half a mile inland from the sea; for this half-mile the river was a tidal ditch with little water in it at low tide, though it had twelve feet of water or more when the tides were at full springs. The problem was studied at the headquarters of Combined Operations and a number of schemes for capturing the lock gates intact were discussed. In the course of this study the matter was referred down to the experts at Cliffe Farm, who put up a proposal that the mines should be neutralized before the invasion was launched by frogmen swimming up the half-mile of the river from the beach.

To neutralize the mines it was necessary to do a relatively simple little electrical job on the wiring near the mine itself, and under water. It would not be sufficient to cut the wires, for circuits of this sort are tested daily and a cut wire would be instantly detected and repaired. Instead, an electric gadget no larger than my little finger had to be wired close up to the mine and in parallel with it; this would ensure that the electrical resistance would remain unaltered under test but that the mine would not go off when the exploding current passed. Such a unit would be very inconspicuous as the mines were under water; if by any chance it were to be discovered by the Germans before 'Overlord' the work that they would have to do would be immediately obvious to the Resistance, who would report to us. We should then have to work out some new means of capturing the gates intact.

The work of fitting this little gadget to each mine would take about ten minutes. Warrant Officer Finch told me that the first suggestion that it should be done by frogmen came from Bill and himself, after they had discussed the matter privately together. They were, perhaps, the best people to advise the Staff upon this matter, for they knew Le Tirage quite well. They had been there twice in the middle of the night to examine the beach defences. They did not consider the German sentries at Le Tirage to be particularly alert, and they were confident that given a dark, windy night and possibly some sort of military diversion they could swim past the sentries at the mouth of the little river and up the half-mile to the lock gates, do their job, and get back undetected to the beach. The gates themselves were unguarded, according to the Resistance, perhaps because they also served as a road bridge and there was a good deal of traffic over them and also, being half a mile inland, the Germans were unable to imagine that we could get at them from the sea.

This plan was considered and discussed at Combined Operations headquarters, and it was decided to adopt it. If it were successful the electrical modification to the firing circuits would be good for many months. It was therefore decided to do the job about a month before 'Overlord' so that if it were detected by the enemy there would be time to try some other way of neutralizing the mines. As regards the diversion, there was a launching site for the V1 weapon about a mile from Le Tirage to the south, and it was arranged to stage a night air raid on this by a few aircraft of Bomber Command at the time when the frogmen were entering the river, to distract the attention of the German defenders from the waterfront.

The electrical gadgets to be fitted to the mines were prepared by the department which specialized in explosive fountain pens and lavatory seats, and Warrant Officer Finch told me that they spent a couple of days practising attaching them to a similar German mine which was in our possession. The latter part of this practice was carried out in darkness under water, working under similar conditions to those under which the operation must be carried out, with men watching from above to see if the frogmen could be detected in the work. When they were perfect in the relatively simple technique that was necessary, a date was set for the operation when there would be half-tide in the entrance channel at one o'clock in the morning and no moon.

These conditions were fulfilled on May 5th, and Sergeant Finch and Bill left Gosport in an MTB at about eight o'clock that evening, with a folboat on board, a sort of kayak built of waterproof canvas on a wooden frame that would carry them ashore on to the beach. They reached the other side at about midnight and lay-to about four miles off shore, and put the folboat in the water. It was arranged that the MTB should lie there for two hours, till 02.15, and she would then stand in towards the town upon a certain bearing if the frogmen by that time had not returned, running on her quiet, low-powered engines. If nothing had been seen of them by 02.45 the MTB would have to return to base.

Sergeant Finch and Bill got into the folboat and paddled it ashore, landing about two hundred yards to the west of the river entrance. Conditions were not too good for their venture. It was a calm, cloudless night and the moon had only just set; there was still moonlight in the sky and visibility was relatively good. They would have preferred a windy, rainy, overcast night, but they decided to go on and do the job. They tied the folboat to one of the beach obstacles, adjusted the cylinders of oxygen upon the harness round their bodies, and entered the water.

Their plan of action was that Bill was to swim in first past the sentries at the mouth of the river and proceed up the half-mile entrance channel. Finch was to follow him five minutes later if all was quiet; if Bill were detected or if there were any firing Finch was to use his own discretion whether to go on or to abandon the attempt. Bill was to go on up to the lock gates and do the job on both mines, and Finch was to stay in support resting in the water at a certain point about a hundred yards from the gates, on the east side of the channel. If the job were not as they expected, or if Bill found himself growing tired before it was finished, he would come back and consult with Finch.

They had timed their movements accurately, for they only had to wait in the water for a couple of minutes off the beach till the air raid on the V1 launching site commenced. Bill then waded forward till the sand fell away below him as he reached the river scour; he then dived and swam in under water, guided for depth by the pressure in his ears and for direction by occasionally touching the channel side. Both swam through the entrance to the river in this way and surfaced quietly well inside, and made their way cautiously up to the lock gates.

Bill came back presently to Finch and paused beside him, whispering in the darkness. He said that he had done the job all right but he had used most of his oxygen, for he had been under water for a considerable time. Finch had plenty of gas left, but they had no means of transferring gas from one man to the other. By that time the air raid was over, and everything was quiet again.

They decided that Bill should swim out first and make his way back to the folboat, postponing the dive under water as late as he dared, to get the maximum distance out from the sentries on his remaining gas. Finch would follow him a few minutes later since he had more gas and could stay under water longer if the sentries were aroused. They were to meet at the folboat if all was quiet and go back to the MTB in that. If an alarm were raised they were to swim out along the bearing that the MTB would come in on to get picked up; they had small electric lamps attached to their suits that they could light for recognition as the ship drew near.

That was the last that Finch saw of Bill. He went off down the channel swimming on the surface; Finch followed him about five minutes later. He did not see Bill dive, but shortly before he reached the point where he had planned to dive himself firing broke out from the shore, directed at the point where Bill would probably have had to surface. Finch dived at once, and swam forward under water.

He swam out of the entrance to the river without difficulty but when the channel scour in the sand petered out and was no longer a guide to him, he lost direction. He thought that he was swimming out to sea, but when his gas was nearly finished he found himself in shallow water. He surfaced very cautiously and breathed fresh air, and found that he was on the beach opposite the town, about two hundred yards to the east of the entrance, on the opposite side to where the folboat lay. He saw nothing of Bill, but searchlights were playing on the water at the entrance and very close to him. He dived again and swam out seawards, surfaced once more for an instant to check his direction, and swam on till his gas was all used up.

He surfaced then for good, and found himself a quarter of a mile from shore. He looked around for Bill and called out once or twice, very cautiously, but got no answer. He jettisoned his harness, gas cylinders, mask, and helmet to make swimming easier. He did not dare to go back to the folboat, for the searchlights were playing all around the entrance and discovery of the boat seemed certain. He set himself to swim out on the bearing that the MTB would come in on, and presently he saw her and lit his lamp for a few moments, till she slowed beside him and men helped him up a scramble net on to her deck.

About that time a searchlight picked her up, and fire was opened on her from the shore. She could not stay to look for Bill, and put on her main engines and made off to sea, in which of course she was quite right.

I think Bill may have been quite close to Finch at one time in the water. His body was picked up by the Germans ten days later floating in the water about five miles out from Ouistreham. He had jettisoned his cylinders and mask, as Finch had done. There was a bullet wound in the left shoulder, but death was due to drowning.

That is how my brother came to meet his end. His body, when it was recovered from the sea, was taken to Caen for examination by the German Intelligence and medical officers, and according to the French it was buried there. Caen, however, was fought over and very largely destroyed a month later, and I have never succeeded in discovering his grave. For a memorial of Bill, who died in the black sea off Normandy a long way from his home at Coombargana in the Western District, let the record stand that when the Canadians took Le Tirage in the assault exactly a month later the lock gates were captured intact and our supply lighters began to use the river immediately.

When I met Warrant Officer Finch at Eastney years later and he gave me that account, he also told me that he had written to Janet Prentice to tell her of Bill's death, and that he had taken the dog Dev to *Mastodon*. I found his letter with some others that she had thought important enough to keep, in her case, at Coombargana, and Viola Dawson told me what had happened to the dog. His letter ran,

4th LCOCU,
C/o GPO

Dear Miss Prentice,

I don't know if you will remember me but I was with Bill Duncan the day the tank was flooded over at Newtown. I'm sorry to say I have bad news for you. We had a sort of operation at a place abroad and Bill did not come back. I am afraid he bought it. That's all I'm allowed to say and I know you will understand about that.

I am very sorry to have to write a letter like this to you but I know that poor old Bill would have wanted one of his friends to tell you, because I know that you and he were such great friends. I am so sorry.

We don't know what to do about his dog Dev that he called after de Valera, could you make a home for him? He said once you had said perhaps you could if he got moved away. The captain said to shoot him and I will do that and see it all done decent for Bill, but before I do that I thought I would ask you if you wanted him and if so I will bring him over to you. Please let me know.

I am so sorry to have to write you a letter like this.

Yours sincerely,
Albert Finch

Viola Dawson told me that Janet gave her this letter to read half an hour after she got it; they must have been very close friends. She said that Janet was dry-eyed and quite composed, though very quiet after she received it. Viola didn't think she cried at all, and she remembered that particularly because it worried her a bit. She explained it to herself, and to me years later, by the reflection that Janet had seen more of death than most Wrens in the Service, and she no longer had the feeling, 'This can't happen to me'. When Viola gave her back the letter with some words of sympathy, she sat silent turning the letter over and over in her hands, looking down at it in her lap. Presently she told Viola very quietly that that was all over and done with, and that she would never marry anybody now. Viola Dawson would have been a great deal happier about her if she had cried.

Presently Janet got up and walked over from her hut to the mansion and asked a wardroom stewardess if she could see Third Officer Collins. Miss Collins was hardly older than Janet herself, and from much the same class. When she came out Janet said, 'Could I see you privately for a minute, ma'am?'

'Of course.'

She led the way down to the office that she shared with another Wren officer in what had been the butler's pantry of the mansion; it was empty at that moment. 'What is it, Prentice?' she asked.

Janet handed her the letter. 'I've had this about a friend of mine,' she said.

The officer read it quickly through. 'Oh my dear, I *am* sorry,' she said. 'Do you want to go on leave?'

Janet shook her head. 'No. I'd rather carry on here. There's nothing to go on leave for. He was an Australian – I didn't know his people, only him. What I wanted to see you about, ma'am, was the dog.'

Third Officer Collins re-read the last part of the letter. 'I see . . .' This was much more difficult than compassionate leave. 'Do you mean you want to have him here?'

'It wouldn't matter, would it? I could keep him out of the way. There's lots of places here, in the grounds I mean, where one could keep a dog.'

The Wren officer hesitated, hating what she had to say. She braced herself to add to the burden of the girl before her. 'I don't believe the Captain would allow it, Prentice. In fact, I know he wouldn't. Second Officer Foster asked the Captain if she could have her dog with her here, and he wouldn't let her. He won't have any dogs in the ship. You see, if you allow it for one you've got to allow it for them all.'

'You mean, he's got to be shot?' asked Janet.

'I only mean it isn't possible for you to have him here, my dear. Couldn't you go on compassionate leave and take him home with you and leave him with your people?'

'They don't want him,' she said dully. 'Daddy's away with

the seaborne Observer Corps, and Mummy couldn't cope with him on her own, on top of all the other things she's got to do. No, he'll have to go. I'll write and tell Sergeant Finch. Thank you, ma'am.'

Third Officer Collins went back to the wardroom, worried and depressed. Lieutenant Parkes, the Ordnance officer, was there reading a copy of *Men Only*. She stopped beside his chair.

'I've just been speaking to your Leading Wren Prentice,' she said. 'Her boyfriend's been killed.'

He looked up at her quickly. 'The Marine sergeant who used to take her out? I say, I'm sorry about that. How did it happen?'

'They won't tell her. He was in that Combined Ops party – you know.' He nodded. 'She's just had a letter from one of his pals.'

His mind turned to the work. 'Does this mean that she's going off on leave?'

'No – she doesn't want to do that.' Third Officer Collins went on to tell him about the dog.

Lieutenant Parkes was very angry indeed. 'I never heard such bloody nonsense,' he exclaimed. 'There's bags of places here where she could keep a dog. I bet this place was stiff with dogs in peacetime. Why, there's a great range of kennels behind the stables!'

She said, 'The Captain wouldn't hear of it when Foster wanted to have hers here'.

He got up from his chair. 'He's not going to hear of it now.'

He was a cigarette smoker, which meant that he did not use the half-pound of duty-free pipe tobacco which he was allowed to draw from Naval stores each month. He had found this useful to him in his duties, because the construction of his armament workshop and the track that led to it had brought him into contact with the head gardener more than once. The house was let to the Admiralty for the duration of the war upon a purely nominal rent, but a clause in the lease required that the magnificent gardens should be kept in order and repair by the owners of the property. Gardens that in peacetime demanded the services of nearly fifty gardeners to tend the hundred acres that they covered still required the attentions of eighteen ancient men even in 1944, and the head gardener was a power in HMS *Mastodon*. Lieutenant Parkes had realized this very early in his appointment and had kept Mr McAlister sweet with an occasional half-pound of Navy tobacco. Burning with indignation, he went straight from the wardroom to the greenhouses.

From there he went to the Wrennery. He stopped a girl going in and said, 'Ask Leading Wren Prentice to come out, will you? I want to see her.'

When she came he was shocked at the stony look of suffering upon her face. He averted his eyes after one glance. 'Look,' he said. 'Third Officer Collins told me that you want to keep a dog.'

She said, 'It's no good, sir. The Captain won't allow it.'

'No,' he replied, 'he won't. But I've just been talking to Mr McAlister, the gardener – you know. He wants a dog to guard the greenhouses. He says the ratings are getting in at night and pinching things. I told him I knew of a good watchdog, and I'd put a couple of ratings on to knock up a kennel. The Captain's got nothing to do with any dog McAlister likes to bring in here to guard his greenhouses, provided that it's McAlister's dog. I've had a word with McAlister. He'll say it's his dog.'

He glanced at the girl before him, smiling, and was alarmed to see a tear escape and trickle down her cheeks. 'Thanks awfully, sir,' she muttered.

He felt that he must cut this very short if she was not to break down in public. 'Get him to McAlister's house,' he said. 'You know where he lives? Let Mac bring him in here – don't you bring him in. Mac's expecting him, and he'll swear blue that it's his dog.' He turned away. 'And look – I'm awfully sorry.'

When I met Viola Dawson she told me a good bit about the dog, both at our first meal together at Bruno's restaurant in Earls Court and later in the course of our many meetings. 'She went crackers over that dog,' she told me once. 'She spent every spare minute that she had with him. I was very glad to see it, as a matter of fact. I mean, it was a sort of outlet for her after your brother's death. Probably did her good.'

Sergeant Finch took Dev to Mr McAlister's house and left him there; he did not see Janet, nor did he want to. 'I couldn't say anything about your brother,' he told me. 'It was all hush, if you understand. It makes it kind of awkward when you can't say anything, and it's not as if I knew her very well. I just left the dog with the gardener like she told me in her letter, and I gave him the packet of letters and the photograph she asked for out of Bill's kit, to give to her, and then I beat it.'

Within an hour Janet had discovered him in the new kennel by the greenhouses that the Ordnance ratings had knocked up for him, and he knew her, and bounded forwards when he saw her, and licked her face. Every Wren in the place knew all about him, of course, and in the galley the cooks set aside a huge plate of scraps for Janet to give him for his supper, for she was popular and they were sorry for her. It was a very well-fed dog that settled down in his new kennel for a good night's sleep.

The Commander of HMS *Mastodon*, an elderly officer brought back from retirement, found him there on the third day and asked about him. The head gardener launched into a tirade in the broadest Scots complaining about the wickedness of ratings who stole flowers that should have graced the wardroom to give to their girlfriends, necessitating the presence of McAlister's own dog to check the depredations. The Commander escaped after a quarter of an hour of earbashing, and Dev became a part of HMS *Mastodon*.

He never did much watchkeeping, because he slept soundly every night. He spent most of the day with Janet in the Ordnance workshop or around the pier. Occasionally she would take him in the boat with her to visit an LCT if she knew he would be welcome, but she did not do this very often for fear that she would meet the Captain of *Mastodon* and be asked about him. On the few weekends that remained before the balloon went up she used to take him for a long country walk on Sunday afternoon, and once Viola went with them, over the moors in the direction of Hythe.

'She'd have been quite happy without me,' Viola said, laughing. 'The dog was company enough for her.'

The last month saw a great transformation of the countryside round Beaulieu, with intense activity in every field and copse. Road gangs were at work with bulldozers and graders ruthlessly straightening and widening the country lanes that led down to the hard at Lepe, tearing down the hedges and pushing them aside into the fields, straightening out corners. Every two or three hundred yards along each lane hard stands were made, which were parking places for tanks and vehicles. Temporary airstrips paved with hessian and steel units appeared almost overnight and crowded thickly one on top of another. The US Air Force moved in to these with Thunderbolts and B 25s, and Lymington became thronged with American soldiers and American trucks. Overhead it was a common sight to see fifty of their aircraft flying in formation at one time.

Every wood and spinney in the district became a dump for stores and ammunition or a parking place for tanks and motor transport. With these came mobile anti-aircraft defence, so that at times it seemed that every hedge and thicket held a Bofors gun in camouflage. But no German aircraft ever appeared by day after the Ju 188 that Janet had shot down; our fighters saw to that. Southampton, where over a thousand landing craft were congregated, suffered a few light raids at night which were beaten off with heavy losses; already the Luftwaffe was growing impotent.

The LCTs came crowding in to the river now; at one time, Viola told me, there were over seventy of them there. Training and fitting out had been hurried, and in many cases the maintenance of ships and guns was poor in the hands of raw, unseasoned crews. The work of the shore staffs grew very heavy; as the days lengthened with the coming of the summer the girls found themselves working sixteen or seventeen hours a day, from dawn till dusk. From time to time the river emptied and the LCTs all sailed away on training exercises, to load tanks and mobile guns and trucks and wading bulldozers at one or other of the hards. They would be gone for two or three days, away down to Slapton Sands in Devonshire perhaps, to assault the peaceful countryside with live shells and rocket bombs, and go through all the motions of a landing on the beaches they had devastated. Then they would come back again, more numerous than ever, crowding in to Beaulieu River and every other river on the south coast of England with a host of defects and deficiencies to be put right.

Through May the sun shone and the ground grew harder after winter rains. The knowledgeable whispered together that the ground was hard enough for tanks to operate, the more knowledgeable whispered back that it wasn't, but both agreed that the balloon would go up very soon. Nobody ever spoke the word invasion, and 'Overlord' was whispered very secretly.

In the last fortnight the work massed up upon the girls to a degree that they had now no leisure time at all, and the sense of tension was so great that they had no desire for leisure. On shore the roads were jammed with tanks and 'priests' and motor transport; every lane was lined with them along one side, their crews bivouacking in the vehicles or underneath them or beside them; there were little cooking fires and khaki figures everywhere. Each new airstrip was crowded with fighters in dispersal in the fields beside it, the pilots and the crews living in tents by the strip. At sea, monstrosities of every sort floated in the Solent, long raft-like things proceeding very slowly under their own power, tall spiky things, things like a block of flats afloat upon the startled sea.

Janet spent most of her time at Lepe Hard, two miles from *Mastodon*, for the time for major exercises was now over and the ships were all engaged in loading, unloading, and refuelling practice on the hards. It was her duty to be there when they were doing that, because when the balloon went up she would become a part of the Hardmaster's team. Her job would be to go on board the LCTs when they came back from France to load up a fresh cargo of tanks or motor transport, to check the ammunition that had been expended and exchange the empty drums for new, full ones that she had loaded on shore, and clean the guns for the tired crews, and make good what deficiencies there might be, all in half an hour while loading and refuelling took place before the craft backed off the hard to sail for France again. To get through all the jobs she had to do in that short time demanded practice and rehearsals, and in those last few days she went through these rehearsals with every LCT in Beaulieu River.

'The captains all knew her,' Viola told me. 'They knew she'd just lost her boy, and I think they liked her because she went on with her job the same as ever.' Through all her private troubles she had gone on just the same, the competent Leading Wren explaining once again to raw, forgetful ratings the meaning of the different colours on the Oerlikon shells and the order in which they should be loaded in the drums, sitting on the deck and working with them with her sleeves rolled up and her hands in a wet mass of grease. 'They had confidence in her,' Viola said. 'I think they felt that if she didn't fold up when her boy was killed, she wouldn't fold when the balloon went up.'

Viola told me that she asked Janet once about her father. 'Is he really going to the party?'

Janet nodded. 'He's finished his training. I got a letter from him yesterday, posted at Wapping. He's got a ship, but he didn't say what her name was. I suppose he wouldn't be allowed to.'

'Good show. How old did you say he was?'

'Sixty-four. He said in the letter that the sailors are terribly ignorant about aeroplanes. He said that none of them could tell a Focke-Wulf 190 from a Thunderbolt even when he pointed out the differences in the pictures.'

'I'm sure I couldn't, either,' said Viola.

'Daddy thinks it's just terrible. He telegraphed to Mummy to come up to London and bring him up his epidiascope and slides, and he rigged it all up in the ship and started giving lectures to the crew. He says they're really quite keen on identification now. He makes them identify every aircraft they see flying over.'

'He must be very keen himself.'

'It's his whole life,' said Janet simply. 'He's been like this about the Observer Corps ever since he joined it at the beginning of the war. Going with the party to the other side is a sort of a reward to him, for all the work he's done in the

Observer Corps since war began. That's how he looks at it.'

At the end of May Janet was transferred on to the Hardmaster's staff, which did not mean a move because the hard was only two miles from *Mastodon*; she was driven down there in a truck each morning and driven back at night. She moved freely from one base to the other in the boats, too, but now her main duty was upon the hard and she reported back to Lepe whenever she was disengaged.

On Saturday, June 3rd, all the LCTs were sailed out of the Beaulieu River and anchored by the stern with their own anchors in the Solent. That afternoon they began coming in in pairs to the hard to load up tanks and 'priests' and motor transport; in the mysterious way in which these things become known in spite of all security, everybody knew that this was it. Janet went through her drill of going on board the craft as they came in and reporting to the No 1, but she had little to do. The crews of the LCTs were all set now for battle; the time for worrying about minor stores deficiencies or rust upon the guns was over. She could have given them anything they wanted on that day without paper work or requisitions, but they wanted little from her. All day she walked from ship to ship upon the cluttered decks in the roar of the tank engines, dodging the men bowsing down securing tackles, chi-hiking sometimes with anxious soldiers uttering strained pleasantries. All day through the loaded vessels backed away in turn from the hard, and went out into the Solent to anchor in flotillas.

The cutter came down river in the middle of the afternoon with Viola Dawson at the helm and Dev standing proudly in the bow. Viola told me that she had taken to looking after the dog in the daytime since Janet was at Lepe all day; he was accustomed to boats and gave the boat's crew Wrens no trouble. Janet crossed an LCT to speak to them as they lay alongside for a few minutes while some equipment for the Hardmaster was unloaded. She climbed down into the cutter.

Viola said, 'This is it, isn't it?'

Janet nodded. 'Everybody seems to think so. It's different, too. Look at all the stuff they're taking with them.' The 'priest' she indicated was loaded high with ration boxes and camouflage netting. On its side was chalked the legend, 'Look out Hitler'. 'This is it, all right.'

Doris Smith looked at the massed vehicles moving by inches down to the hard, at the helmeted soldiers, and voiced all their thoughts. 'I wish one could *do* something more,' she said. 'One ought to be able to.'

Janet said, 'There'll be plenty to do when these start coming back for another load.' She bent and fondled Dev's ears.

She went on all that afternoon and evening visiting the LCTs as they loaded. Food came to the Hardmaster's hut from time to time, dixies of tea and thick meat sandwiches and biscuits and jam; as the evening went on Janet went and foraged for any food that happened to be going at the moment when she was free. The loading went on till seven o'clock, when it was suspended for a time by the low tide; at dead low water it was difficult for landing craft to manoeuvre in the narrow river on to that hard. It began again at half past eight and went on uninterrupted as night fell; floodlights were lit and the landing craft continued to come in to the hard, load up with tired soldiers and their vehicles, and back away again.

By midnight Janet was tired out, but there was no respite for men or Wrens. She had done enough during the day to justify her presence on the hard; she had replaced two damaged ring sights, supplied about five hundred rounds of ammunition for the Oerlikons, and a large quantity for the Sten guns. She had helped the gun crew of a 'priest' by giving them a can of grease and a great armful of cotton waste. Much of her day had been spent in futile walks from ship to ship, trying to locate the officer she had to report to and finding in the end that nothing was required.

Loading finished at about two in the morning, when the last LCT of the first assault backed off the hard and the floodlights were doused immediately to screen the hard from any German aircraft that might venture over in the night. There was no transport to *Mastodon* because the crowded vehicles upon the roads prevented any traffic backwards from the hard. Janet and May Spikins wrapped themselves in their duffle coats and lay down on a pile of camouflage nets, and slept a little. There Doris Smith found them at five in the morning, and woke them up, and took them back up river to the pier; they walked wearily to their quarters and turned in at six in the full light of day.

Janet got out of her bunk at ten o'clock, and Viola got up with her. Outside the Wrennery the sky was overcast and grey, and the wind was rising, whipping the tops of the tall elm trees. They stood at the window in pyjamas, looking at the weather in consternation. Viola said, 'It's going to be a pig of a day'. And then she dropped her voice. 'They can't go in this, surely?'

Janet asked in a low tone, 'When do they go – when is it? Do you know?'

Viola whispered, 'I think it's tomorrow morning. They're supposed to sail this evening. But half of them will be swamped if they go out in this. It must be blowing quite hard in the Channel.'

They dressed and got some breakfast; then Janet set out in her duffle coat to walk down to the hard. She got a lift in a small Army truck and reached the hard at about eleven in the morning. It was a dirty grey day with a stiff westerly wind; out in the Solent the LCTs were anchored by the stern in rows, pitching uneasily in a short, breaking sea. One or two of them had dragged and fouled each other, and were struggling to free themselves and to turn back against the wind to regain their berth. She found the Hardmaster and reported to him. 'I hope I'm not late, sir,' she said. 'You didn't say any time.'

'That's all right,' he replied. 'You might have stayed in bed. It's been postponed for twenty-four hours. They'd never have got across in this.'

She stayed down at the hard for a couple of hours and had her dinner with the Wrens in Lepe House, but there was nothing for her to do. The Hardmaster released her for the day then, warning her to stay on call in *Mastodon*, and she walked back to the great house that was her ship. Back in her quarters she felt tired and strained; she took off some of her clothes and lay down in her bunk, and slept uneasily for a time. At about five o'clock she got up and went and found

Dev in his kennel, and got his supper for him from the galley and sat and watched him eat it; then she got her clothes brush from her quarters and gave him a grooming with it, not before time. It was better to do that than to sit about in tension, thinking of the battle that was coming.

That night when she went to bed there was half a gale blowing, with squally, driving rain. Few of the Wrens in Janet's hut slept much that night; all were young, and most of them had boyfriends, fiancés, or even husbands in the LCTs that lay tossing and dragging their anchors in the black night in the Solent. They lay listening to the wind and to the rain beating on the window, thinking of their men wet and cold and in some danger, struggling to keep their loaded, cranky ships afloat until the weather moderated enough for them to sail across to France to battle with the Germans on the beaches on the other side.

All night Janet tried to sleep, but sleep eluded her till just before dawn. She was sick with a great apprehension, with fear of what was coming. She was seized with the presage of a huge, impending disaster. She did not worry much about her father; it was clear to her that the merchant ships would not be brought to the invaded coast until the enemy had been driven well back inland. She was filled more with a dread that the whole enterprise would fail and end in a shambles of defeat upon the beaches. Mixed up with this was a sick memory of the airmen she had killed in the Ju 188, the smashed bodies that she had seen lying in the field where she had shot them down, men who were friendly to us, on our side. A great sense of guilt lay heavily upon her which was to remain with her, I think, until she died, and over all was the memory of Bill, my brother, who had loved her, whom she would have married, who had vanished without trace out of her life leaving only the bare word that he was dead. She had killed seven airmen wantonly and so Bill had been taken from her, because Judgement was inexorable.

She slept a little before dawn, a restless, nightmarish, unhappy sleep.

When the petty officer roused out the hut the sun was breaking through the clouds; at breakfast it was evident that the wind was falling. Janet went down to the hard and reported to her officer; he told her that the indications were that the operation was laid on for the next morning, June 6th. He employed her on a variety of minor jobs in the forenoon and at lunchtime he dismissed her for the day; there would be plenty for her to do when the landing craft came back from France to reload.

In the evening Janet went down river in the cutter with Viola Dawson and Doris Smith to embark a party of RN officers at Lepe and to take them across the Solent to Cowes. She had no business to be in the boat upon a trip like that; it was a joyride for her, but she had become so used to going up and down the river in the boats by that time that she ranked practically as one of the boat's crew. The officers were mostly of commander's rank; she did not know it, but these were the headquarters naval staff of *Juno* sector, changing ship. They were serious-faced, silent men. They crossed to Cowes in the sunset and one of them directed Viola to an unpretentious steamer called *Hilary* lying in the roads, studded all over with radio and radar aerials. *Hilary* had been the headquarters ship at the invasion of Sicily and at Salerno, and now she was to serve the same function at *Juno* beach of 'Overlord'.

They turned back to Beaulieu as the sun was going down, and now they saw the whole fleet getting under way. The whole stretch of water between the Isle of Wight and the mainland was crowded with landing craft and ships of every sort, and all in turn were getting short their anchors, weighing, and moving off. In the deep channels were the Infantry Landing Ships, cross-Channel steamers and small liners with landing craft hanging on their davits; in the shallows were the LCTs loaded with vehicles and tanks and men, moving off towards the eastern entrance of Spithead in great flotillas, shepherded by their MLs. Coming down South-ampton Water was a great fleet of Tank Landing Ships, big American vessels with a double door that opened in the bow. Overhead the fighters circled in the evening light, the inner patrol positioned to catch any German aircraft that penetrated the outer guard of fighters over the Channel. The evening was thunderous with the roar of engines on the sea and overhead.

Viola slowed the cutter to half-speed and they lingered over the return to Beaulieu, silent and wondering, conscious that they were looking at a mass of ships that nobody might ever see again assembled in one place. Viola told me that she tried to count the ships that were in sight that evening; she counted over four hundred and then failed to separate the hulls massed together in the east down by Spithead. Gradually as they crossed the Solent, weaving in and out between the landing craft, the Western Solent cleared. The craft that had been lying between Lymington and Beaulieu passed them going to the east, and by the time they reached the river entrance there were few left to the westwards. The girls stood talking in half-whispers as the cutter steamed up river, as if to speak out loud of what they had just seen would break security and put the men in peril.

In the Wrennery it was another sleepless night. Aircraft were passing overhead all night hindering the restless girls from any sleep they might have got; if drowsiness came through the sheer weariness of anxiety a wave of bombers from some aerodrome nearby would pass over, climbing in fine pitch, and they would be wide awake again. They were too young to have acquired a knowledge or the habit of sedatives, too much accustomed to a healthy life, too little used to feminine megrims. Through most of the night one or two of them were out of bed, whispering together. Towards dawn a little knot of them in pyjamas collected at the open door, listening in the quiet of the summer night. Far to the south beyond the Isle of Wight the faint reverberations of explosions came a hundred miles over the sea; they stood there tense, and cold, and rather sick, listening to the distant echoes of the bombardment.

One of the signal Wrens from Lepe House whispered, 'The airborne party go in about now . . .'

Janet got practically no sleep at all that night. The tension in the Wrennery was contagious, and for forty-eight hours now she had had little to do. Before, the work had been continuous and exacting since she had shot down the Junkers, since Bill had been killed, and had given her little time for thought; she had slept well every night in an exhaustion of fatigue. Now in her idleness and tension the sense of guilt was heavy on her. She had killed seven men who were not Germans, but Poles and Czechs, trying to escape to fight upon our side. She had smashed them into the pathetic, sodden, mutilated things she had seen lying in the field. She had done that in her pride and folly, for she had seen the wheels come down and had been so exultant in her skill with the Oerlikon that she had not paused to consider what that meant. God was a just God, and she must take her punishment. He had taken Bill from her to Himself as a judgement for what she had done, but was that punishment enough? Perhaps there was more coming, for she had murdered seven friendly men and Bill was only one. One life could not atone for seven. Perhaps she had made some terrible mistake that would kill six more of her friends. Perhaps a ready-use ammunition locker on the deck of some craft she had tended would explode and kill six of her friends through some mistake that she had made, because God was a just God, and His judgement was inexorable. She racked her brains to think what her mistake could be.

She lay awake in silent agony all night.

The Wrens were up at dawn next morning clustering around the radio in their recreation room, listening to the news of the invasion put out by the B B C. Janet went down to the hard at Lepe after breakfast, but there was nothing to do there except listen again to a small wireless set, talk interminably about the position on the various beaches, and wait for the landing craft to come back for another load. There was little chance that any of them would return before nightfall; at dinner time the Hardmaster dismissed his staff till seven o'clock, advising them to get some sleep.

Janet took three aspirins and lay down in her bunk in the Wrennery, and pulled a blanket over her, and slept till six. It was the last spell of heavy, refreshing sleep she was to have for several days.

At half past ten that night the first LCTs came back to Lepe. They came from Nan beach in *Juno* sector, near the small town of Courseulles in Normandy. Janet heard something of their landing from a tired young rating as they lugged a box of Oerlikon ammunition on board together. 'They got landmines, old shells, anything to make a bang, tied on them beach obstacles,' he said. 'Three of ours got it and sank in about two foot of water on the beach; I don't think anyone got hurt. Time we come to go in the Jerries was a bit back from the beach; I reckon they're a mile or two inland by this time. They didn't put up much of a fight, not in our sector. I did hear it was worse for our chaps at Bernieres and down that way.'

About German aircraft all he had to say was, 'One or two come over, strafing the chaps on the beach. Everybody had a bang at them, but I never see one come down.' He had fired off two and a half drums; while the LCT was embarking vehicles and refuelling Janet helped him to grease the rounds and reload the drums. May Spikins was working at the same jobs on another LCT on the other side of the dolphins that ran down the middle of the hard; Janet finished her work and crossed to help May out with hers, and while she did so the first LCT backed off and was replaced by another empty one. Officers and ratings in these ships kept watch-and-watch, taking what rest they could while the flotilla was on passage.

Reloading, refuelling, and re-arming that flotilla took five hours. When the last ship backed off the hard at half past three in the morning there was a pause. Janet and May went wearily to the Hardmaster's hut, where there was tea brewing, and bully sandwiches. There was no indication when the next flotilla would arrive though it was expected soon; the tanks and motor vehicles were jammed tight down the lane leading to the hard. The Wrens wrapped themselves in their duffle coats and lay down on the camouflage nets at the back of the hut, and slept.

They were roused again at six and came out bleary-eyed in a cold dawn to see another lot of LCTs from France at anchor in the Solent, and the first two craft slowly nosing their way in to the hard. The Wrens gulped down a cup of tea and went to work. At eight o'clock the Hardmaster called them off for breakfast for half an hour; then they went on with the job. The last craft of the flotilla backed away at noon but there was another flotilla already anchored in the Solent waiting to come in to load; the Wrens swallowed a hasty dinner in the hut, brushed the hair back from their foreheads with filthy hands, and went to work again.

That was Wednesday, June 7th. That afternoon Viola Dawson took the cutter down the river to Lepe and lay alongside one of the LCTs for a few minutes, using it as a quay while they unloaded some equipment they had brought down to the hard. Janet broke off, and went over to the boat. 'Viola, be a darling. You'll be back at *Mastodon* tonight?'

The Coxswain nodded. 'As far as I know. Can I bring you down anything?'

'It's not that. Viola, I shan't be able to get up to see Dev till Lord knows when. Will you see he gets his supper tonight? Look, ask that Leading Wren in the galley – Rachel Adams – ask her if she'll see he gets his food for the next few days, while I'm down here. She knows what he has.'

'I'll look after him, old thing. Would you like us to bring him down here in the boat one day, or don't you want to be bothered with him?'

Janet said, 'I couldn't look after him with all this going on – he'd better stay up at *Mastodon*. But I'd love to see him if you could bring him down and take him back again.'

Viola said, 'Okay, I'll do that. Hope it lets up soon, Janet.'

'It's going on for ever, by the look of it,' Janet told her. 'I don't mind. It's the build-up that's important. Commander Craigie says the Jerries are four miles inland now – that's in *Juno* sector.'

She left the cutter, and went aft to the wardroom to find the first lieutenant of the ship.

All day and night through Thursday, Friday, and Saturday the build-up continued. The flotillas came in to load irregularly and without previous notice; so long as the flow of tanks and 'priests' and trucks kept coming down the road, directed by the Army, so long the LCTs would keep on coming to the hard. The girls ate and slept irregularly in the Hardmaster's hut, taking food and sleep as they offered, working in a daze of fatigue. Troubled, the Wren officers from *Mastodon* offered relief to the Ordnance Wrens; as there was no one else to do their job the Ordnance Wrens refused. 'I'm quite all right, ma'am – it's nice down here. I had a lovely sleep last night, and another one this morning.' Working in a daze of exhaustion they went on with their job.

The boat's crew Wrens brought Dev down to the hard each day standing proudly in the bow of the cutter; he would jump on board the LCT as they came alongside and frolic in and out among the tanks and trucks till he found Janet; then he would be all over her. She would give him biscuits and knock off for a few minutes to play with him, fondling his ears; then Viola would take him back into the boat and Janet would go on, cheered and refreshed by the short interlude with her dog.

On the morning of Saturday, June 10th, Third Officer Collins rode her bicycle from *Mastodon* down to the hard, her pretty young face troubled and upset. She leaned the bike against the hut and went in to the Hardmaster. 'Where's Prentice, sir?'

He pointed at an LCT loading on the hard. 'In that one, I think.'

'Could you send for her, do you think? I've got to see her, and I'd rather do it here, not in the ship.' She hesitated. 'We got a message from her mother. Her father's been killed.'

When Janet came, wondering, to the hut Miss Collins said nervously, 'Prentice, I want a word with you. Come out here.' She led the way down on to the strip of beach below Lepe House. 'I'm afraid there's been some bad news, Prentice,' she said. 'It's about your father.'

Janet said quickly, 'Has Daddy bought it?'

'Well – yes, I'm afraid that was what the message was, my dear. Somebody rang up trying to get hold of you, speaking for your mother.'

'He's killed, is he?' Janet asked directly.

'I'm afraid that's what the message said.'

Janet walked on in silence for a minute. In the back of her mind she had been ready for this, because God's judgements were just and she deserved His punishments. Ever since she had heard that motor transport ships had been beached upon the coast of Normandy on Wednesday to unload their trucks with their own derricks on to the sand, she had known that her father was not far from the German Army. She was too tired to grieve, too dazed with work and little sleep, too much obsessed with the thought that she had left her job with the breech out of the port Oerlikon and, as like as not, without her help the rating wouldn't be able to put it together again. Daddy had bought it; when she was rested perhaps tears would come and she would want to go to church. Now it was just a matter of brushing off Third Officer Collins and getting back on to the LCT to put that breech back.

She said quietly, 'Thank you for telling me, ma'am. It was good of you to come down.' She stopped, turned round, and started to walk back towards the hard.

The officer said, 'I've arranged forty-eight hours leave for you, Prentice. I'll just see the Hardmaster; then you can come up to *Mastodon* and change, and go off on the 14.00 ferry. You can take my bike and go on ahead, if you like. You'll find your pass and warrant on my desk; if they're not there, ask Petty Officer Dowling for them.'

Janet said, 'I don't want to go on leave.'

The Wren officer was nonplussed. 'They said on the telephone that you're her only child in England – that's why we put it through. Of course you must go, Prentice. You must go home and see your mother.'

'I couldn't go till this flap's over,' Janet said stubbornly. 'Not unless you can get me a relief.'

'Don't you think Spikins can carry on alone, just while you go home for forty-eight? You're working independently; she can carry on without you.'

Janet said, 'It's just a question if she can carry on *with* me, ma'am.' She quickened her pace towards the hard. 'She's just about all in. No, honestly, I'll be all right. There aren't any reliefs. Is it true that it's all coming to an end tomorrow?'

'Tuesday, I think,' Miss Collins told her. 'There's a buzz that there'll be no more loading here after Tuesday.'

Janet said, 'Well then, I'll go home on Tuesday.'

'You'd better telephone your mother, anyway, Prentice.'

Janet hesitated. 'I would like to do that,' she said. 'I must go back on to that LCT now, ma'am, because I've got the port gun dismantled; the seal was very dry and sticking down. They'll be casting off any time now. I must just get on board and see to that. Do you think I might make the call from here after I've done that?'

'I'm sure you can,' the officer said. 'I'll go up to Lepe House and see if I can get a post-office line for you. Come up there directly you've finished on this ship.'

A quarter of an hour later Janet, stony-faced, dry-eyed, her hands black with ingrained grease, was speaking to her mother. 'Mummy dear,' she said, 'I don't know what to say. I just can't realize it yet. How did you hear? . . . Oh, how kind of him. I know – well, I'd better not say that over the telephone. Look, Mummy, who's with you now? . . . Will she be able to stay over the weekend? Mummy, I want to come home but I just can't leave here before Tuesday. It's the invasion, Mummy – I haven't been to bed for four days. We're going on day and night. I think I'll be able to come home on Tuesday . . . Oh yes, I'm very well . . . We sleep all right but it's in little bits, you know, between the flotillas . . . I'll tell you when I come home. I'll try and get some long leave as soon as this is over, Mummy, but I can't come till Tuesday. Daddy wouldn't want me to. I'll tell you when we meet. On Tuesday. Look after yourself, Mummy. I'll be home on Tuesday, probably rather late. I'll ring you up again tomorrow or on Monday.'

She had been speaking from a room on the ground floor that had been the office of a captain, now vacated because Captain J3 was on the other side of the Channel. She sat for a moment, weary, after putting down the telephone. From the window she could see another LCT nosing in to the hard below, and a long line of loaded trucks and Bren carriers waiting to embark. Presently she got up stiffly and went out into the corridor. Third Officer Collins was watching for Janet from the wardroom opposite, and came out to meet her. 'You got through all right?' she asked.

Janet said, 'Yes thank you, ma'am. Thank you for letting me use that room and make the call from here. Do you think I could possibly speak to her again tomorrow?'

'Of course, Prentice – I can fix that for you. What time do you want to call her?'

'I think about teatime would be best. She's always in then.'

The officer said, 'I'll come down here at about four o'clock and see that everything's all right for you. You wouldn't like to come back to *Mastodon* and rest a bit?'

'I'd rather go on here, if you don't mind. There's another LCT just coming in.'

She went back to her job, her mind in a daze. In the roaring of engines as the trucks and carriers backed in to the LCT she started working with the ratings to get the ammunition on board. There was a short pause half an hour later while that ship backed off the hard and another one came in to load, sufficient time for her to smoke a cigarette but not to grieve. Then she went on again. That flotilla was finished by three o'clock in the afternoon and she went up to the hut and had a couple of bully sandwiches and a piece of jam tart with two cups of tea for her dinner; then she lay down to rest till she was needed again. She was too tired to think clearly, too weary and dazed to cry. She lay in unhappy suffering for a time, and presently she slept.

The Wrens were called to work upon another flotilla at about eight o'clock that evening, and they worked on till one in the morning. They had a short sleep then, but another flotilla came in with the first light of dawn, at half past four, and they went on again. They finished that one at about nine in the morning and had breakfast; by the time they had finished eating, a fresh pair of LCTs were nosing their way in to the hard, and a mixed lot of tanks and carriers and 'priests' was waiting in the lane to be embarked.

About the middle of the morning the cutter came down river with Dev standing proudly in the bow; Viola brought her alongside the LCT that lay at the west side of the hard dolphin. Janet was working on the other ship, on the east side of the dolphin. Dev, who knew his way around, jumped on to the LCT and from there to the hard, and began running round on the hard amongst the tanks and trucks looking for Janet. Presently he got under a Sherman.

Viola was still down in the cutter, and she never learned exactly how it happened. She heard a sudden shrill, agonized yelping above the roaring of the engines and the grinding of the tank tracks on steel decks, and put her head over the side of the LCT. She saw Janet running from the ship on the east side. The Sherman moved on backwards to the ramp, probably quite unconscious of what had happened. On the hard Janet found a small, concerned group of Army NCOs and privates grouped around the dog, struggling on his forepaws with both hind legs broken, yelping in agony.

Janet cried, 'Oh Dev, *darling*!' and dropped down on her knees beside him. He knew her and stopped screaming for a moment, and sniffed her hand, but he screamed again when she touched him. She raised her eyes from him in distress and saw a revolver belted at a knee, and looked higher; it belonged to a young Army captain.

'Please,' she said. 'Please, will you shoot him?'

The young man hesitated. 'Who does he belong to?'

'He's mine,' she said. 'Please shoot him for me.'

He glanced around; the hard was paved with concrete, and crowded with men and tanks and trucks. 'I can't do that here,' he said. 'We'll get a ricochet. We'll have to move him, I'm afraid.' He touched her on the shoulder and made her get up. 'Look, go up to the top of the hard and try not to listen. I'll look after this for you.'

She took one last look at my brother Bill's dog, then turned away and went up between the tanks and trucks, tears streaming down her face. She heard the agonized screaming of the dog as the soldiers moved him to the soft sand of the beach, and then two shots. With those two shots her service in the Wrens came to an end.

Years later Viola Dawson told me about that day, as we lingered over coffee in the restaurant in Earls Court after dinner. 'I couldn't wait then,' she said. 'I had to take some officers back up the river. I managed to get down to Lepe again early in the afternoon, and when we'd moored the cutter I went on the LCTs looking for Janet, but she wasn't there. I found May Spikins, and asked where Janet was.'

'She's not here,' she said. 'She's gone sort of funny, Viola – crying all the time. Look, be a dear and find her – she's somewhere about. Take her back to *Mastodon* with you. She'll have to report sick.'

Viola found Janet sitting at the head of the beach about a

couple of hundred yards from the hard, the tears streaming steadily and quietly down her face. She had borrowed an entrenching tool from one of the soldiers and buried the dog there in the soft sand. Viola said, 'Come on, old girl. It's no good sitting here.'

Janet sobbed, 'I ought to be working but I can't bloody well stop crying.'

'Of course you can't,' said Viola. 'I'm going to take you back up river in the cutter to the Wrennery.'

'I can't leave here. May Spikins can't do all these ships alone.' She wept again.

'Of course she can,' said Viola. 'They're not using any ammunition. They haven't fired a round for the last two days, and you know it. Besides, there's no more loading here after tonight.' She offered her own handkerchief, rather dirty. 'Here, take this. I'll go and see the Hardmaster and tell him.'

She found him on the hard outside the hut. 'Leading Wren Prentice seems to be a bit upset, sir,' she said. 'Could she have the rest of the day off? I could take her back up river in the cutter, to the Wrennery.'

He nodded. 'I'm sorry about her dog, but it was silly of you and her, to bring it to the hard. Yes, take her back with you. She's put up a good show, and loading finishes tonight, I think.'

'It was her dog getting killed that put the lid on it,' said Viola, seven years later. 'Funny, that, wasn't it? She stood up quite well when your brother got killed and when her father got killed, but when the dog got killed it finished her. I suppose she felt responsible or something.'

'I suppose she did,' I said. 'What happened after that?'

'I took her back up to the Wrennery, and when Third Officer Collins saw her she made her report sick,' she said. 'There weren't any naval surgeons left in *Mastodon* – they were all in "Overlord". There was an American Army doctor there, Lease-lend, and he sent her on sick leave.'

'Was she away long?' I asked.

'She never came back,' Viola told me. 'She messed about for a couple of months under a Navy doctor in Oxford. I went and saw her when I was on leave but she was sort of –

well, funny. She was still crying quite a lot, and very nervy. As a matter of fact, there'd have been nothing much for her to do in the Navy after the invasion. She went up to a board in London some time in August and they gave her her discharge, on compassionate grounds I think, to look after her mother.' Viola paused, and then she said reflectively, 'I suppose the truth is that she wasn't any good to the Navy any more.'

CHAPTER SIX

WHEN I went back to Oxford in 1948 I spent much of my time in trying to trace Janet Prentice. I soon discovered that her mother had died in the year 1946 and that Janet had left Oxford. The house in Crick Road had been sold and there had been a sale of furniture; everything seemed to have been converted into ready cash. I managed to trace the agent who had sold the house but he had no address for the girl, though he told me the bank into which he had paid his cheque. I went and saw the bank manager and he confirmed what I had already learned, but the account had been closed and he had no address. The balance had not been a large one, for the house had been mortgaged and large houses in those days had sold badly. He said that he had an idea that Miss Prentice had gone abroad.

When I found May Spikins, then May Cunningham, she remembered the name Mr Grimston as Professor Prentice's companion when he had joined the Seaborne Observer Corps, and Viola Dawson confirmed that name shortly afterwards when I mentioned it to her, though she could not recall the name till she was prompted. I went to the head-quarters of the Royal Observer Corps in Oxford and I found that Mr Grimston was still a leading member in the local organization, much looked up to for his maritime war experience. I went to see him one afternoon at the chain-store grocery that he manages in Cowley, and he made me stay until the store closed and then he took me round to his small house for tea.

He remembered the visit of Janet Prentice to the Royal Bath Hotel, but he was unable to tell me where she went to after she left Oxford on her mother's death; he did not know the family and had only met Janet on that one occasion. He was able to give me a full account of the Professor's death, however, and what he said was this.

Dr Prentice had been drafted to a ship called the *Elsie Davidson*, one of the Davidson line of coastal cargo steamers. She was a vessel of about four thousand tons, chartered for the invasion of Normandy and loaded with motor transport in the London Docks. She sailed in convoy from Southend on June 5th and reached the coast of Normandy off Courseulles about midday on D-day, June 6th. She anchored still in convoy well off shore and remained there for the afternoon and evening, being in no great danger because already the Germans in that sector had retreated well inland.

It had been the original intention that these motor transport ships should unload their cargo on to Rhino Ferries. The vehicles that they carried, with their Army crews, were loaded principally with gun ammunition for the tanks and 'priests' in the front line and were, of course, most urgently required on shore. The Rhino Ferry was a great steel raft a hundred and fifty feet long or more, built up of rectangular steel caissons bolted together and powered by two sixty-horsepower petrol engines at the stern. The vehicles were to be lifted bodily down on to the Rhino Ferry by the ship's derricks and the ferry would then convey them to the beach, where it would ground in about two feet of water, that being its very shallow draft. The vehicles would then drive off it by means of a ramp, drive through the shallow water and up the beach to make their way inland to the guns.

The Rhino Ferry, however, proved to be unmanageable in the bad weather of D-day though it had functioned well in trials; it was swept by the seas and with its low power it could make no headway against the wind. This had been foreseen as a possibility and an alternative means of unloading the motor transport from the merchant ships had been planned. At dawn on D plus 1 the ships were steamed in to the beach and grounded on the sand an hour after high water, so that when the tide fell and left them high and dry they could lower the trucks down on to the sand beside them with their own derricks, and in this way they unloaded every truck in safety.

It was a bold expedient to beach big steel ships in this way because the ships were needed urgently back in England for the build-up of the Army, and if they had been damaged on the beaches the whole venture might have met disaster a week later for lack of supplies. However, the planners knew their job and the ships suffered very little damage; they floated off in the evening and sailed for England to load up again.

The SS *Elsie Davidson* beached with the others of her convoy soon after dawn, and by midday all her motor transport cargo had been unloaded on to the wet sand beside her and had driven away. By that time the Germans were several miles inland so there was no particular danger to the ships upon the beach, though a few snipers left behind in ruined buildings were still giving trouble and had not yet been cleaned up. At intervals, however, a solitary mortar bomb would sail up from some point inland and would land upon the beach and go off, and the Army were having a good deal of difficulty in locating this trench mortar.

Nobody in *Elsie Davidson* had had much sleep since they left London, and when the motor transport had been unloaded and six or seven hours must still elapse before the ship could float, the officers and crew of the ship mostly went to their bunks to get a little badly needed rest before commencing the return passage. There had been no enemy aircraft over during the day, but the captain left the guns manned, the gunners mostly curled up on the deck asleep beside their guns. Dr Prentice would not have gone below on this the great day of his life, for his duty of aircraft identification kept him on the bridge and in any case the scene unrolled before him on the beach was far too fascinating for him to leave, but the captain had provided him with his deck chair. When all the motor transport had been unloaded and the last soldier had left the ship they went to dinner, and after a quick meal the don sat down beside the canvas dodger in a corner of the bridge and presently he slept, a worn, ageing man rejoicing in the part that he was privileged to play in war.

Soon after three o'clock one of the occasional mortar bombs came over, fired at random, and exploded on the bridge of the SS *Elsie Davidson*, only a few feet from the old sleeping man. As luck would have it a steward was bringing

147

him a mug of tea, and this man was killed instantaneously on the ladder leading to the bridge. Dr Prentice died a few minutes later, probably without regaining consciousness.

The soldiers searched all day to find that mortar, for it was evidently firing from a point well behind our line. Shortly before dark they found two girls who had been sitting on a stile in a hedgerow all day, waving at the soldiers passing down the lane in trucks or tanks and chi-hiking with the few who passed on foot. They were pretty girls and wore tricolour ribbons in their hair and waved little French flags at the passing trucks, but in fact they were German and had the mortar and its ammunition hidden in a bed of stinging-nettles just behind the hedge. When everything was quiet and there seemed to be nobody about they would pop one of the projectiles down the spout and get up quickly on the stile again and watch it sail away towards the beach, looking as if butter wouldn't melt in their mouths. When finally the troops located this trench mortar and arrested the two girls they could hardly move for laughter, it went as a tremendous joke on a grim day.

That is how Professor Prentice came to meet his end. I asked Mr Grimston when I met him at his house in Cowley if Janet Prentice ever heard the rather grotesque details, and he was inclined to think that she hadn't. He had heard the facts himself from one of the other aircraft identifiers who had been in another ship which had remained stranded on the beach for some days till they could get her off, and had got the details from the beachmaster's party. Mr Grimston had debated whether he should tell Mrs Prentice the whole story and had decided not to, thinking that it would only distress her needlessly. He was doubtful if anybody else had told her.

As I have said, I never met Janet Prentice again. I wanted to, but in the pressure of war it wasn't possible. I wrote to her at *Mastodon* in August 1944 as soon as I had time to turn round after the mass of work that came upon me at the invasion and I suggested a meeting, but I never got an answer to my letter. It may never have reached her, for by that time she was out of the Navy and in and out of various institutions, for her nerves were in a bad way. Viola Dawson remembered the name of one of these places, and I went to see the matron of the Mary Somers Home at Henley when I was in England, who remembered the case. Janet Prentice had been there for about two months in the autumn of 1944. The matron remembered her as a listless girl, obsessed with a sense of guilt for something that she fancied she had done in the war, and inclined to be suicidal. They did not regard her as an acute case but one more in need of occupation and psychological help, and, as she had a mother to look after, the psychologist attempted to direct her mind towards an ideal of service and regeneration through work. It is just possible that my letter was purposely withheld from her, in that home or some other, as being likely to produce a psychological setback.

I knew nothing about this at the time, of course; I only knew I hadn't had an answer to my letter. By the time that might have troubled me I was back on operations in the RAF and I had closer and more intimate troubles and excitements of my own to occupy my mind.

I dropped a rank to squadron leader and got away from Fighter Command in September 1944, and went to Aston Down to convert on to Typhoons. I can't say that I liked the new machine with its thick wings and its enormous Sabre engine, but the day of the Spitfire was practically over in Europe. In that last stage of the war the Luftwaffe was better equipped than we were and our fighters and our fighter bombers were having a rough time in France; the Focke-Wulf Ta 152 was a better fighter than anything we had till the Tempest became operational, and in the Messerschmitt 262 jet fighter they were streets ahead of us, though this machine was reported to be killing more Germans than English in its first months of operations due to its high landing speed and its unreliable engines. Still, there it was, and if you met one in a Typhoon or a Spitfire it was likely to be curtains unless you had a great numerical advantage.

I went to Belgium at the beginning of November 1944 and took command of my Typhoon squadron on Evère aerodrome just by Brussels. The squadron was armed with eight rockets on each aircraft and was principally employed on shooting up railway trains, bridges, and flak positions; the last duty was murder, for the German flak was accurate and intensive in those days. True, the range of the rocket enabled a breakaway to be made sooner than if the attack had had to be pressed home with cannon, but even so casualties had been very heavy in the squadron in the months since the invasion. In my squadron of fifteen machines, casualties had been running at the rate of over two a week for months on end, and only one pilot who had landed in France with the squadron in June now remained, though two others had completed their tour of operations and had been relieved. Three replacement pilots for my squadron crossed to Brussels with me in the Anson.

It was an anxious and a trying time for me at first. Morale in the squadron was not good, and everyone was well aware that their new squadron leader had been off operations for a year – none more than me. In that year fighter-bomber tactics had progressed enormously and I was definitely out of touch; the saving grace was that I knew that myself. I had a frank talk with the Group Captain the day after I arrived, taking my stand perhaps upon my DFC and bar. I told him that for the first ten days he mustn't expect a great deal from my squadron and that the fault would be mine; after that he would get good results from us. He bellyached a good deal but he took it, and for a week I played it very, very safe. In that week I got the squadron pulled together a bit, and after that we went to town upon our sorties.

Shooting up flak positions, I discovered, is a matter of planning the attack beforehand and good discipline; one can keep down the casualty rate if the right machines start firing in the right direction at the right time. We got our casualty rate down quite a lot and at the same time did our job as well as anybody else. We got more railway trains than Huns. I got one Messerschmitt 109K certain and another probable in my six weeks of operations, but we never mixed it with the German fighters if we could avoid it, for with rockets on we were no match for them and without rockets our main duty was to get home in one piece. We had a fighter cover normally who fought for us.

It all came to an end for me on New Year's Day, 1945. That was the day when the German fighters made their massive attack upon our aerodromes and did enormous damage to the RAF and to the USAAF. They concentrated everything they had and came over at dawn with about 650 Focke-Wulfs and 450 Messerschmitts in three formations, and within an hour most of the aircraft dispersed on our aerodromes were blazing ruins by the runways.

We had a show on that morning, and we were in the process of scrambling when the Jerries came over. I had just taken off with Red Two beside me and I had my head down in the cockpit at about two hundred feet as I got the undercart up, throttled back, and set the pitch. I looked up, sensing there was something wrong, and saw a burst of tracer flying past me; there was a violent shock as one smacked into the armour at my back. I got my seat down in a hurry and saw a Focke-Wulf pass just underneath me, and another one, and then the air was full of them and our own flak everywhere. My radio went dead, and I saw Red Two go down and crash in flames upon a house.

The air was full of aircraft, all unfriendly, and the cloud base far above. I stuffed my Typhoon down to deck level, breaking to port. On the ground the Fortresses and the Dakotas and the Typhoons and the Spits all seemed to be burning in rows; the Jerries certainly had made a mess of us. I got a Focke-Wulf fairly in my right sight for a moment and pooped off all my eight rockets at him, more to get rid of them than anything else, and two of them got him on the port wing and broke it off. The wing flew past, mercifully without hitting me, and the rest of the machine went down and rolled along the ground in a flaming ball.

I went on turning putting all my strength upon the stick, practically blacked out, probably at about three or four hundred feet, but I hadn't got a hope; there must have been hundreds of them. Somebody got me from the side with a big deflection shot; there was a crash between me and the engine, half the instruments leapt from the panel and crashed into my face, there was a frightful pain in both my feet and a hot waft of burning rubber that told me I was on fire. I shoved the throttle through the wire to emergency full and shot straight upwards for the clouds, and by the mercy of God at that moment there was nobody upon my tail. I jettisoned the hood as I went up and wrenched away the oxygen and radio, and with each hand in turn I managed to draw my damaged legs close up to me in spite of the pain. Then I pulled the stick back and turned her over, waited an instant and pushed it forwards and got thrown out cleanly, probably at about two thousand feet. I had enough sense left to pull my parachute and then I think I may have passed out, because I can't remember anything about the descent or landing. The next thing I remember is sitting on the snow with some chaps of the RAF Regiment about me putting tourniquets upon my legs; one of my feet wasn't there at all, and the other was a mess. There was a Bofors gun nearby; I was very lucky to have got down so near help for I was bleeding like a pig. Then a doctor came and gave me a shot in the arm and I passed out again.

That is how my service in the RAF came to an end.

A couple of days later I was flown in a Dakota direct from Evère to an aerodrome near Shrewsbury in the west of England, and I spent the next four months in the RAF hospital there. They operated three times because they tried to save the left foot but weren't able to. I was very depressed in those months, because it's not funny to lose both your feet when you're thirty years old. You don't realize that in time you'll get accustomed to the disability, that in years to come you may have just as much enjoyment out of life as you had before, though in a different way. I was passionately fond of winter sports and ski-ing as a young man and all that was over for me now, and swimming also, and long walks over the hills. I had black moods when I was in the hospital that lasted for days on end, cursing myself for an idiot that I had ever baled out. I should have had the guts to take it.

Outside the RAF I had few friends in England, and as the months went on my Service friends were all dispersed. I didn't want to see anybody, anyway. I am ashamed to say that in those months I thought little about Janet Prentice; when I did so it was in cynical reflection that she had not bothered to answer the letter I had written to her. I'm not very proud of those months of self-pity, but that's what happened.

Presently I was moved to the Orthopaedic Hospital at Clifton just outside Bristol, and I was there till November 1945. We had considerable freedom as patients in that place while we were being fitted with artificial feet and learning to walk on them, for part of the treatment was that we should get used to taking part in normal life. I had of course, as much money as I liked to ask my father for, for wool was already high and Coombargana was doing well in spite of the rabbits; I was far better off than most of the other chaps. The obvious thing for me to do was to buy a car to get around in, but there were difficulties and frustrations all around that one. No new cars were available and the six-year-old one that I bought gave constant trouble which I wasn't really fit to cope with, for I couldn't stand at first on my new feet for more than a few minutes at a time. The petrol allowance I could get, though generous by British standards in those days, was far too small to let me range widely over England, and I was allowed no new tyres at all. There was little that was healthy, therefore, for me to spend my money on and it mostly went on drink and rather dreary parties with the nurses; I suppose I was already too old to take much pleasure in a wild time with the girls.

By the time I left the Orthopaedic Hospital tottering on my new feet I was disenchanted with England, and only anxious to get back to Coombargana, my own place, where anyway the sun would be shining and petrol and new tyres would be available for me to travel on, whatever the regulations might say; I knew that much about my countrymen. I booked a passage home by sea for February, not caring to fly, and got enough black-market petrol to drive my car to Newhaven. In France there was unlimited petrol for anyone who had the money to pay for it and freedom of movement was restored to me, and by the time that I got south of Lyons the sun was shining. I spent a pleasant couple of months exploring the South of France and Italy as far as Rome, and in those months I got back some of my mental poise again.

The ship did a good bit to dispel it. I returned to London a few days before sailing for Australia and sold my car, but I was hamstrung without it. While I had the car I was a free man, able to travel and enjoy life like other people, but without it on the ship I was a pitiful cripple. I had a couple of falls in the rough weather of the Bay, one in the dining-room in front of everybody, and everyone was very sorry for me, which made me furious. I spent most of the rest of the voyage in my cabin, having my meals there, wondering if I was a fool to go back home to Coombargana if I could never ride a horse again. Up till the time I had left home, of course, the whole of the work about the property was done on horses.

There was a Queenslander from Rockhampton on board, a chap called Petersen who had lost a leg at Arnhem; he had been a paratrooper and had spent the rest of the war in a German prison camp. He was in much the same state physically and mentally as I was, and we used to drink and talk about the war each night in my cabin or his, and sometimes we would get a crowd together for a poker game, playing pretty high. I don't think I went to bed entirely sober any night of the voyage or before two in the morning; I used to lie in bed till about noon and then get up and sit around in the cabin trying to read and drinking a good bit, till evening came and all the women out on deck went in because it was getting cold, and I could go out for a breather without people staring at me or being sympathetic. Then would come dinner in the cabin and the serious business of the day, which was talking about the war and drinking.

We got to Fremantle at last and there my father met me. He had booked seats for us on the airline to Adelaide but I didn't want to fly; I had a scunner against flying at that time which took about two years to fade. So Dad came round to Adelaide with me in the liner, and I must say he was good. He saw that I was drinking pretty hard and set himself to drink with me, matching scotch with scotch; when I talked about my war he'd start talking about his. We both got shot together each night on the way round from Adelaide and he won a lot of his own money off me at poker. He made my homecoming far easier than I had thought it would be, because when we got back to Coombargana and he laid off the grog because of Mother it was easy for me to play along with him and go slow on it too.

Dad had met Harry Drew during the war and had brought him to Coombargana when they got demobilized and made him foreman; Dad was always a good picker of men. Mother was already getting disinclined to travel on her own, so Harry brought the old Bentley they had bought before the war to Adelaide to meet us at the ship, and we drove home in that. I drove it most of the way and it was a delight to be at the wheel of a decent car. In a car I could regain my freedom of movement and be equal to anybody once again.

At Coombargana I found that Dad had come back from the war with some pretty advanced ideas about the mechanization of the property. Before the war Coombargana ran almost entirely upon horses in the traditional style. I don't think we had more than one truck on the station; we had an old kerosene tractor but I don't remember that it was used much, and we conserved little fodder. I remember that we used the tractor for ploughing firebreaks before the war but I don't think we ever ploughed up a paddock; we grazed entirely on the natural grasses of the district. All the real work of the property was done with riding and draught horses; all told we had about eighty horses on the place, to the ten or eleven we keep now.

Dad, however, had spent much of the war in the Northern Territory in close contact with the highly mechanized American Army; he had seen a thousand miles of first-class bitumen road made at an incredible speed between Alice Springs and Darwin; he had seen vegetable farms to feed the Army created from the bush by modern agricultural machines, producing the vegetables in a matter of months. He had watched all this carefully with his mind on Coombargana, sifting out what was likely to be useful to us from what was not. When I got home in the Australian autumn of 1946 I found that he had brought a number of disposal vehicles on to the station, most of which proved useless to us in the end because they had been designed for other service but which gave us valuable experience. The Bren carrier lies rotting in a brier thicket now because it didn't really do anything we wanted and we couldn't get spares for it, but we learned from it that a tracked vehicle was necessary to us in the winter and our big diesel crawler is the outcome of that knowledge. We still use a couple of the four-wheel-drive Chevrolet trucks he bought, but the disposal jeeps have long since given place to Land Rovers.

I found that Dad was still using his horse to get about the property, though he had a sneaking affection for a jeep and was starting to drive where he had ridden formerly. When I got home I made a conscious effort to take an interest in the station though it all seemed terribly small and insignificant after the business I had been engaged in for the last six years. A horse was impossible for me, of course, or at any rate pretty unsafe, and at an early stage we got a jeep for my personal use about the property. With his Army associations Dad could get to know what was coming up for sale, and he managed to produce a nearly new jeep for me that would give no trouble.

It was a pity that it had to be a jeep, although we neither of us realized that at the time. A man in my condition depends so much upon his car; it means far more to him than a car would to any normal person. This jeep was identical in every respect with the many jeeps that I had driven in the war; it made the same noise, was painted the same colour, had the same soiled canvas seats; the gear lever came to hand in the same place, the steering was the same. It made too strong a link with the war days to be quite healthy; continually it brought back memories that had better have faded with the different scene and with the passage of the years. When I had had a drink or two I would be driving in the darkness round the perimeter track towards our Typhoons at dispersal with Samuelson and Driver and Jack Carter in the jeep with me, Jack Carter who was to collide with Driver over the target an hour later and fall together with him in a flaming mass, and Samuelson who was to pull out far too low over the train so that the flak got him and he crashed on the line ahead of the ruined engine, belching smoke and steam and cinders high into the air. There was the little clip above the instrument panel that I never learned the use of, in which Jack Carter left his pipe before we went to the machines, in which I found his pipe when we came back. Once or twice at Coombargana when I was a bit tired I reached out to take that pipe out of the clip, and it wasn't there.

Helen was living at home when I got back, though she was making plans to go to England in the spring and straining at the leash to get away. She was six years younger than I was and might have been good company for me if things had been different, but mentally we lived in different worlds. I think the war made bigger chasms between Australian young men and women than in England, where girls were called up and had to serve in the Armed Forces like the men. In Australia war service for girls was on an easier basis, and Helen and her friends had had no difficulty in avoiding it and in pursuing their lives more or less uninterrupted through the war; indeed the pretext of doing war work in Melbourne had made it easier for them to leave the country and take a flat in town. For these girls the war had little reality; no bomb fell within two thousand miles of them, no death came near them, no military discipline forced them into contact with girls of another class; they came out of the war in much the same state of mind as they went into it, avid to get to London and to Paris, to the seats of fashion and of culture that the silly nuisance of the war had stopped them visiting before.

Most Australian men returning from the war accepted their girls for what they were, reflecting perhaps that men are different from women and girls are like that. I couldn't do it. Perhaps my disability had made me bitter and critical, but I had spent six years in daily contact with English-women in the RAF who had shared many of my own experiences, had been scared stiff when I was scared myself, had known the same discipline, had grieved for friends when I had grieved, had turned to cigarettes and grog to hide the grief as I had turned myself These Englishwomen spoke the same language that I spoke and thought in the same way; compared with them Helen and her friends seemed shallow and trivial to me, people of no account incessantly pre-occupied with details of their clothes and personal adornment, and their unending, foolish parties.

On her part, Helen found me much changed by the war, and changed for the worse. I had gone to it a pleasant, affable, and intelligent young man, a good dancer and skier, popular with her friends. I had come back from it an unpleasant, soured cripple, contemptuous of her friends and their way of life, a man with a sharp, bitter tongue, and a fairly heavy drinker. I think my return put the lid on it for Helen; like most young Australians she wanted to get out into a wider world, and by the time I had been home a month it would have taken a dog collar and a chain to keep her at Coombargana.

She sailed for England in December 1946; we had a reconciliation when she went for I had behaved badly to her, and we parted on better terms than we had been since I came home. After she went I saw no more of her friends and it was lonely at Coombargana; I did not care for them but, in the words of Barrie, they were like a flight of birds, and when they went it seemed that they had taken away the sun in their pockets. I met very few young women after that. I was conscientiously trying to learn the business of the property but I couldn't make it a full-time occupation. I had been brought up at Coombargana in the wool business and, in fact, there wasn't a lot left for me to learn; running a station isn't as difficult as all that. My father was still active and able to make quick decisions, not yet ready to turn over management to me. We have an interest in a cattle station in the Northern Territory, a property of about fifteen hundred square miles about three hundred miles north of Alice Springs near Tennant Creek, and I used to go up there for him once or twice a year for a few days. I wasn't much good up there because I wasn't really safe upon a horse and I couldn't walk very far; in the bush I had to have one of the stockmen with me all the time, because if I had fallen from my horse I couldn't have caught him again and I could never have walked out back to the homestead. However, I was able to look through the books and talk to everyone, and this saved my father a good deal of travelling.

I used to go to Melbourne fairly frequently from Coombargana and stay at the Club on some pretext such as visiting the Show or a machinery exhibition, or to buy something that we needed for the property that could have been bought just as well by correspondence. I could not fill my time, however, and presently for lack of any other occupation I got out my Law textbooks and began to read up what I had been studying at Oxford before the war, and that I had half forgotten. As the quiet months went on at Coombargana I gradually became accustomed to my disability and learned what I could do and what was dangerous for me, and as I grew safer on my feet I think perhaps I grew a little better in my temper.

It's rather lonely in the Western District, because to see any of your friends you've got to get into your car and drive a good long way. Few girls came my way, understandably perhaps, and I had too little in common with the ones that did to seek their company. As time went on I found my thoughts turning more and more to England. I had been irritated with England when I came away and only anxious to get out of it and back to Coombargana; now that I was home it seemed to me that I was something of a misfit in the Western District, and that after six years of war in England I was more in tune with their austerity than with the ease and the prosperity of my home. England was a place of strain and relative hardship, but it was a place where real, vital things were happening, where people thought about things as I thought.

If Bill had lived and had come home with Janet Prentice it would have been different, for then there would have been three of us, a little island of three people who had shared the same experience, but now I was alone. As the months went on I became uneasy about Janet Prentice. I had written to her and I had received no answer, but I began to feel that I couldn't leave it there. So far as I knew she was the only girl that Bill had ever been in love with. She had been very good for him at a time when he was tired and strained and not far from his death, and for that Coombargana owed her a good deal. I could not keep from thinking of the grey-eyed, homely, competent girl in jersey, bell-bottoms, and duffle coat in the grey-painted fishing boat, whom Bill had loved. I felt I should have made a greater effort to keep in touch with her; she should have been a friend of the family, because she had deserved well of us. I had not told my mother or my father anything about her, but now it seemed to 'me that they should know about her.

I didn't say anything to them, because the girl might be married to someone else and happily settled, but in October 1947 I wrote her a letter. It was a chatty sort of letter that began with an apology for not getting into touch with her more energetically after Bill's death, and telling her about my crash and disability, and my life since then. I asked her to forgive the long gap in our friendship and said that we should keep in touch, and I asked what she was doing in these post-war years.

I had a little difficulty in addressing this letter. I knew she lived in Crick Road, Oxford, but I didn't know the number, so for safety I put my own address upon the envelope and sent it off by airmail. Three months later it came back to me by sea mail in an official envelope; pencilled across it were the words, GONE AWAY – ADDRESS UNKNOWN.

I was a bit troubled when that letter came back. I opened it and read what I had written three months previously. It seemed to me all right, so I added a few words at the bottom and sent it off again, addressed to Miss Janet Prentice, c/o Dr Prentice, Wyckham College, Oxford. Again I put my own address on the back of the envelope.

It came back to me again, by sea mail, after about two months. A short covering note came with it, from the Bursar of Wyckham. He said that I was evidently unaware that Dr Prentice had been killed on war service in the year 1944. After the death of her mother the year before last Miss Janet Prentice had left Oxford, and he had been unable to find out her present address. In the circumstances he had no option but to send back my letter.

All this took a considerable time, and it was March when this letter came back to me again. It worried me more than I cared to admit. While I had been sunk in my abyss of self-pity, Bill's girl had had a packet of bad luck. Not only had she lost Bill, but her father had been killed on service in the same year. She had told us that he was going on the party as an aircraft identifier in a merchant ship; had he been killed then? I thought he must have been, but in that case she had lost Bill and her father within a month of each other. In a very few weeks she had lost both men who were important in her life, a shattering blow to any girl, even to so level-headed and competent a girl as Janet Prentice. Now came the news that she had lost her mother two years later, and that she had gone away, and lost touch with her father's old friends and associates at Oxford.

I had little sleep for some nights after getting this letter. Bill had loved her, and at Coombargana we should have stood behind her in her trouble, and we hadn't, because I had been lazy and self-centred. I didn't know quite what we could have done to help her, but we should have tried. We had one thing at any rate that might conceivably, somehow, have been used to make her troubles easier for her, and that was money. She didn't know it, but if she had married Bill she would have married into a fairly wealthy family. I knew that my father and mother, if they were to hear of her exist-ence and were to hear what she had meant to Bill, would feel exactly as I felt; that she was virtually one of us, a daughter of the house.

I wrote a pretty candid letter back to the Bursar of Wyck-ham, for I had nothing to lose by putting my cards on the table. I thanked him for returning my letter, and told him that Miss Prentice had been engaged to my brother in the Royal Marines, who had been killed in 1944, apparently shortly before the death of her father. I told him something about myself in explanation why I had lost touch with her, and said that we were really most anxious to make contact with her. I asked him to make what in-quiries he could to find out her address. If he preferred to put her into touch with us instead, would he give her my address and pass a message to her asking her to write to me.

I got a letter back from him by airmail some weeks later. He said that he had delayed answering my letter till he had been able to make some inquiries, but he was sorry to say that he had had very little luck. The Prentices apparently had no relations living in Oxford. Dr Prentice, he thought, was born in London and had become a don at Wyckham about thirty years ago. He had a brother who had been upon

161

the faculty at Stanford University in the United States, but this brother was thought to have died some years ago. Another daughter, a sister of Miss Janet Prentice, was thought to be married and in Singapore but he had been unable to discover her married name. He had, however, been in touch with a charwoman called Mrs Blundell who had worked two mornings a week for Mrs Prentice up to the time of her death, in October 1946, and Mrs Blundell said that Janet Prentice had then told her that she was going to live with an aunt in Settle. Settle was a small town in the West Riding of Yorkshire, about forty miles north-west of Leeds. He had written to the postmaster of Settle to inquire if there was any such person living in the district, but had received the reply that nothing was known about any Miss Janet Prentice in that district.

It was of course possible, he said, that Miss Prentice had married and was living in the district under her new name, but in view of the nervous breakdown that she had suffered after the war he thought that was unlikely. He was very sorry not to be able to offer more assistance. As a colleague and an old friend of the late Dr Prentice he was anxious to do everything he could to help his daughter, and he hoped I would not hesitate to call upon him if he could do anything further in the matter.

This letter reached me at the beginning of May 1948, and it was very bad news. This girl who had deserved so well of us was in trouble, for she had had a nervous breakdown after the war. I knew enough about university life to know that the daughter of a don would probably inherit very little money at the death of her parents, and for civil life she probably had little earning power. She had left school before qualifying for a job and in the war she had learned automatic guns, no great qualification for civil life. Without the breakdown she would have got by upon her native wit, and with her competence she would have made her way in peacetime; as things were she had apparently become a housekeeper or a companion for some aged relative, living no doubt in circumstances that were far from affluent in England. I felt very strongly that she was a part of Coombargana, that we were responsible for her and should look after her. Coombargana could do better for her than that. She was Bill's girl, and in trouble.

I thought about it for a day or two, restless and unhappy. The memory of the clear-eyed, competent Leading Wren at Lymington was very vivid in my mind; in love with Bill, she had been a very lovely girl that day and I had thought he was a very lucky man. It was a terrible idea that she might no longer be like that, that trouble and poverty perhaps had aged her, made her different, uncertain of herself where she had been direct and positive. Not many years had passed, however, though much had been crammed in to them. She was only four years older now than she had been when we had met and picnicked in the motor boat. With help and money and kindness she could regain a great part of her youth. Somehow we must let her know that people still cared a great deal about Bill, and so cared for the girl he loved and would have married.

It was difficult, if not impossible, to find her and do any-thing to help her from Coombargana, but difficulties can be broken through. There was nothing to keep me in Australia because my father could get on perfectly well without me, and if I wanted to go to England I could go. In fact, nothing could be easier or more convenient, because I was still a Rhodes scholar only halfway through his course at Oxford, and Oxford was probably the place where I could find a thread that would lead me to Janet Prentice. Presumably I was still entitled to go back to the House and finish my scholarship and take a degree in Law, and in doing so I felt that I would certainly be able to find Janet Prentice.

I didn't tell my parents anything about her, possibly be-cause I was ashamed to tell them of the part that I had played, or had not played, in the affair. I was reluctant to tell them anything about her till I had located her and found what she was doing; they couldn't do anything to help, and it all seemed so private. When finally I found her she might well be married and happily settled in life, and in that case there would be no point in interesting the older generation in her; probably better not to. It would be time enough to tell my parents if I found they could do anything to help her.

I raised the question of going back to Oxford with my father two days after the letter arrived. 'I'd like to finish off my scholarship and take a degree, and perhaps get called to the Bar,' I said. 'It's something that I started, Dad, and that I'd rather like to finish. There's not a great deal here for me to do till you get older, is there?'

He nodded. 'You mean, there's not enough work for two?'

'That's right,' I said.

'I hoped when you came home that you'd get married and have a place of your own,' he said. 'Your mother and I both hoped that. But it doesn't seem to be working out that way.'

I smiled. 'Too bad. I suppose I'm too restless.' I paused. 'I don't feel an invalid any longer, like I did when I came home. I want to get out and do something.'

He nodded. 'That's reasonable,' he said. 'After all, you're still a young man. How old are you, Alan? Thirty-two?'

Dad was never very good at figures. 'Thirty-four,' I said. 'I'd like to get around a bit before settling down for good, and this seems the right time to do it.'

'We shall miss you here,' he remarked, '—your mother and I. But I think you're right to want to travel while you're young. You haven't seen anything of Europe, really, have you?'

'Only from on top while I was trying to smash it up,' I said. 'I had two months in France and Italy when I got out of hospital, but I really wasn't fit to notice anything much then.'

'You'll start off by finishing your scholarship?' he asked.

'That's what I'd like to do.'

It didn't prove quite so easy as I had supposed. The scholarship was still there waiting for me though it wouldn't have mattered if it hadn't been. Oxford, however, was still full of post-war undergraduates and there was no place for me in college till October 1949. I exchanged several letters with the Secretary to the Trust in Oxford and with the Dean of Christ Church to see if I could get digs for the coming year within a short distance of college, but the place was still so crowded that they could not offer me accommodation nearer than North Oxford. For a normal man this might have been no great impediment, but I was still unable to walk much more than a mile without a good long rest and for me this meant that I should be very largely cut off from the life and benefits of the university.

I chafed at the delay, but there seemed to be nothing for it but to wait a year and go to Oxford when I could get in to college. I thought this over for a week and then decided that I wouldn't wait; I was confident that if I were in Oxford I could find somewhere to live within a stone's throw of the college even if I had to buy a house to live in, and Janet Prentice might well be in trouble that would brook no delay. My father generously fixed up money for me in England on a basis that was virtually unlimited, and I sailed for England in the *Orontes* in August 1948.

I got to Oxford about three weeks before term began, and put up at the Randolph, and immediately began my search for somewhere to live. I traded on my disability and my war record shamelessly, but at the lower levels I'm afraid the money helped. By the time term began I was very comfortably installed in rooms in Merton Street conveniently close to college, which may well have been the most expensive lodgings ever to be rented by an undergraduate. However, there I was; I bought a nearly new car dubiously at an inflated price from a young doctor who had got it on a priority licence, and started in to look for Janet Prentice.

I shall pass over the details of my quest quite shortly, because it ended in a complete dead end. I went and had a talk with the Bursar of Wyckham, who remembered my letter, of course, and was very helpful. He introduced me to the Provost and three other dons who had been friends of Dr Prentice, but they knew nothing that would help me. Settle seemed the best line of inquiry, and I went up to that little town in Yorkshire just before the Oxford term began, and stayed there for three days. I went and saw the police, the postmaster, the stationmaster, the headmasters of two schools, the vicar, the Roman Catholic priest, the Methodist minister, the Town Clerk, and a chap in the Food Office who issued ration cards. Nobody that I spoke to had ever heard of Janet Prentice, and there seemed to be no young married woman in the town who answered the description in any way.

I went back to Oxford disappointed.

At that time in England everybody had to have a registration card, which was, theoretically at any rate, a means of tracing anyone at any time. As I took up my legal studies once again in Oxford, an elderly, battered undergraduate somewhat out of tune with his surroundings, I started an inquiry into registration cards with the Ministry of Labour. This led me to the Admiralty. I discovered then that Leading Wren Prentice had been given a compassionate discharge from the Navy in September 1944, for the purpose of looking after her mother, who was recently widowed and in bad health. A civilian registration card had been issued to her on her discharge from the Navy, and I got the number.

All this correspondence took time, because a good many letters were involved and no British Government department seemed to answer any letter in less than a fortnight in those days. It was near the end of term when I finally got the number of the identity card and wrote to the Ministry of Labour to ask where she was.

They took a month to answer, creating something of a record in this correspondence, and then wrote back and gave me the address of the old Prentice home in Crick Road, Oxford.

I had, of course, been there at a very early stage and made inquiries up and down the road, with no result. It was just before Christmas when I got this letter. I had stayed in Oxford to await it, cancelling a project I had had to go down to the South of France for the vacation, because I could not bear to waste time in my quest. I went to London directly Christmas was over and stayed at the Royal Air Force Club, of which I was an overseas member, and spent a morning in the Ministry of Labour. In the end I found an affable young man who went to a good deal of trouble in the matter, and produced some information that surprised me.

The registration card had been handed in at Harwich on November 14th, 1946, when Miss Janet Prentice left England for Holland. At that time the regulations stated that if a

British subject were to go to live abroad the registration card had to be handed in on leaving the country and a new one taken out when he came back and wanted ration cards again. No new registration card had been issued to Miss Prentice, so presumably she was still abroad.

By this time the trail was growing very cold, but I could not give up until I had done everything within my power to find Bill's girl. I went to the steamship company and succeeded in discovering from their records that a Miss Prentice had, in fact, crossed as a passenger from Harwich to Rotterdam on that November day two years before, travelling tourist class, but they could provide no clue as to her destination. More to fill in time during the vacation than with any real hope of success I went to Rotterdam and saw the British Vice-Consul, to try to learn if any British subject of that name were living in the district, perhaps with an old lady, perhaps in some town or village with a name that resembled Settle. He had no information for me, but suggested that the British Embassy at The Hague had fuller information covering all Holland, so I went on there. They knew of nobody in Holland that corresponded with my description, but the Third Secretary discovered a small village or hamlet called Settlers about sixty miles north of Pretoria, in the Transvaal, in South Africa. It was a desperately long shot, but the Transvaal is closely linked with Holland and when I got back to Oxford I addressed a letter to the postmaster of Settlers. Too long a shot, because I never got an answer.

So, for the time being, my search for Janet Prentice came to an end. Two years previously she had vanished into Europe and had left no trace behind her.

CHAPTER SEVEN

A MAN with my disability has to make new interests and amusements, and while I was in England motor racing became mine. It began, I think, in 1949 when I joined the London Aeroplane Club and took up flying again, more for mental discipline and to show myself I wasn't afraid to than because I really got much kick out of a Tiger Moth. I set myself to do about fifty hours solo flying to rehabilitate my skill; I think I had vaguely in my mind that having once flown I should retain the ability in case we ever wanted to use aeroplanes on our Australian properties.

At the flying club I found a number of enthusiastic motor-racing types, young men of all social classes united in a common love of the internal combustion engine, who appeared at the aerodrome on stripped-down motor bikes or ancient racing cars. None of them had much money, most of them spoke with a slight London accent not unlike my own, and all seemed to have cheerful and attractive young women perched athletically on their uncomfortable vehicles. I found their company congenial and their enthusiasms contagious, and I went with them upon a number of excursions to races and hill climbs, and once in a chartered Anson to the Tourist Trophy races in the Isle of Man.

Early in 1950 I got so far involved in this amusement that I bought a little racing car myself, a Cooper, which I raced once or twice without distinction in the miniature class. I found that, while I could still fly an aeroplane all right, I hadn't really got the nerve for motor racing. Perhaps I was too old, but with my dummy feet it took a matter of minutes to wriggle in or out of the cramped little single-seater cockpit, so that I was continually troubled by the thought of fire. After a few races I gave up and handed it over to a young friend of mine at the club, John Harwood, content to be the backer and pay the bills, and watch him win races on it. It served its turn well, did that little car, because John developed into a very fine driver and now races for various firms continually, all over Europe.

I took Schools at Oxford in May 1950 and got a second in Law, and went to Mr A. N. Seligman's chambers in Lincoln's Inn with a view to getting called to the Bar. There wasn't a great deal of sense in it, perhaps, because the Bar wasn't going to be much help to me in running Coombargana, but by that time I was interested in Law and legal processes and there was no need for me to go home just yet. I got a flat in Half Moon Street quite handy to my club and settled down to live in London for a time, retaining my associations with the flying club and with my motor-racing friends, of course. Petrol was de-rationed shortly after I came down from Oxford, so I got a ten-year-old Bentley and began to explore England.

I had visited the Admiralty soon after my return to England and I had got an account of my brother Bill's death which was rather scanty, though all the essential facts were there. The Second Sea Lord's office were helpful in the matter, however, and they suggested that I could get a fuller account from Warrant Officer Albert Finch of the Royal Marines, who had been Bill's companion on the night when he was killed. Warrant Officer Finch, however, was serving a tour of duty on the China Station and was due home in November 1950. I wrote to Finch and got rather a laboured letter in reply because he evidently wasn't a very easy writer and had difficulty in telling a story on paper, and I arranged with him that we would meet when he got home to England.

In the years when I was at Oxford I met a good many young English women, particularly in the motor-racing crowd. They were cheerful, sensible girls mostly, but I didn't get involved with any of them. The best of them had a little of the same quality of forthrightness and community of interests that I had admired so greatly in Bill's girl and that had made me so glad to have her as a prospective sister-in-law, the indefinable quality of being easy to live with. None of them approached the Leading Wren that Bill had loved, in my opinion; the more I saw of these others, the more they reminded me of Janet Prentice, the more my mind turned back to all the details of that day at Lymington.

It was to be August 1950 before I got any further in my quest for her, however. There was a race meeting on the perimeter track of the old Goodwood aerodrome, and I had entered the Cooper for two events with John Harwood driving it for the first time; he had put in a lot of work upon the car in his mews' garage in Paddington and had got her in good nick. I sent the Cooper down upon a truck and left London at about five in the morning with a carload of my friends and two other cars with us, a party of fifteen or sixteen of us all told. It was a glorious summer morning and we made quick time down to West Sussex, and got the Cooper unloaded and filled up before nine o'clock. We pushed John off for a few trial circuits so that he could get the feel of her; he took her round easily for two or three laps as we had arranged and then trod on it and did a lap at seventy-eight, timed by my stopwatch, which seemed good going for a car of only 500 cc. He came in to the paddock and said he could do better than that, so we pushed her into a corner and went to breakfast.

We had brought a lot of food down in baskets and a Primus stove to boil a kettle, and the girls got breakfast for us on the grass beside the cars in the warm sun. There was a girl there I hadn't met before, Cynthia Something – I forget her surname. Somehow the talk turned to the war, as it so often does; she evidently knew all about me, but I knew nothing about her. She looked about twenty-seven and so had probably seen service of some sort, and I asked her casually, 'What did you do in the Great War, Mummy?'

'Mummy yourself,' she retorted. 'I was in the Navy.'

I had had this once or twice before, but it had never led to anything. 'In the Wrens?'

She nodded, her mouth full of cold sausage.

'What category were you in?' I asked.

'Boat's crew,' she said. 'First of all at Brightlingsea and then Portsmouth – in *Hornet*.'

'When were you at Portsmouth?'

'1944 and 1945,' she said. She took a drink of tea to wash the sausage down. 'I was demobbed from HMS *Hornet*.'

I lit a cigarette, for I had finished eating and it was warm and pleasant sitting on the grass in the sun, listening to the engines revving up. 'Did you ever meet a Leading Wren Prentice?' I inquired. 'Janet Prentice. She was an Ordnance artificer, I think, at HMS *Mastodon* in the Beaulieu River.'

She checked with her cup poised in mid-air. 'You mean, the one who shot down the German aeroplane?'

I stared at her. 'I never heard that.'

'There was a Leading Wren Prentice who shot down a German bomber with an Oerlikon,' she said. 'At Beaulieu, just before the invasion.'

'It's possible,' I said. 'I never heard that about her, but it could be. She was engaged to my brother, but he was killed about that time. I've been trying to get in touch with her, but she seems to have disappeared.'

'It must be the same,' she said. 'There couldn't have been two Leading Wrens called Prentice at Beaulieu, at that time.'

'Did you know her?' I inquired.

She shook her head. 'I never met her. There was a lot of chat about it in the Service – naturally. It never got into the newspapers, of course. Security.'

I nodded. 'I wish to God I could find somebody that knew her and kept in touch with her,' I said. 'I believe she's out of England, but she must have some friends here. I've been trying for two years to find out where she is.'

She chewed thoughtfully for a minute. 'She was engaged to your brother?'

'That's right. I met her once, at Lymington, early in 1944, just before Bill got killed.' I paused, and then I said, 'She was a fine girl.'

'Viola Dawson would be the best person,' she said thoughtfully. 'Viola must have known her.'

'Who's Viola Dawson?'

'She was another Leading Wren,' she said. 'She was in boats with me at Brightlingsea, and then she went to Beaulieu. Viola must have known this Prentice girl.'

'Can I get in touch with Viola Dawson?'

'I know Viola,' she said. 'She's got a flat in Earls Court Square. She's in the telephone book. If you like, I'll give her a ring tonight and tell her about you, and say you'll be calling her.'

'I wish you would,' I said. 'It's the first time I've been able to find anybody who might know something about Janet Prentice.'

'I'll do that,' she said. 'I'll tell her who you are.'

'What would be a good time to ring her?' I inquired. 'Does she work?'

'She works in a film studio,' she said. 'At Pinewood or some place like that. She does continuity, whatever that may mean. I should think you'd get her any evening at about seven o'clock – unless she's out, of course.'

I thanked her, and at seven o'clock next evening I rang up Viola Dawson. 'Miss Dawson,' I said. 'You won't know me – my name's Alan Duncan. I met a girl—'

'I know,' she broke in. 'Cynthia rang me. I've been expecting to hear from you, Mr Duncan.'

'Good,' I said. 'What I really wanted to find out from you is if you know anything about Janet Prentice.'

'I knew her quite well in the war,' she said.

'You haven't seen her recently?'

'I haven't,' she replied. 'I'm not sure even where she's living now.'

'I don't think she's in England,' I said. 'I've been trying to find someone who could put me in touch with her.' I paused, and then I said, 'She was engaged to my brother, before he got killed.'

'I know,' she said. 'I remember that happening.'

'You do?'

'Oh yes. Janet and I were together at Beaulieu. We were great friends in those days, but I'm afraid I've lost touch with her now.'

'Look, Miss Dawson,' I said, 'there's a lot I'd like to ask you about Janet. I never knew much about her, and I'm very anxious to get into touch with her if I can. Could we have a meal together, do you think?'

'I'd like to,' she said.

'What about tonight? Have you eaten yet?'

She seemed to hesitate. 'No – not yet. Yes, I could come tonight, a bit later on.'

'Suppose I call for you in about half an hour?'

'Give me a little longer – I've got some work I want to finish. Come about eight o'clock and we'll go out somewhere. Somewhere simple; I shan't have time to change.'

'All right. I'll be with you about eight o'clock.'

'Top flat,' she said. 'Right up at the very top, in the attic.'

I went round in a taxi an hour later, and climbed the stairs of the old four-storey terraced house converted into little flats, up to the very top. It was such a place as any working girl in a good job might live in, decent but not affluent. I rang the bell, and she opened the door to me.

If her face hadn't been quite so lean, her jaw quite so definite, she would have been a very beautiful woman. She had very fair hair and a beautiful complexion, slightly tanned or sunburnt. That she had been a boat's crew Wren was in the part; I realized directly I saw her, with the knowledge of her Service that I had, that she would look exactly right at the wheel of a motor boat. Perhaps her dress may have put that into my mind, for she wasn't ready for me yet. She was wearing a dark-blue linen overall coat, and she had an artist's brush in her hand.

'Come in, Mr. Duncan,' she said. 'I'm going to ask you to sit down and wait a few minutes while I finish off, before the light goes.'

The door opened directly into her sitting-room, which was half studio; apparently her interests were artistic. Various canvases were propped up on chairs or bookcases or stacked against the wall, and sketches and sketchbooks littered her table. She was working at an oil painting upon an easel, and she went back to this without more ado, picked up her palette, and began work again. 'Find somewhere to sit down for just a minute,' she said. 'That's sherry in the bottle on the tray – help yourself. I ought to have got this place all tiddley before you arrived, but it's such a pity to waste the light.'

'Don't bother about me,' I said. 'I'll sit and watch. Cynthia didn't tell me that you were an artist. She said something about working in the movies.'

'That's what I do,' she said. 'Continuity and set design. I do this as a spare-time job, for fun. Give yourself a glass of sherry and give me one. I won't be very long.'

I did as she told me, and took her glass to her before the easel, and saw the picture she was painting for the first time. The easel stood beneath a skylight in the roof which gave it a north light, probably why she lived in that flat. The canvas was a fairly large one, perhaps twenty-four by twenty. It showed a brightly camouflaged motor torpedo boat ploughing through a rough sea at reduced speed, under a lowering sky with a break at the horizon giving a gleaming, horizontal light. The curved bow of the vessel was lifted dripping from the water in a trough showing a fair length of her keel; there was vigour in the painting and life in the pitch and heel of the boat, and in the gleaming, silvery light.

I gave her the sherry and stood back behind her, looking at the picture. 'That's good, isn't it?' I asked. 'I mean, that's what it must look like.'

'I hope so,' she said equably. She stood back for a moment, then bent forward and added a deft, sweeping stroke to one of the grey-green waves of the foreground, giving it form and texture. 'You don't know much about painting, do you?'

'Not a thing,' I said.

'Then there's a pair of us,' she remarked. 'I've never had a lesson and I'll never be any good, but I like doing it.'

I stared at the painting. 'Never had a lesson?'

'Not in painting,' she said. There was a pause while she changed brushes, dabbed on the palette, and added a stroke or two. 'At school, of course – drawing. And then night classes after the war to learn to do a monochrome wash drawing, for the sets, you know, for the stage carpenters to work to. I'm not sure that lessons in colour would be much good, anyway.'

'I like that,' I said. 'I like it very much.'

There was another pause while she worked. 'Journeyman stuff,' she said at last. 'I'll hang it on the wall and look at it till I've outgrown it. Then I'll sell it, and some stockbroker who was RNVR in the war 'll give me twenty quid for it and love it for the rest of his life.'

I glanced around the room, taking in the other pictures. Most of them seemed to have to do with naval matters, studies of ships and landing craft, and one or two portraits of naval officers. One recent painting showed white-painted yachts moored in a harbour; this was principally a study of water reflections.

'Are most of your things naval?' I asked.

'Most of them,' she said. 'I'm beginning to get it out of my system now.' She worked on in silence for a time, and then she said, 'It seemed so much the normal way of life after the war that one didn't do anything about it. And then one day I woke up – we all woke up – and had to realize that it had all been quite unusual; it would never come again. Not for us, not in our lifetime. We should be too old, or married – out of it. And then I felt I had to work and work and put it all down on canvas, everything I'd seen, before I forgot what it was like.' She worked on in silence, and then she said, 'It's very hard to realize that it will never come again. To realize we've had it.'

'I know,' I said. 'I think we all feel that.'

She laid the palette down and wiped the brush upon a bit of newspaper. 'You were in the RAF, Cynthia said.'

'That's right,' I replied.

'I remember Janet telling me about you,' she said. 'Didn't she pinch one of the boats and take you out in it, one Sunday?'

'That's right,' I said again. 'I went out with her and Bill, to a place called Keyhaven.'

She scraped the palette with a palette knife and wiped it with a cloth. 'She said you were the hell of a chap,' Viola remarked. 'Fighter Command, three rings, and a chest full of ribbons.'

'That was then,' I said quietly. 'Now I'm a fat cripple walking with two sticks, living on wool and only interested in Law.'

She went on tidying up her things, for the light was failing and her work was over for the evening. 'It comes to all of us,' she said. 'You think a thing's going on for ever when you're young, and then you wake up and you find it doesn't, and you've got to find something fresh to do. New interests.'

She finished putting her things away, gave me another sherry, stood for a minute looking at her painting, and then went through to another room to wash and get ready to come out to supper. I sat down off my feet and rested, pleasantly lulled by her sherry, studying her pictures. She had made a better job of adapting herself to Peace than I had.

She came out presently, pulling on a raincoat over her blouse and skirt. 'There's a little restaurant just round the corner that I go to,' she said. 'In the Earls Court Road. Will that be all right for you?'

'Anywhere you say,' I replied.

She turned to a cupboard, opened it, and stooped down on the floor rummaging among the contents. 'There's something here I'd like to show you,' she said. She pulled out a big, floppy sketchbook, discarded it upon the floor beside her, pulled out another and another, and finally stood with one in her hand. 'I think it's in here.'

She flipped the pages through and turned the book back, and laid it on the table before me. It was a vigorous drawing of a Wren firing an Oerlikon at an aeroplane flying very low towards her. The drawing was in sepia crayon. The Wren was a broad-shouldered, dark-haired girl, hatless, leaning back upon the strap that held her in the shoulder rings, tense, unsmiling, intent upon the sights. I had only met her once six years before but she was unmistakable to me.

'Janet Prentice,' I said.

She nodded. 'I did that the same evening, in the Wrennery. I was in the boat alongside when the thing came over.' She paused. 'I think that's pretty well what it looked like.'

'Cynthia told me she had shot a Junkers down,' I said. 'I never heard the details. I think that must have been after I met her.'

'Probably it was,' she said. 'I think it was after your brother got killed – no – I'm not sure about that. I can tell you what happened, though.' She paused, and then closed the book. 'Let's go out now and have supper.'

She took me to her restaurant and I ordered dinner. They had no very good wine because it was a cheap little place, but they produced a bottle of claret, very *ordinaire* and probably Algerian, the sort of wine we would pay seven and six a gallon for at home. The wine helped, no doubt, and I found Viola Dawson easy to talk to, so that when we were sitting smoking with a cup of coffee I had no difficulty in speaking to her frankly about Janet Prentice.

'I want you to understand where I stand in this matter,' I told her. 'I only met her once, that day when she took Bill and me to Keyhaven in the boat. I don't think they were engaged, but they were pretty near it.'

She nodded. 'They were never engaged,' she said. 'She wanted to be. They were waiting until after the balloon went up.'

'I know,' I said. 'Bill told me that. He was my only brother, you know. We were very close.'

'He thought a lot of you,' she said. 'Janet was afraid of meeting you that day because Bill had told her about you. Three rings, DFC and bar, Fighter Command and all the rest of it. She wasn't a bit happy when she went off with the boat that morning. She was afraid she wouldn't make the grade with you.'

I stared at her. 'I'd never have thought that . . .' I paused, and then I said, 'She made the grade all right. I told Bill afterwards. You see, my father and mother came into it. They'd have wanted to know about her if Bill had got married in England. I thought she was a fine girl, and she'd have made Bill a good wife. I told him that I'd write and tell them so at home.'

'She was quite happy when she came back to the Wrennery that night,' Viola said. 'She wasn't worried after that. The only thing is, I think she was a bit puzzled.'

'What about?'

She smiled. 'About what she was marrying into, if she married Bill. She thought he was a sheep farmer's son. She'd got herself accustomed to the idea that she might be marrying – well, a little bit beneath the way she'd been brought up. She didn't worry about that because she was in love with your brother, but she knew she'd have to make adjustments, that she might find her new relations a bit raw.' She paused. 'Your brother was a sergeant, of course. Then you came along and it turned out you were a Rhodes scholar, which rocked her a bit, and then it seems you told her that both you and Bill had been at some school in Australia – I forget the name. She found out afterwards that it was a sort of Eton in Australia, and rather expensive. Then she didn't know what to think.'

'Bill was telling her the truth,' I said. 'We *are* sheep farmers. But there are little ones and big ones in Australia.'

'You're one of the big ones?'

'Yes.' I paused for a minute to collect my thoughts. 'She was very good for Bill,' I said. 'I thought that day that he was feeling the strain a bit – the work he had to do.' She nodded. 'She was just the right person for him, as I saw it. I was grateful to her then,' I said. 'I'm grateful to her now.'

'They should have given him a rest,' she remarked. 'The trouble was, of course, there were so few of them that had the skill to do the job, and so much to be done before "Overlord".'

'I know,' I said. 'They were expendable. The thing that matters now is this. She made Bill very happy in his last weeks. I should have kept in touch with her, and I didn't. She should have been a friend of the family for the remainder of her life, but it's not worked out that way. I tried to get in touch with her three years ago and I've been trying ever since. All I've succeeded in discovering has been bad news. Things haven't been too good for her. That's what's worrying me now.'

I went on to tell her why I hadn't kept in touch with Janet Prentice, about the snow at Evère aerodrome, about my time in hospital, about my self-centred preoccupation with my own affairs before I went back to Australia. 'Not so good,' I said quietly at the end. 'But that's what happened.'

'I lost touch with her, too,' said Viola. 'I'm just as bad, I suppose, because she needed her friends after the war. But – one can't keep up with everyone.' She glanced at me. 'You know that she was trying to get back into the Wrens?'

'No,' I said. 'I never heard that about her.'

She thought for a minute. 'I went and saw her just after the invasion, at Oxford,' she said. 'I was on leave. She wasn't up to much then – sort of weepy and very, very nervous. It was just before she got her discharge from the Wrens and she knew that it was coming. She took it as if it was a sort of disgrace, I think. The Junkers she'd shot down was worrying her, too.'

'I don't know anything about that Junkers,' I said. 'What was it that she did?'

She told me as much as she knew. I called the waiter and ordered a fresh pot of coffee, and lit another cigarette for her. At last I was learning something real about Janet Prentice.

'It was all a bit depressing,' Viola said at last. 'She'd been such a fine person a few months before, and now she was all to pieces.'

I said nothing.

'I saw her again in the summer or autumn of 1946,' Viola said. 'I can't remember what month. I saw her mother's death in the *Telegraph*, and I was driving to Wales or somewhere so I wrote to her and fixed up to have lunch with her in Oxford on my way through.' She paused. 'It was just after the funeral and she was packing up the house and selling everything. Her one idea was to get back into the Wrens.'

'Why was she so keen on that?' I asked.

She shrugged her shoulders. 'Why do any of us look back on our war service with such pleasure, in spite of everything?' she demanded. 'Answer me that. You'd be glad to be back in the RAF in another war, and you know it. If it happened again, I'd be back in the Wrens like a shot.'

'Did she get back into the Wrens?' I asked.

She shook her head. 'They wouldn't have her.'

'Why not? She must have had a very good war record.'

'I know.' There was a pause, and then she said, 'They're very, very careful who they take in. Even in peacetime there are many more girls trying to get into the Wrens than they want. They can afford to be choosey.'

'I see,' I said.

'I know a girl who stayed on in the Wrens,' she told me. 'She's a second officer, in the Admiralty. She tells me that they won't have anyone back, however good, if there's the slightest hint of any nervous trouble on the record. She says they get a lot of cases like that, and they turn them all down, just on principle. They want girls with untroubled minds, who sleep soundly at night.'

We sat in silence for a minute. 'When you saw her in 1946,' I asked presently, 'was she really bad? I mean, I'd like to know.'

'She wasn't raving, if that's what you mean,' Viola said, a little sharply.

'I want to try and understand,' I told her.

'I know,' she replied, more gently. 'She was very lonely, for one thing, I think. She was missing her mother, of course, and she didn't seem to have any relations left in England to speak of. She didn't seem to have made many friends, either.'

'She didn't make friends easily?'

Viola shook her head. 'She did in the Service, but that's different. When you're sleeping thirty in a hut you just can't help making friends. But in civil life, living at home and looking after her mother – I don't think she would have done. She was rather shy, you know.'

'I'd never have thought that of her,' I remarked.

'You only saw her in the Navy,' Viola said. 'It's so totally different, living with men and working alongside them. You can't do a job in the Navy and be shy. But it can come back afterwards.'

'Was she still nervous?'

She shook her head. 'Not in the way she was when I saw her before, the time I saw her just after the invasion. She'd got herself under control. I don't think anything was very real to her that had happened since she left the Wrens, though.'

'Was she still worrying about the Junkers?'

Viola nodded. 'It was still very much upon her mind – that, and your brother's death. But what really did worry me was the way she talked about the dog.'

'What dog was that?' I asked.

'Your brother's dog,' she said. 'He had a dog that he called Dev. I thought you'd have known.'

'I know he had a dog,' I said. 'A sort of Irish terrier. They had him with them in the boat that day. What about him?'

'Bert Finch brought him over to her after your brother's death,' she said. I sat in silence while she told me about Dev.

Ten minutes later I said, 'It was that that really finished her? When the dog got killed?'

She nodded. 'You see, it wasn't just a dog that she'd got fond of. It was your brother's dog. She told me in the Wrennery that evening that she'd let your brother down by not taking more care of his dog. Of course, I didn't pay much attention to that at the time, because she was in a sort of a breakdown and going off on leave next day. But after her mother's death, more than two years later, she told me the same thing. I tried to tell her it was my fault as much as hers, that I shouldn't have let him out of the boat on to the hard. But it didn't register with her. She seemed to have got a sort of horror and disgust with herself that she hadn't looked after Bill's dog better.'

'She never had another dog, after the war?'

Viola shook her head. 'Oh no – I shouldn't think so.' There was a pause, and then she said, 'Something broke in her when that dog got killed that took a lot of breaking, and would have taken a lot of building up. And it never got built up ...'

She looked at her watch presently, and it was half past ten. 'I must go,' she said. 'I've got to work tomorrow.'

I paid the bill and we left the restaurant. We walked slowly together the short distance to her flat, and paused for a minute on the pavement outside before I left her. 'There are one or two other people who might possibly know where she is,' she said. 'There's a girl called May Spikins, the other O A Wren who worked with her. I think I might be able to get you her address. You ought to see Bert Finch, too.'

'I've been in touch with him,' I said. 'He's in China, or on his way home now. I'll be seeing him before Christmas – about Bill.'

She nodded. 'Of course. I think you might find he knows

something about Janet Prentice. Anyway, I'll find out about May Spikins for you.'

I saw a good deal of Viola Dawson after that. She rang me up a few days later to give me information about May Spikins, who was May Cunningham by that time, and when I suggested that we might have lunch together she seemed pleased. She was almost as anxious as I was to find Janet Prentice, for having been close friends in the war Viola was genuinely worried to find that they had drifted so far apart that she had lost all touch with her. On my part, I soon found that Viola knew a great deal about Janet Prentice that had not come out at our first meeting – not important things, for she had told me all of those, but little touches, little incidents that happened in their Service life together that helped me to build up a picture of the Leading Wren that Bill had loved.

I went to see May Spikins in her new house in the new town at Harlow, and she put me on to Petty Officer Waters in his tobacconist's shop in the Fratton Road at Portsmouth. Then, about Christmas time, Warrant Officer Finch came home and I went down in January after he came back from leave and saw him in his mess in Eastney Barracks. From him I got the account of Bill's death, and in the long vacation of 1951 I went to France and spent some time endeavouring to find out where Bill had been buried. As I have said, I failed, but it wasn't very important to know that in any case.

At each step in this matter Viola and I used to meet to talk things over, often at a restaurant in Jermyn Street. Presently she began coming with me to motor-race meetings, and I visited her film studio and spent an afternoon upon the set with her, and had lunch with her in the commissary. She was a very easy person for a man like me to go about with, for we had the Service background as a link. I found presently that I was telling her about my life in the RAF, almost unconsciously, a thing that I had never been able to talk about to anybody, and I woke up one day to realize uneasily that we were getting very close, that she knew more about me, probably, than anybody else in the world. It was a year after we had met for the first time that I woke up to that, and the realization troubled me. I liked Viola, and I didn't want to hurt her.

It all came to a head next winter, either just before or just after Christmas. She had been to Switzerland ski-ing for a fortnight and had come back with a lot of action photographs, and from these she had been working up a painting of a chap on a snow slope doing a fast turn. It was part of her artistic development that she was getting away from naval subjects now; at long last, perhaps, the preoccupation with her Service life was beginning to fade. She had asked me to come round to her flat to have a look at this picture, and I went with slight reluctance. At some stage I would have to hurt her, and I didn't want to do it.

I went one afternoon at a weekend, intending to take her out to a movie and dinner. The painting she was working on was a good, vigorous action picture; if anything, I think she was a better draughtsman than painter and her action drawings were unusually good for a woman. We talked about the picture for a few minutes, and then she went through to her kitchenette to make tea, and I dropped down upon the sofa.

She had been rummaging in the cupboard where she kept her old sketchbooks, and the big, floppy things were all out upon the floor. I turned them over till I found the one that I thought contained the sketch of Janet Prentice firing the Oerlikon, and turned the pages. It was full of pencil sketches of Naval craft and Naval scenes, with a number of rough portrait sketches, a sort of commonplace book that she had kept with her throughout her service in the Wrens. Presently, turning the pages, I came upon a pencil sketch of Janet Prentice.

It was a head-and-shoulders portrait, exactly as I had seen her in the boat at Lymington, as I remembered her. She wore a round Wren cap and a duffle coat, the hood thrown back upon her shoulders. I sat there looking at the square, homely face that I remembered so very well, thinking of that day. Viola came in as I sat motionless with the book upon my knee. She asked, 'What have you got there?' and looked over my shoulder.

'Portrait of Janet Prentice,' I said. 'Can I have it?'

'What do you want it for?' she asked. There was a sharpness in her tone, so that I knew there was trouble coming. It had to come some time, of course.

'It's very like her,' I said quietly. I wanted a picture of her very badly. 'I'd like to have it, if you can spare it.'

She did not answer that at once. She crossed to the table and put down the teapot and the plate of cakes that she was carrying, and stood silent for a minute, looking into the far corner of the room. Then she said, 'You think you're in love with her, don't you?'

'I don't think anything of the sort,' I replied. 'She was Bill's girl. If he'd come through she'd have been my sister-in-law. We ought to have a picture of her.'

'It's absolutely crazy,' she said dully. 'You only met her once for a few hours nearly eight years ago.'

'It would be absolutely crazy if I was,' I retorted. 'You're imagining things.' I paused, and then I added weakly, 'I'm just trying to find her.'

She turned to me, suddenly furious. 'And when you've found her, what then? Do you think she'll still be the same person as she was eight years ago? Are you the same person as you were in 1944? For God's sake be your age, Alan, and stop behaving like a teenager.'

She was quite right, of course, but I wasn't going to stay and have her talk to me like that. I got to my feet. 'About time I beat it, after that,' I said. I put on my raincoat and picked up my sticks. 'I'm sorry, Viola, if I've done anything to hurt you. I didn't mean to.' And I made for the door.

She stood watching me go, and I half expected the embarrassment that she would call me back and ask me to stay, and so prolong the inevitable. But she didn't do it, and I closed the door behind me and made my way slowly down her stairs for the last time. It's no good looking backwards; one has to go on. It's no good trying to be happy with the second best. She had said that I was absolutely crazy, but I had known that myself for some considerable time.

Two days after that I got a note from Viola; it enclosed the little pencil sketch of Janet Prentice, cut from her sketchbook. It said simply,

My dear Alan,

Here's your sketch, as a peace offering. I've fixed it, but you'd better frame it under glass.

I think you're mad as a March hare, and I don't want to see you any more, so please don't ring up or write and thank for this.

Good luck,
Viola

London wasn't much fun after that. I had grown to depend on Viola more than I quite realized for company, and when it all came to an end I didn't know what to do with myself. I had my work in chambers, of course, and I had the Club and motor racing still, but as 1952 progressed I began to take less interest in these things, and to feel that a time was approaching when I should have had England. Reports from home weren't too good, either; both my father and my mother were beginning to fail in health and to find the work of the station a burden, and a wistfulness was starting to creep in to their letters when they mentioned my plans. I saw Helen from time to time and she was obviously fixed in London with her Laurence, and I began to feel that I should be at home. My search for Janet Prentice seemed to have petered out, and it was only a chance now if I ever heard of her again. In the uncertain climate of the English spring and summer I began to think with longing of the warm settled weather of the Western District in summer, and the drenching sunshine of our property at Tennant Creek.

I had another year of keeping terms and eating dinners to do before I could be called to the Bar, and there was no urgency for me to go home till that had been achieved, but I began to make my plans to go home in the autumn of 1953. I didn't really want to stay in England for another year, and it may well have been the really big mistake of my life that I did so. But having set myself to one of the learned professions it seemed silly to abandon it when it lay within my grasp, and though I was growing tired of London there was nothing imperative to take me home. I went to Spain for a month in the summer and to Greece, Rhodes, and Cyprus for a couple of months in the winter, garnering all the experience that an Australian likes to take back with him to the Antipodes when he knows it may be many years before he comes to Europe again, if ever.

I achieved my ambition and was called formally to the Bar in September 1953. I had booked a passage home by sea to leave England at the beginning of October, and in the last month I was winding up my affairs in England and saying goodbye to all my friends. I was troubled about Viola Dawson, the best friend I had made in London, and uncertain if I ought to see her to say goodbye to her or whether that would only upset her and so be an unkindness. But she solved the matter, because ten days before I sailed she wrote to me. She said,

Dear Alan,

I hear I've got to congratulate you on being called. I'm so glad. And Cynthia tells me that you're sailing on the 5th. I want to see you before you go, and it's about Janet Prentice so you'll probably come.

I shall be dining at Bruno's, the little restaurant I took you to the first night we met, next Thursday at eight. Will you come and dine with me there? Don't come to the flat.

Yours,
Viola

I was waiting for her in the little restaurant when she came, at a table by the wall. She was paler than usual, I thought, not looking very well. She seemed pleased to see me, and I ordered sherry while we discussed what we would eat. I asked her what she had been doing, and she said, working.

'No holiday?' I asked, for it was autumn and the weather was still warm.

She shook her head. 'There seems to have been such a lot to do.'

The waiter took our order and went away, and then she turned to me. 'I've got news for you,' she said. 'Janet Prentice.'

'What about her?' I asked.

'She's living in Seattle, or she was about a year ago.'

'Seattle – in America?'

She nodded. 'On the West Coast somewhere, isn't it?' She smiled faintly. 'It was Seattle she was going to, when she left Oxford, not Settle. The charwoman got it wrong.'

'What on earth's she doing there?'

'Didn't you say that she was going to live with an aunt in Settle?'

'That's what the charwoman said.'

'She had an uncle who was on the faculty of Stanford University in the United States,' she reminded me. 'Is that in Seattle?'

'I think it's on the West Coast somewhere,' I said slowly. 'I always thought it was near San Francisco.'

'Anyway, she's living in Seattle now,' said Viola. 'I've got her address for you.' She picked up her bag and opened it, and took out a folded slip of paper, and passed it to me across the table. 'That's what you've been looking for,' she said quietly.

I opened it, and it read: Miss J. E. Prentice, 8312 37th Ave, NW, Seattle, Washington, USA. I stared at it for a minute, and then asked, 'How did you get hold of this, Viola?'

'Dorothy Fisher got it for me,' she said a little wearily. 'The girl I told you about, who stayed on in the Wrens. Second officer, in the Admiralty. Janet's been writing in every few months, ever since the Korean War started.'

'Trying to get back into the Wrens?'

She nodded. 'She wrote in when the Korean War broke out and there was nothing doing, and she wrote in again about six months later. Then about eighteen months ago she put in an application to rejoin the Wrens through the Naval Attaché in Washington, and that went to the Admiralty, of course. They were getting a bit fed up with her by that time, so they wrote her rather a sharp letter, saying that her application was on the file and would be considered if and when the expansion of the Service justified the re-engagement of ex-Naval ratings in her category. They haven't heard from her again.'

'That was eighteen months ago?' I asked.

'About that. I think their letter to her was dated some time in April.'

The waiter came with soup, and I sat silent, thinking rapidly. I could scrap the passage I had booked by sea back to Australia and fly home through the States, but I should have to wangle a few dollars. A little thing like that wasn't going to stop me. Buy a set of diamond cuff links and sell them in the States, perhaps . . .

The waiter went away, and Viola said, 'I suppose you'll write to her.'

'I'll do that,' I said slowly, 'but there won't be time to get an answer before I go. I'm booked to leave in a few days. I think I'll cancel the sea passage and go back through the States. I'll be in Seattle in a few days' time, pretty well as soon as my letter.'

'I thought you'd probably do that,' she said. 'Mad as a March hare.'

I didn't know what I could say to that without hurting her more, and so we sat in silence for a time. The waiter came with the next course and woke me up from the consideration of the detail of my change in plans, of airline bookings, visas, vaccination certificates, travellers' cheques, and all the other impedimenta to air travel. I became aware that I owed Viola a lot. It must have cost her a great deal to give me what she had.

'I'm very grateful to you for all this, Viola,' I said clumsily. 'I don't think I'd ever have got in touch with her without your help.'

'We were good friends in the war,' she muttered, looking down at her plate. 'She's had a bad spin since, and I'd like her to be happy.'

Instinctively I sheered away from the difficult subject. 'Do you think she'd be happy if she got back into the Wrens?'

She raised her head and stared across the room. 'She might. It's difficult to say. She only knew the Wrens in wartime, and it's very different now.'

'What she wants is a Third World War,' I said, half laughing.

'Of course.' She sat silent for a moment, and then she said, 'Until we're dead, we Service people, the world will always be in danger of another war. We had too good a time in the last one. We'll none of us come out into the open and admit it. It might be better for us if we did. What we do is to put our votes in favour of re-armament and getting tough with Russia, and hope for the best.'

I stared at her. 'Is that what you really think?'

She nodded. 'You know it as well as I do, if you're honest with yourself. For our generation, the war years were the best time of our lives, not because they were war years but because we were young. The best years of our lives happened to be war years. Everyone looks back at the time when they were in their early twenties with nostalgia, but when we look back we only see the war. We had a fine time then, and so we think that if a Third War came we'd have those happy, carefree years all over again. I don't suppose we would – some of us might.'

'We're getting older every year,' I said. 'Perhaps more sensible.'

She nodded. 'That's one good thing. Most of us are gradually accumulating other interests – homes, and children, and work we wouldn't want to leave. It's only a few people now like – well, like Janet, who've had a bad spin since the war, who are so desperately anxious now to see another war come – for themselves.' She sat in thought for a moment. 'But for our children – I don't know. If I had kids, I'd want them to have all I had when I was young.'

'If you had daughters, you'd want them to be boat's crew Wrens?' I asked.

'Yes,' she said. 'Yes, I'd want them to have that. I'd want them to have all I had when I was young.' She turned to me. 'Your father served in the First War, didn't he?'

I nodded. 'He was at Gallipoli, and afterwards in France. He served in the last war, too.'

'Was he shocked and horrified when you and Bill joined up?' she asked relentlessly. 'Or was he glad you'd done it, for your own sakes?'

I sat in silence. 'I see what you mean,' I said at last. 'I never thought of it like that.'

'When you and I are dead, and all the rest of us who served in the last war, in all the countries,' she said, 'there'll be a chance of world peace. Not till then.'

'Get a nice atom bomb dropping down upon Earls Court tonight,' I said. 'That 'ld get rid of a good many of us.'

She smiled. 'Maybe that's the answer. But honestly, war's always been too pleasant for the people in it. For most young people it's been more attractive as a job than civil life. The vast majority of us never got killed or wounded; we just had a very stimulating and interesting time. If atom bombs can make life thoroughly unpleasant for the people in the Services, in all the countries, then maybe we shall have a chance of peace. If not, we'll have to wait till something else crops up that will.'

'Actually, in the last war, people in the Services in England had a better time than the ones who stayed at home, working in the factories,' I said.

'Of course they did,' she replied. 'That's the trouble. You'll never get rid of wars while you go on like that.'

It was better for us to go on talking so rather than to get back to Janet Prentice, and we went on putting the world right throughout our dinner till the coffee came and I lit her cigarette. She drank her coffee quickly. 'I must go back soon,' she said. 'I've got some work to do upon a script before tomorrow morning.'

I knew that she was making an excuse to cut our meeting short. 'This 'll have to be goodbye for the time being,' I said awkwardly. 'I don't know when I'll be in England again.'

'Not for some years, I suppose,' she said.

I nodded. 'I ought to have gone home a year ago. My father and mother are both getting pretty old, and there's the property to be looked after.'

She said, 'Maybe that's as well, Alan, for both of us.' She ground her half-smoked cigarette out into the ashtray and said, without looking up at me, 'Are you going to ask her if she'll marry you?'

'I don't know,' I protested. 'I may be mad as a March hare, but I'm not as mad as all that. Nine years ago, and only for a few hours then. We'll both have changed. You said that once yourself.'

'You'll marry her,' she said, 'and you'll be very happy together. And I'll send you a wedding present, and stand godmother to one of your kids.' She raised her eyes to mine, and they were full of tears. 'And now if you don't mind, Alan, I think I'm going home.'

She got up from the table and went quickly to the door of the little restaurant, and I went with her. In the doorway she turned to me. 'Go back and pay the bill,' she said. She put out her hand. 'This really is goodbye this time, Alan.'

I took her hand. 'I've done you nothing but harm, Viola,' I said, 'and you've done me nothing but good. I'm sorry for everything.'

She held my hand for an instant. 'It wouldn't ever have worked,' she said. 'I see that now. You're what you are and she would always be between us, even if you never see her again. We're grown-up people; we can part as friends.' She let my hand go. 'Good luck in Seattle.'

'Goodbye, Viola,' I said.

She turned away, and I stood in the doorway watching her as she went down the street, irresolute, half minded to go after her and call her back. But presently she turned the corner and was lost to sight, and I went back to pay the bill, sick at heart. Whatever I did with my life seemed to be wrong and make unhappiness for everyone concerned. I tried to kid myself it was because I was a cripple, but I knew that wasn't true. You can't evade the consequences of your own actions quite so easily as that.

I went back to my flat in Half Moon Street and sat down to write a letter to Janet Prentice. I slept on it, tore it up, wrote it again, slept on it next night, and wrote it a third time. When I was satisfied and posted it by airmail I had cut it to about one half of the original length. I just reminded her of our meeting in the war and said that while I was in England I had met Viola Dawson, who happened to have her address. As I was flying back to Australia in a week or so it would hardly be out of my way to come to Seattle to see her, and I would give her a ring as soon as I got in.

It took me a fortnight to rearrange my passage to Australia by air through the United States and to comply with all the formalities, maintaining the old adage – 'If you've time to spare, go by air'. It was not until October 14th that I finally took off from London airport for New York. I was leaving behind me in England a great deal that I admired and valued, but as I settled down into the Stratocruiser's seat I was absurdly and unreasonably happy. Of course I was going home after an absence of five years, and that probably accounted for a little part of my elation.

I had one or two friends in New York and I had never been in the United States before, so I went to a hotel and spent three days there, seeing my friends and being entertained and seeing the sights. I couldn't spare more time than that for the greatest city in the world because I had a date to keep in a smaller one. On the night of the nineteenth I was sitting in a Constellation on my way across the continent to Seattle; we got there in the morning and I checked in at a big hotel on 4th Avenue.

I didn't want to rush at this, so I had a bath and went down to a light lunch in the coffee shop. Then I went back up to my room and looked for Prentice in the telephone directory. It was there, all right, with the same address, though the name was Mrs C. W. Prentice. I stared at it in thought for a minute. There had been mention of an aunt that she was going to live with. This would be the widow of her uncle, the one who had been on the faculty of Stanford University. Widow, because if the husband had been alive the telephone would have been in his name.

I put the book down presently and sat down on the edge of the bed, and called the number.

A woman's voice answered, with a marked American accent. I said, 'Can I speak to Miss Prentice?'

'Say, you've got the wrong number,' she replied. 'Miss Prentice doesn't live here now.'

A sick disappointment came upon me. I had been counting on success this time. 'Can you tell me her number?' I asked. And then, feeling that a little explanation was required I said, 'She's expecting me. I'm on my way from England to Australia, and I stopped here in Seattle to see her.'

I don't think my explanation impressed the woman very much, because she said, 'She left here more than a year back, brother, after the old lady died. We bought the house off her. Did she give you this number?'

'No,' I said. 'I looked it up in the book.'

'I'd say that you'd got hold of an old book. Did you say she was expecting you?'

'I wrote to her from England a few days ago to say that I'd be passing through Seattle, and I'd ring her up,' I explained.

'Wait now,' she said. 'There's a letter came the other day for her from England. I meant to give it to the mailman and I clean forgot. Just stay there while I go get it.' I waited till she came back to the phone. 'What did you say your name was?'

'Alan Duncan.'

'That's correct,' she said. 'That's the name written on the back. Your letter's right here, Mr Duncan.'

I asked, 'Didn't she leave a forwarding address with you?'

'A forwarding what?'

I repeated the word.

'Oh, *address*,' she said. 'You certainly are English, Mr Duncan. No, she didn't leave that with us. A few things came in after she had gone, and we gave them to the mailman.'

I thought quickly. There was just a possibility that the woman might know more than I could easily get out of her upon the telephone, or possibly the next-door neighbour might know something that would help me. 'It looks as if I've missed her,' I said. 'I think the best thing I can do is to come out and collect that letter.'

'Sure,' she said affably. 'I'll be glad to meet you, Mr Duncan. I never met an Englishman from England.'

I laughed. 'You've not met one now. I'm Australian. Would it be all right if I come out this afternoon?'

'Surely,' she said. 'Come right out. The name's Pasmanik – Mrs Molly Pasmanik.'

I drove out in a taxi half an hour later. It was quite a long way out of town, in a district known as North Beach; the house was a street or two inland from the sea at Shilshole Bay, a decent suburban neighbourhood. The taxi driver didn't want to wait, so I paid him off and went in to the open garden to ring the bell of the small, single-storey house.

I spent an hour with Mrs Pasmanik, who produced a cup of coffee and some little sweet cakes for me, but I learned very little about Janet Prentice. She had lived there with her aunt until the aunt had died, but Mrs Pasmanik could not tell me how long she had lived there; they had themselves come to Seattle very recently from New Jersey. She really knew very little that was of any use to me.

I could not find out from Mrs Pasmanik that Janet made friends in the neighbourhood, and in that district houses seemed to change hands fairly frequently. The neighbours on the one side had left two months before my visit, and on the other side had come shortly before Janet had sold the house, and they knew nothing of her. The aunt had died in May 1952 and the Pasmaniks had bought the house from Janet in June. They had not seen much of her as the business had been handled by an agent; they had an idea, however, that she was going down to San Francisco to live there. There had been one or two legal complexities about the sale of the house because she was an alien in the United States, inheriting the estate of the aunt who was a US citizen. They had never had any address for the forwarding of letters, but had given everything back to the mailman. She thought the post office would have a forwarding address. The aunt had been cremated and the urn had been deposited in a cemetery at Acacia Park.

There was nothing more to be done there. Janet Prentice had been here, had lived here for some years, but she had gone on. I said goodbye to Mrs Pasmanik and walked slowly three or four blocks up the street to the Sunset Hill bus that would take me back to town. These were the streets she must know very well, the surroundings that had formed her in the years that she had spent in this district while I searched for her in England. Here were the stores where she had done the daily shopping for her aunt, the A & P and the Safeway, far from her home in Oxford, far from the Beaulieu River and from Oerlikon guns. As I drove in to town in the bus we crossed a great bridge and I saw masses of fine yachts and sturdy, workmanlike fishing vessels ranged along the quays and floats, and I wondered if the ex-Wren had found solace there, some anodyne related to her former life.

Somewhere along that waterfront there might be somebody who knew her, some fisherman or yachtsman, but how to set about such an inquiry in a foreign country was an enigma.

I sat in my hotel bedroom that evening brooding over my problem, which seemed now to be as far from a solution as it had ever been. True, I had caught up with her in time and I was now no more than fifteen months or so behind her, so that the memories of those who might have known her would be fresher, but to balance that she had disappeared into a foreign country, if a friendly one, of a hundred and fifty million people. I had dinner in the dining-room of the hotel, and then I couldn't stand inaction any longer and went out and walked the streets painfully until I found the inland water I was looking for, with infinite quays and wharves packed with small craft. I must have walked for miles that night beside Lake Union. I walked till the straps chafed raw places on my legs, and hardly felt them, but it was like looking for a needle in a bundle of hay, of course. Once, crazily, I stopped an old man coming off a little run-down fishing boat and asked him if he had ever heard of an English girl who worked on boats, called Janet Prentice.

'Never heard the name,' he said. 'There's a lot of boats in these parts, mister, and a lot of girls.'

Finally I came out to a busy street and hailed a taxi and went back to the hotel. I didn't sleep much that night.

There were still a few faint threads to be followed up that might possibly lead to her. I went and saw the British Vice-Consul in the morning; he knew of her existence but thought she had returned to England. I went to the head post office and saw a young man in the postmaster's department, who told me that it was against the rules to give out forwarding addresses and suggested that I should write a letter to the last known address, when it would be forwarded if any forwarding address existed. I hired a car after lunch and went out to the cemetery and talked to the janitor, who showed me the urn containing the ashes of the late Mrs Prentice and told me that the urn had been endowed in perpetuity at the time of the funeral. I had hoped that annual charges of some sort would be payable which might lead to an address, but there was nothing of that sort.

With that I had shot my bolt in Seattle, but there remained one faint hope of contact in America. I flew down to San Francisco next morning and got a room in the St Francis Hotel. That afternoon I got a car and drove out to the beautiful Leland Stanford University, and called on the Registrar as a start, who passed me on to the Dean. He remembered Dr Robert Prentice, an Englishman who had joined the faculty about the year 1925 and had worked with the Food Research Institute; he had left Stanford about seven years later to take up an appointment with the University of Washington at Seattle, where he had died about the year 1940. They had no records that would help to trace his niece. I thanked them, and went back to the hotel.

That evening I booked a reservation for the flight across the Pacific to Sydney. I had followed a dream for five years and it had got me nowhere. Now I must put away the fancies that I had been following and, as Viola had once remarked, stop behaving like a teenager. I was a grown man, nearly forty, and there was work for me to do at Coombargana, my own place. I dined that night in a restaurant at Fisherman's Wharf looking out upon the boats as they rocked on the calm water of the harbour. I must put away childish things and get down to a real job of work. I was content to do so, now that it was all over. I knew that I should never quite forget Janet Prentice, but that evening I felt as though a load had slipped down to the ground from off my shoulders.

CHAPTER EIGHT

It was nearly two o'clock in the morning in my bedroom at Coombargana in the Western District before I could bring myself to begin upon a detailed examination of the contents of her attaché case. I had been reluctant to violate her privacy when she was impersonal to me, a housemaid that had been engaged while I had been away. Now she was very personal, for she had been Bill's girl. She had come here for some reason that I did not understand after the death of her mother and her aunt, and she had looked after my mother and father in my absence more in the manner of a daughter than a paid servant, all unknown to them, till finally she had died by her own hand. Why had she done that?

If I had been reluctant to violate her privacy when she was a stranger I was doubly reluctant now. I laid the contents of her case out on the table, putting the letters in one pile, the photographs in another, and the bank books and the cheque book in a third. There remained the diaries, eleven quarto books of varying design. I had opened one and shut it again quickly; her writing was small and neat and closely spaced. Those books, I had no doubt, would tell me all I had to know, and I didn't want to know it.

There was no need to hurry over this, I told myself. I made the fire up, took off my dirty trousers and pullover and changed back into my dinner jacket, sat staring at the fire for a time, wandered about the room. Twice I roused myself and drew a chair up to the table to begin upon the job and each time my mind made excuse, and little trivial things distracted me from the job I hated to begin. I remember that I stood for a long time at the window looking out over our calm, moonlit paddocks stretching out beyond the river to the foothills. Already one hard, painful fact protruded, the first of many that her diaries must contain. She had made an end to her life on the eve of my return home, presumably because I was the only person who could recognize her and disclose her as Bill's girl. I had arrived earlier than I had been expected; if I had come by sea as they all thought, she would have been buried by the time that I arrived and her secret would have been safe.

If I had stayed away from Coombargana, if I had gone on as an expatriate in England as my sister Helen had chosen to do, Janet Prentice might have lived. In some way that I did not want to understand, I was responsible for her death.

I came to that conclusion at about two in the morning, and I think it steadied me. My mother had said earlier in the evening that she had failed the girl and made her terribly unhappy without knowing it so that she had taken her own life, and she couldn't understand what she had done. It now seemed quite unlikely that my mother had anything to do with it at all. It was my homecoming that had precipitated this thing, and I must face the facts and take what might be coming to me. If only for my mother's sake I had to read these diaries.

I sat down at the table, put all the other papers on one side, and started to examine the eleven quarto books. I glanced at the first page of each and arranged them in order of date, beginning with the first.

It started in October 1941, when she had joined the Wrens. In that first volume the entries were daily to begin with and largely consisted of reminders about Service routine, leave dates, corresponding ranks in the Army and the RAF to indicate who should be saluted and who not, and matters of that sort. As the volume went on, the entries ceased to be daily and became rather more descriptive and longer; some power of writing was developing in her, as might have been expected from her parentage, and the diary began to show signs, which were to become more marked in the later volumes, that it was assuming the character of an emotional outlet.

An entry in August 1942 is fairly typical:

Saturday. Went to movies in Littlehampton with Helen

and a lot of boys in W/T. Community singing in truck on the way home, Roll me over. Air-raid alarm as soon as we got back about 11.45, went down to the shelter. A lot of bombs dropped and one near miss, a lot of sand came down from the roof and our ears felt bad. Waves of them were coming over and a lot of Bofors firing. All clear about two-fifteen and very glad to come up on deck, a lovely starry night but a lot of stuff on fire better not say what. Shelter No 16 got a direct hit and some of the boys were killed, and Heather Forbes, engine fitter. Alice Murphy was buried but dug out and sent to hospital, not very bad. A crash by the transport park and three bodies on the ground beside it, but they were German. One of the Bofors got it rooty-toot-toot. They let us lie in, but I got up for breakfast and Divisions was as usual.

Another entry read:

Tuesday, September 15th. We always test the guns at the butts before fitting them in aircraft of course, but last night at the dance Lt Atkinson asked if I had ever fired one from the air and when I said I hadn't he said it was a shame and he'd take me up. We aren't supposed to fly but of course lots of the Wrens go up for joyrides when nobody's looking. He got me a flying suit and helmet and saw me properly harnessed in to the back cockpit of the Swordfish and we went up with four drums to be pooped off before coming down. It was awful fun. We went out over the sea somewhere by Bognor, a bit to the east of Selsey, until he saw a packing case floating, and then he came down to about five hundred feet and told me to pull the plug. The first drum was pretty haywire all over the shop but he went on circling round with the Swordfish standing on its ear and told me to keep on trying, and about the middle of the second drum I seemed to get the hang of it and it suddenly came right and I began to shoot it all to bits. He made me try some big deflection shots then flying straight past at about a hundred feet. He said he'd have my bloody hide if I shot his wing tip or his tail off. They weren't a bit easy, but I got one or two hits

199

towards the end of the last drum. We landed back at Ford after about an hour. It was a lovely morning.

There was nothing of any particular significance in the months she spent at Ford. When she went to Whale Island for her conversion course on to Oerlikons the diary assumed the nature of a technical memorandum book and was filled with details of the lubricants, their Service designations, how they were drawn from store, the colours painted on the shells, and matters of that sort. There must have been official publications available to her containing all this information, and I can only think it made it easier for her to remember if she made notes in this way in her own diary. The only entry of any importance related to her meeting with the First Sea Lord, and that was very short.

Thursday, July 1st. Last day of eye-shooting on the grid. They had an experimental shoot first at a towed glider target but they weren't very good. Then the Chief put me on to shoot and I fluked a hit. They sent for me to go up to the tower and there were more admirals there than you could shake a stick at, all brass up to the elbow. They asked a lot of questions that I didn't understand. The Chief gave me another coconut and we ate it in the Wrennery.

She went to *Mastodon*, and there is not a great deal of interest in the diary in her first nine months or so at Exbury. She was getting out of the habit of daily entries, and now she only wrote in it when something unusual happened that interested her emotionally. There is a gap of five weeks at one point, filled only with a detailed list of the various types of landing craft and the armament and ammunition stowage upon each.

She wrote a full account of her first meeting with Bill and the incident of the flooded Sherman tank. I have used that earlier in this account and I am not going to repeat what she had written in her diary. She was very much in love with Bill, right from the first. I had to read her diary entries myself but I shall see that nobody else does. In the succeeding weeks they were almost wholly concerned with Bill, and with what Bill and she had done together. I pass those over, till my own name comes in:

...Tomorrow, brother Alan. I wish we could go on as we are, sergeant and Leading Wren, but of course we've got to meet each other's relations some time if we're going to go on together. When we come back from the Lake District we may have to get married pretty quick! I'll have to take Bill to meet Daddy and Mummy and of course Alan comes in because he's about Bill's only relation on this side of the world. Bill thinks such a lot of Alan that I'm really a bit windy. Still, it's got to be.

Sunday evening. Bill was quite right, of course, brother Alan really is something rather terrific. He turned up in a car with a WAAF driver all dolled up with half an inch of stuff on her face, making me look like twopennyworth of sump oil. Three rings, wings, and five medal ribbons including the DFC and bar. He's the sort of person who seems to have been everywhere and done everything, and yet he's quite quiet about it all. You can see the likeness to Bill, but an older and more mature Bill; they're evidently very fond of each other. Bill hadn't told me that Alan was a Rhodes scholar or that he was at the House; I must ask Daddy if he ever met him. They both went to a school they call Gellong Grammar or some name like that, that evidently means a lot to them. I must ask Daddy if he ever heard of it. I suppose it's where the farmers send their sons to school, but I'm getting a bit puzzled. I suppose boys born on farms in England turn into people like Bill and Alan, only one doesn't know that they were born on farms. I really did like brother Alan, and I'm not a bit windy now about Bill's people. They can't be so different to us as I thought.

Very soon after that came the Junkers incident.

Saturday, April 29th. I shot a Junkers down today and it was all wrong. Everyone in it was killed, and it seems they were friendly, Czechs or Poles, trying to get over to our side. Everyone else was firing at it, but I actually got it, I think. I can't sleep and I don't know what to do and Bill's away somewhere.

I went down to 968 with Viola this morning to put some Sten guns on the LCTs and while I was on board this thing came over and they started firing at it from the Isle of Wight but didn't hit it. It got quite low down over the Solent, I should think about a thousand feet and started wandering about more or less out of range of all guns. We thought it was taking photographs. 702 was lying alongside 968 and all the gunners were on leave and the sub too wet to do a thing, so I manned the port Oerlikon. Lieutenant Craigie took the starboard gun on 968 but when it turned towards us he got blanked off by the bridge because we were moored bows upstream, so he shouted out to me to take it. It came right at us at less than a thousand feet; one simply couldn't miss, no layoff at all sideways, I just fed it down the rings at six o'clock and hit it three times in the cabin, and then the wheels came down. A Bofors hit it after it passed over us and it crashed in a field at the edge of the marshes. We went and saw the wreckage, it was awful. Seven of them, all sergeants in the Luftwaffe.

I got sent for by the Captain after dinner and put on the mat; there was an RAF officer there, Intelligence I think. He said they thought that it was trying to make a peaceful landing and surrender, but they didn't really know for certain. They tried to make me say the wheels came down before I fired, but honestly I don't think they did. They may have put them down when I began firing but I think I shot away some bit of the controls and they just fell down or something. The Captain gave me the hell of a ticking off for firing at all.

I don't know what to do. I ought to have known it was too easy, I suppose. A hostile aircraft wouldn't fly straight over a ship at seven hundred feet like that, going slowly, too. I ought to have known better, but everybody else was firing at it when it was in range. I can't get to sleep, and I'm feeling so ill. I'd like to put in for a posting up

North or somewhere, but they'd never let me go before the balloon goes up. I don't know what to do.

The diary remains blank after that for several days, and then comes a long entry describing her visit to the Royal Bath Hotel at Bournemouth where her father was in training for the Seaborne Royal Observer Corps. I have used that information earlier in this account, and only the last sentence or two need be quoted here:

... I meant to tell Daddy about the Junkers but I didn't. He was so full of fun, and having such a glorious time.

There was another gap of several days, and then came an entry about Bill.

May 7th. I got a letter from Bert Finch this morning. Bill is dead. He went off with Bert on some job over to the other side, and didn't come back. Bert's not allowed to say what happened, and I don't specially want to know.

I can't seem to realize that it's happened. I thought people went all soppy and cried, but I don't seem to feel like that. I've been going on with the work all day because there's such a lot to do and no time to sit and think. It's almost as if it had happened to somebody else.

I'm glad I never told Mummy or Daddy about Bill. I couldn't stand anybody being sympathetic. What happened between Bill and me was just ours and nobody else's, and if it's over now it's still ours and nobody else's just the same. I couldn't bear to have anybody else knowing about us.

Bill never told any of his people at home about us, only brother Alan of course. I know he didn't because we decided that we wouldn't tell anybody till we were quite sure ourselves, till after the balloon had gone up and we'd been away together and really got to know each other, out of uniform. I wrote and told Bert Finch that Bill's people in Australia didn't know about us, and asked him to look through Bill's gear and send me back any letters he found, and the photograph we had taken together. Bert's a

203

good sort, and I think Bill would have wanted it like that. When a thing's done, it's done. I couldn't bear to have strangers butting in and being sympathetic from the other side of the world, even Bill's people.

The only complication now is Dev. Bert said he was told to shoot him if I couldn't have him, but I couldn't bear that. I went and told Third Officer Collins about it and asked if I could have him here, and she said I couldn't. But then half an hour later Lt Parkes came to the Wrennery and said he'd fixed it for me, and he was to be Mc-Alister's dog. I cried for about ten minutes, in the heads, when I got back into the Wrennery. It's awful when people are so kind as that, but I suppose it does one good to let go. I felt better afterwards and went down river with some Bofors ammunition for the LCGs. I'm so frightfully tired.

There are no more entries in the diary after that until the middle of June. Only a very few weeks remained before the invasion, and in those weeks she was working at high pressure. She had the dog to look after, too, and Viola told me that she spent every minute of her spare time with Bill's dog. Probably in those weeks there was no need for the emotional outlet of a diary, for the dog Dev provided that. Perhaps it is significant that the next diary entry was written on the evening of the day that Dev was killed.

Tuesday, June 11th. Dev is dead, and I made a fool of myself and broke down on the hard, in front of everyone. He got under a Sherman because I wasn't looking after him properly. He was in such pain and it wasn't possible to do anything for him, so I got an Army officer to shoot him. Then everyone was sympathetic and that put the lid on it, and when I started crying I couldn't stop.

Viola was a brick; she came back with the cutter as soon as she could and got me out of it and back to the Wrennery, and Collins came over and told me to go and see the surgeon and report sick. All the RNVR surgeons have gone off on 'Overlord' and there was an American Army doctor there, a Captain Ruttenberg, quite a young fair-haired man. I was so glad it was a stranger because there wasn't anything the matter with me but I couldn't get a grip of myself, and I was so ashamed.

I think he was frightfully good as a doctor or psychologist or something because he didn't do anything at all. He made me sit down in a chair and got a couple of cups of tea from the wardroom and gave me a cigarette and started talking about himself. He said it was his first visit to Europe and he's only been here for about three weeks; his name is Lewis and he's got a wife called Mary and a little boy of three called Junior and a baby called Susie and they live in a place called Tacoma. He says he runs a 1938 Ford sedan, I think that's a saloon, and they all go camping in the mountains in it with a tent in the summer because he likes trout fishing and his wife likes riding a horse. I dried up after a bit and presently he got me talking about myself and I told him about Bill and the Junkers, and Daddy, and Dev. I must have been in with him for an hour and a half before he got busy with his stethoscope and blood pressure and all the rest of it, and started making notes about my length of service and all that. And then he said that there was nothing wrong with me except I was tired out so he was sending me on a month's leave. He took two solid hours to get around to that. Lewis C. Ruttenberg. He must be very clever because he didn't seem specially concerned about me, but after a bit I just wanted to tell him all about it and I think it did me good to spill it. He says I've got to have ten hours' sleep each night for the next three nights, and he's given me three little yellow capsules to take when I go to bed, on each night. I've never had anything like that before. I hope they don't make you dream like I've been dreaming lately; I couldn't stand ten hours of that.

Oh Bill, I'm sorry about Dev. Do please forgive me. It was all my fault.

There was a long gap then of about six months, and the next entry is headed December 16th, 1944:

The last of those foul children went away today, thank God. I told the billeting officer a month ago when I came back from Henley that my mother couldn't cope with them any longer but he didn't do anything and they just stayed on. I went and saw him on Thursday and told him that I'd murder one of them unless he took them away, and I think he saw I meant it, and I did. So they all went away today and the house is our own for a bit, and we've got a nice black mark against us at the Town Hall. Unpatriotic. We'll have to have somebody with three spare rooms, and I said adults – no children and no babies. My God, I'll be glad when I can get back into the Wrens.

The first thing is to keep out of the hands of the bloody doctors, of course. I'm never going to see a doctor again in all my life, and I'm not going to any more homes. I'm not a looney and I never was. They don't understand that some people do things that they've got to be punished for. God looks after that, and it's fair enough, because if you kill seven people wantonly just to show how good you are with an Oerlikon you've got to be made to suffer for it. The trouble is that all the proper doctors are in the Services and the ones left aren't any good. If you try to explain about punishment they think you're crackers and send you to a looney-bin like Henley.

Mother not at all good. She gets tired so quickly and she doesn't seem to be interested in anything. I took her to the pictures yesterday because she liked going with Daddy before the war, but she didn't seem able to follow the plot, and a bit bored with it all. I wish we hadn't sold the car now, because she never gets out at all and if I could take her out into the country now and then I think she'd like it. One couldn't go far on the basic ration, but it would be something. But God knows we needed the money. If I don't get back into the Wrens soon I'll have to take a job because there's not much left of the car money and our capital won't last so long if we go selling out to live on it. PGs would help, of course, but not those ghastly children.

The war looks like going on for a long time now, at least another year. They're bound to call me up again before long. May Spikins has been drafted to Brindisi;

they're starting up an Ordnance depot there. With all these Ordnance Wrens going out to the Med they must be getting very short of them at home.

There were several entries in a similar tone in the early months of 1945, showing a great sense of frustration, of being out of active service in the war and fretting over it. Then came the armistice.

May 9th. The war in Europe seems to be over, though the war against Japan is still going on. Fighting has stopped in Europe, Hitler is supposed to be dead, and everyone is starting to talk about getting demobilized.

I can't believe it's true. The war against Japan will go on for years, and it must be a Naval war. They must need Ordnance Wrens all the more out in the East. Now that the fighting has stopped an awful lot of girls will be getting married and leaving the Service, and I don't suppose they'll be training any more. I believe if I wrote in now they might take me back.

I don't know what to do about Mother. She doesn't seem to pick up a bit, and I don't know that she could manage by herself now if I went back to the Wrens. I suppose we'll have to go on as we are for a bit till things get easier, unless they write and call me up again, when of course I'd have to go. They might do that, because I've had a long spell at home, nearly a year, and I'm perfectly fit now.

I went and saw the bank manager and told him to sell out enough of the Associated Cement to give us £200 in the bank. At the rate we're going the capital won't last more than five years, though it would be better if I got a whole-time job instead of this half-time one. The trouble is with Mother in bed so much that isn't going to be very easy. I've got a feeling sometimes that if the money lasts five years it may be long enough. Poor old Ma.

She never got back into the Wrens, of course. She was writing fairly regularly in the diary again, with an entry every three or four days, but there was nothing particularly notable about the entries in the fifteen months that were to elapse before her mother's death. They were a record of small, daily frustrations and austerities, and of her rebellion against the circumstances of her life. The coming of peace meant no joy or release to her; it meant rather a continuation of a prison sentence. Freedom to her meant life in the Navy in time of war.

Her mother died in August 1946 and I pass those entries over, and I turn on to one of more significance.

September 7th. Viola Dawson turned up this morning in her little car. It was lovely seeing her again, but I hardly recognized her in civvies. It's funny how different people look. We went and had lunch at the Cadena and talked till about three in the afternoon.

She's got a job with a film company, not acting, but doing something with scripts and sets; she's making eight hundred a year. Of course, she can draw awfully well, and that helps in the set design. She's such a splendid person, I do hope she marries someone who's really up to her. I did enjoy seeing her again.

I told her about Mother and selling the house, and about my letter to the Admiralty. It's five days since I posted it so I ought to be getting an answer any day now. She was a bit discouraging about getting back because she says they're cutting the Navy down so much, but Wrens get paid less than ratings so it's obviously economical to use Wrens on Ordnance duties when they can. If I can't get back I suppose I'll have to take a job in a shop or something. I don't believe I'd ever be able to do shorthand well enough to make a living as a secretary.

Viola asked if I ever had another dog, and when I said no, she said I ought to have one, and that it wasn't my fault that Dev got killed. I told her I still pray for Dev every night, because I think dogs need our prayers more than people. We know that God looks after people when they die and that Daddy and Mummy and Bill are all right, but we don't know that about dogs. Unless somebody keeps on praying to God about dogs when they die they may get forgotten and just fade out or something.

Some day Bill and I will get together again but it wouldn't be complete unless Dev was there too. I let Bill down so terribly by not looking after Dev, but if I keep praying for him it will all come right.

May Spikins is married to her boy, the one who was a PO in *Tormentor*, and they live in Harlow. It was nice seeing Viola again.

The next entry reads:

September 16th, 1946. So that's over, and they don't want me back in the Wrens. The only person who wants me is Aunt Ellen in Seattle. I can't remember her at all, although she says she met me on their trip to England in 1932. I've a vague recollection of an American woman coming to see Daddy and Mummy once when I was at school. Perhaps that was her.

I think I'll go and stay with her for a bit anyway. It's an awfully long way and a very expensive journey; it's rather sweet of her to offer to send money for the fare but I've got enough for that. I don't suppose I'll like America but it's time I got out of my groove here, I suppose, and I don't have to stay there longer than a month or two.

One can go all the way to Seattle by sea, through the Panama Canal. Cook's are finding out about passages for me, in case I should decide to go when the house has been sold. They seemed to think a Dutch ship would be best, as there's a regular line of cargo ships that carry a few pass-engers from Rotterdam to San Francisco and Seattle, and it's cheaper to go that way than by Cunard to New York and then across America by train. I'd like it much better, too, going by sea all the way.

I pass over a few entries, mainly concerned with the sale of the house in Oxford and the furniture. The diary at this point becomes filled with rather muddled notes about her finances; she was not very good at accountancy, but when everything was realized she seems to have possessed about seventeen hundred pounds, of which she was spending about a hundred and twenty on her passage to Seattle.

November 15th. Rotterdam. In a ship again, and it's simply grand. The *Winterswijk* only carries ten passengers, and I've got a lovely single cabin right under the bridge, beautifully furnished. We're still in dock, but there's the same old smell of salt water and oil and cabbage cooking, and the moon on the water, all ripply. I brought my duffle coat and my Wren bell-bottoms, and I've been leaning on the rail looking at it all and taking it all in, hour after hour. We sail about two in the morning, so I shan't get much sleep tonight. I don't quite see how they're going to get her out of this dock even with a tug, because I'm sure there's not room to swing her. I believe they'll have to take her out backwards.

I'm sorry to have left England, and yet in a way I'm glad. It will be good to get away and have a change from Oxford. There's been so much unhappiness. I'll come back in a year or so because I don't think I'd want to live anywhere else, but it's a good thing to snap out of it and see new places for a time.

They've started up a donkey engine on the forecastle, heaving in on something. I must go and see.

November 18th. We're out of the Channel now and heading out into the Atlantic, rather rough. I felt a bit funny at first and didn't want breakfast, dinner or tea, and spent most of the first day lying on my bunk reading a grand book by Hammond Innes. I'm fine now and spend most of the day on deck. When Captain Blok saw my duffle coat he asked me where I got it and when I told him I was in the Wrens he invited me to go up on the bridge any time I liked. So I spend most of each day up there now, keeping as much out of the way as I can in case they find it a nuisance having me up there and stop it. We go north of the Azores and we shan't see anything at all till we pass Puerto Rico in about nine days' time, and after that Panama. If only there was a gun to be looked after it would be as good as being back in the Wrens.

I pass over several more entries in the diary that describe her voyage. It was obviously very good for her; the entries are balanced and cheerful. She was keenly interested in everything that related to the management of the ship, and at one point she listed the names and addresses of all the officers and stewards, and many of the men. She was less impressed by the Panama Canal than one would have expected; to her it was mere inland steaming, rather hot and humid and less interesting than being at sea. She went on shore at Colon and at Panama, where they refuelled, but didn't like it much and was glad to get back on board. The last shipboard entry in her diary reads:

December 12th. We dock tomorrow at Seattle, and it's cold and misty. It was clear this morning and we were quite close in to the coast and could see snow-covered mountains a good long way inland. Of course, it's winter now and we are pretty far north, almost as far north as England in latitude. The Captain says it doesn't get very cold in Seattle in the winter because of the sea, not like the inland cities of America, but they get a lot of fog and mist.

It's been a lovely month, and I'm sorry to be leaving the ship. They make four trips a year between Seattle and Rotterdam and I shall try to go back in her, probably in three months' time. They're such a good crowd to be with.

I wonder what Aunt Ellen will be like.

She got on well with Aunt Ellen but found her rather a sick woman with mysterious internal pains. In fact, she was dying though she took five years to do it and at the time that Janet went to Seattle they neither of them thought that there was very much wrong. Her aunt-by-marriage proved to be about sixty-five years old, in fairly easy circumstances. There was a seven-year-old Pontiac car that had done little mileage which Aunt Ellen no longer cared to drive herself, and a Boxer dog, and a cat.

Janet Prentice lived with her aunt in Seattle till she died, in May 1952. It was the logical thing for her to do, of course, and she seems to have been fairly contented with a very quiet life in that suburban district. I think the dog and the cat provided her with the emotional outlet that she needed, for there are many references to them in the early pages of the diary. Later on, the diary entries become infrequent, as had happened once before when she had Bill's dog to look after.

Rather curiously, I found no mention in the diaries that she had ever made contact with fishermen or yachtsmen in Seattle, or had been to sea in a boat in all the five years that she lived there. From my mother's account of her life at Coombargana she seems to have developed into a very reserved girl, and there is little in the diaries to indicate that she made any friends of her own at all while she was in Seattle. She seems to have been content to go on quietly in the daily round of housekeeping for her aunt. If she couldn't get back into the Navy she had no particular ambition for another form of active life. When friendships had been forced on her in the close quarters of the Service she enjoyed them and treasured them, but she was too reserved to make friends on her own.

An entry in her diary about six weeks after she reached Seattle is of interest.

January 29th, 1947. Tacoma is only thirty miles from here and of course that's where Dr Ruttenberg lives. I looked him up in the telephone book and he's there all right, Lewis C. Ruttenberg. He's got an office in the city and a residence at Fircrest. I would like to see him again because he was so awfully nice at *Mastodon*, but I couldn't bother him unless I was ill. Today a friend of Aunt Ellen's came for lunch, a Mrs Hobson who lives in Tacoma, and I asked her if she knew Dr Ruttenberg. She didn't know him herself but she had heard about him; she says he's got a very good reputation as one of the up-and-coming young doctors, and that he takes a tremendous amount of trouble over his patients. It *is* nice to know he's here within reach. Almost like having a bit of *Mastodon* here in Seattle.

Apart from that, I do not think that there is anything worth quoting from the diaries till the Korean War broke out, more than three years later.

June 29th, 1950. There's a full scale war on in Korea now, and the Americans are being forced back southwards. Everything is just tearing in to action here — troops embarking for the East, tanks and guns on the quays, destroyers in Lake Union. Everybody says that it's the beginning of the Third World War.

I wish I was in England now. They're bound to want a lot of Ordnance Wrens back into the Navy, because they're calling up reserves. I've been an awful fool, because the Admiralty don't know where I am; they probably still think I'm at Crick Road. I wrote airmail at once, of course, and posted it yesterday, saying that I could pay my own passage home if they wanted me, or else join up in Canada, at Esquimault or somewhere. It will be about a fortnight before I hear, even if they reply airmail. I should think they'd probably cable, though.

I think Aunt Ellen would be all right. She's got her family in Denver; one of them would have to come over and look after her, Janice or Frances. It's not like it was when Mummy was alive. If they want me in the Wrens I'll have to go.

Six weeks later she got a letter from the Admiralty, delivered by sea mail, saying that there was no requirement at the moment for ex-Naval personnel in her category and that she would be notified in due course if vacancies for re-engagement should arise. It was a disappointment to her, though I think she must have been getting used to disappointments by that time. She put in another application to the Admiralty in December 1950 when the Chinese Communists had intervened in Korea and were driving the United Nations forces southwards, and the Third World War seemed really to have begun. Again she got the same type of reply.

She would have found it difficult to leave her aunt by that time if the Wrens had wanted her, however, for Aunt Ellen was a very sick woman.

February 17th. Aunt Ellen had the operation this morning, and it all went off quite well. I saw her for a few minutes in the hospital this afternoon and she seemed quite cheerful, but still very dopey. I took some chrysanthemums but the sister wouldn't let her have them in the room today, but I saw some lovely carnations in a flower store and I'll take her some of those tomorrow. I saw Dr Hunsaker for a minute or two in his office at the hospital and he says she stood the operation very well and thought she'd be home in about a fortnight, but when I asked him if it was malignant he sort of dodged the question and said that at this stage it was difficult to make an accurate prognosis. Doesn't look too good. Billy isn't at all well; he wouldn't eat anything yesterday or today. It's rather lonely in the house without Aunt Ellen. I went out to the movies last night, but it was a stinker.

Billy was the Boxer dog, now getting very old.

The operation did little to relieve Aunt Ellen of her complaint, and throughout the year 1951 her infirmity increased. Again trouble and overwork were massing up on Janet Prentice, for by the end of the year her aunt's spells of pain were practically continuous and were only kept in check by drugs and analgesics. The dog Billy was dying, too, and in September he had to be put away, and from that point onwards a note of tired despair begins to creep into the diary.

November 13th. I persuaded Aunt Ellen to stay in bed again today; it's two days since she ate anything solid. Dr Hunsaker came this morning and he's going to see if he can get a nurse to come in every day for a couple of hours. I asked him what was coming to us and he couldn't hold out much hope, but said she might go on for a long time. In the end she'll have to go into the hospital.

I suppose this is what happens at the end of life and it's normal and nothing to do with the Junkers. But this is the fourth, or if you count the dogs, and I think you ought to, it's the sixth. There were seven people in the Junkers, so there's only one more due. I suppose that will be me.

I think she misses Billy a great deal, and I do too.

* * *

The nurse was living permanently in the house by January, and by the beginning of March Aunt Ellen was removed to the County Hospital, where Janet used to go and see her every day.

April 7th. It's very lonely in the house now. I've been starting to pack things up a bit, because I don't think there's a chance now that Aunt Ellen will ever come back. Janice is coming from Denver to stay for a few days; Aunt Ellen was always very fond of her. I'll talk it over with her and decide what's to be done with all the things.

When it's all over I'm going to make a real effort to get back into the Wrens. I think I'll write to the Naval Attaché in Washington. I believe that's the right thing to do for a British subject living in the United States. I simply don't know what I'd do if they won't have me back. But the war in Korea is so serious now I think they're bound to want more Ordnance Wrens.

May 2nd. Aunt Ellen died today at about five in the morning. Janice saw her yesterday but she was so much doped she didn't really know anything. Poor old dear. They rang up from the hospital to tell us, but we'd been expecting it of course.

Well, that's over. The house is to be sold and all the clothes and stuff. Janice is staying here for another week to help me sort it all out. There's a tremendous lot of stuff that we shall have to give away or pass on to the garbage man including all the drugs and medicines except the ones I've pinched. Janice says that she made a new will about two years ago and that the house has been left to me, but I wouldn't go on living here. I shall post my letter to the Naval Attaché tomorrow.

May 11th. Janice left today; she's been away from the family too long as it is. She asked me to go and stay with them in Denver when everything has been cleaned up here, but I left that open. I told her that I felt rather bad about the will, getting the house, because I'm not really a relation at all, but she said they were all agreed about it at

215

the time the will was made and they were grateful to me for doing what I had in the last five years. So that's that. I put the house in the hands of the agent yesterday and some people called Pasmanik came and looked over it today; I think it should sell fairly easily. The furniture goes to the saleroom on Wednesday of next week and I've booked a room at the Golden Guest House from Monday. I do hope I hear soon if they want me in the Wrens. I don't know what to do if they don't.

May 28th. I got a letter from the Admiralty today, and they still don't want me. Not a very nice letter. I suppose that's the end of it and in a way I'm glad. It's been so miserable sitting here and doing nothing, just watching for each post. I'm glad in a way it's over and I know something definite.

I suppose I'll have to go back to England now, but I don't know what I'd do. I'm beginning to think the best thing now might be to finish it all here or somewhere in America, where nobody really knows me and there won't be any scandal or any trouble for anyone. Most women have something to hang on to that makes going on worth while – children, or a husband, or relations, but I've got nothing like that. If I go on I'll have to start from now and build up a new life, almost like being born again, and I don't think I want to. I feel too tired to face up to that. It's not worth while.

It would be terribly easy to do, because I've got enough of Aunt Ellen's stuff to kill a horse. You'd just go to sleep and never wake up. It would make the seventh, and that must finish it. All the people that I've loved, Bill most of all, and then Daddy, and Dev, and Mummy, and Billy, and Aunt Ellen. I'd make the seventh, and all the people in the Junkers would be paid for then.

The only thing is that it seems so cowardly, as if you can't face up to things because you haven't got the guts.

Perhaps the drugs that had been provided for Aunt Ellen were not wholly menacing to her, because the next entry reads, two days later:

May 30th. I couldn't sleep again last night, just miserably tired and depressed, and about midnight I got up and took one of Aunt Ellen's things as an experiment, with a glass of water. It was a knock-out drop all right because I didn't wake up till half past nine – clean out, like a log. I got up feeling fine and it was a glorious morning, sunny and bright and fishing boats on the blue sea in Shilshole Bay. I was too late for breakfast here so walked up to the drug store on West 85th and had a cup of coffee. I'd been so miserable the night before and I was feeling so good that I thought perhaps all I needed was a tonic. And then, rather on the spur of the moment, I rang Dr Ruttenberg's office in Tacoma from the drug store and told his nurse he'd treated me before in England during the war, and asked for an appointment to see him. She said to come along at two-thirty, so I drove over in the Pontiac and had lunch in Tacoma and saw him in the afternoon.

He didn't seem to have changed much in eight years, hair a bit thinner, but he looked as young as ever. He remembered me, and he really did because when we got talking he mentioned Bill and Daddy, and he even remembered Dev's name – pretty good to remember the name of a dog all these years when he'd only seen me once. I asked how he did it and he said that he'd been very much interested in the case because it was the first he'd come in contact with, where a woman had been exhausted and worn out in Service life, and he'd always been sorry that he hadn't been able to follow the case up. It was just like it was before at *Mastodon* and I told him everything, about Mummy and Billy and Aunt Ellen and how miserably ill I'd been feeling and that I wanted a tonic. He started asking me things then, about love affairs of which there aren't any, probably that's bad, and I was getting too tired to keep up a front any longer and told him about the Junkers and the expiation that had to be made, and there'd been six already and the last one would be me. I said I didn't know when that would happen, but if I didn't get a hefty tonic it would happen pretty soon.

He said of course that there was no future in that, and that all that was wrong with me was that I'd been spending myself and got myself worn out again, like I had in *Mastodon*. He said the expiation angle was baloney, that I seemed to have the instinct of a nurse in doing things for people, but a nurse didn't talk about expiation and go all suicidal after a hard case when her patient died. He said he wanted to see me again and made an appointment for next Tuesday at the same time, and gave me a prescription to get made up at the pharmacy. I did like seeing him again; he gives one such confidence. I was with him for about an hour.

Before her next appointment the doctor wrote her a letter which influenced her a great deal. I found the letter itself among her correspondence, and it reads:

1206, S 11th St,
Tacoma.

June 1st, 1952

Dear Miss Prentice,
    I have been giving your case a great deal of consideration in the last two days and would suggest a line that you may care to consider and talk over at our next appointment.
    Medically your case is not a complicated one, and as you are aware your trouble is more of a psychological nature. As such it may be somewhat beyond my province, but as a friend can I suggest that you might think over the following.
    I do not think that you have taken sufficiently into account the family of the young man Bill Duncan whom you would have married. If he had lived you would have become a part of that family, and you would have owed duties to your new relations by marriage. I can readily understand that in the circumstances of 1944 you did not wish your love affair to become known to strangers, but the circumstances of 1952 are very different.
    As I understand the matter your recent bereavement has given you a small independence so that you are under no immediate necessity to look for paid work. In these

circumstances I would say you might seek out the Duncan family and satisfy yourself that they are well and are in no need of help from you, even if this should mean a journey to Australia. From what you have told me both now and in the year 1944 these people are farmers. If with increasing age the father or the mother of your friend Bill should be in any distress it may be that you could assist them, and in doing so achieve a purpose and new interest in your life.

If this suggestion should entail a sea voyage of several weeks from this country to Australia I presume that this would be an interest and an enjoyment to you. From the medical point of view I could advise nothing better for you in your present circumstances.

I look forward to seeing you again on Tuesday next.

Sincerely,
Lewis C. Ruttenberg

The next entry in her diary reads:

June 2nd. I got a letter from Dr Ruttenberg this morning. It's given me an awful lot to think about. When Bill got killed it was the end of everything for me. I never thought about it being the end of everything for other people, for his mother, for one. What Dr Ruttenberg says is absolutely right, of course. If it had happened six months later, after Bill and I were married, say if he'd been killed at Arnhem or something like that, then I'd have been one of his family. My name would have been Mrs Duncan. I couldn't have slid off then and kissed my hand to them and never seen them again. Bill wouldn't have thought a lot of me if I'd behaved like that, and I don't suppose I'd have wanted to anyway. But that's about what I did. We'd have got married if he'd lived a few months longer, after the balloon went up. And now I don't know anything about his father and mother, and I haven't cared. I've been wrapped up in my own affairs and my own grievances, very selfish. I'm so sorry, Bill.

It's going to be a bit difficult finding out. They may be fit as fleas and perfectly all right; after all I suppose they've got brother Alan to look after them and the sister, Helen. I can't just write and say, well, here I am. You've never heard of me, but how are you getting on? I think the doctor's right, as usual; I'll have to go to Australia and snoop around, and come away if everything's all right. Perhaps if I went there I might find brother Alan and have a talk with him. I think he'd understand.

I've been wondering what sort of place a sheep farm in Australia can be. I suppose it's very hot and people riding round the desert in big hats on horses, and boomerangs, and black people. And billabongs whatever they may be, like in the song. I don't think I'd be much good in a place like that, but I'd feel now that I was letting Bill down if I didn't go and see if I was needed there at all.

Anyway, it'ld mean another month on a ship. I've been down to the library looking at an atlas. Honolulu, Fiji, New Zealand, Sydney, I should think. It would be a marvellous trip, anyway.

On the next page of the diary she had totted up her financial situation to the best of her ability. Her aunt's house had sold to the Pasmaniks for eighteen thousand dollars. Unravelling her somewhat tangled accountancy and putting together the money from the sale of the house and her English capital, she seems to have possessed a total of about eight thousand pounds in English money, a sum which she considered as indecent riches.

She saw Dr Ruttenberg again, but there is only a short mention of that meeting in the diary.

June 4th. I saw Dr Ruttenberg again today. He gave me a medical check-up, stethoscope and blood pressure and all the rest of it and we had a talk about things. I told him I was going to take his advice and take a sea trip to Australia and perhaps meet brother Alan and find out how Bill's parents were, but I wasn't going to barge in if everything was quite all right as it probably will be. In that case I should come back to Seattle because I'll have to come back here, because it will take the lawyers about six months to settle up Aunt Ellen's estate and they can be doing that while I'm away. He asked me to come and see him when I got back. And then he said that in his experience a woman without family duties was generally an unhappy woman until she got adjusted to what was an unnatural condition, and that was really all that was the matter with me. I suppose he's right. He generally is.

I went to the shipping office this morning. There's a ship called *Pacific Victor* loading bulldozers and earth-moving machinery for Sydney which is due to sail in about ten days' time. She has accommodation for four or five passengers, and they don't think she's full up but they're not sure. They've given me a letter of introduction to the captain. She's in a dock on the East Side somewhere by Lander St. I couldn't go today because of seeing Dr Ruttenberg, but I shall go and find her tomorrow and see if she's got a berth.

June 17th. We sailed from the East Waterway this morning. This isn't half such a nice ship as the *Winterswijk* was, much older and dirtier and slower, not so well kept. However, I've got a two-berth cabin to myself and it's lovely being at sea again. It's two thousand four hundred sea miles to Honolulu and we do about ten knots, so it will take about ten days.

There was nothing of any particular interest in the diary until she disembarked at Sydney. At Suva a young married couple called Anderson came on board for the passage to Sydney; they were English born but resident in Australia for many years. From them she learned a good deal about the country that was useful to her.

August 2nd. We docked today and I got a taxi and went to the Metropole. The Andersons say that anyone can get a job of any sort in this country and it certainly looks like it from the situations-vacant columns in the paper. They say that lots of English girls come out and work here, usually in pairs, flitting about from job to job and seeing the country. I believe that's the best line. Travelling by bus.

Sydney is rather like Seattle, a bustling sort of place with bits of sea all round. Tomorrow I shall have to find out about buses, and probably leave here on Monday. I asked the Andersons where the Western District of Victoria was, and they said west of a place called Ballarat. I got a map today and found Ballarat. It looks as if it would be best to get to it through Melbourne.

She had a talk with the chambermaid in the Metropole Hotel and learned of the acute staff shortage experienced by all hotels in Australia, and of the considerable wages that were paid. She left Sydney by bus early in the morning a few days later and reached Albury on the borders of New South Wales about the middle of the afternoon. She found Albury to be a prosperous country town, an attractive place with a number of hotels, good shops full of fine fabrics and Swiss watches, and a general feeling of well-being about it. She parked her suitcases in the office of the bus company and strolled out down the street to look for a job. Within half an hour she was a waitress in Sweeney's Hume Hotel at a wage of twelve pounds a week, sharing a room with a Dutch girl who had been in the country for about three months. An hour and a half later she was serving dinner.

August 5th. When Mrs Sweeney asked me what my name was I said, Jessie Proctor. It went down all right, and it matches the initials on my case. I want to find out about Bill's people but if everything's all right I don't want to be bothered, and Alan probably told them about me so that they'll know the name. Everything's a bit more under control this way.

She stayed in Albury for a fortnight before giving up the job and going on. It was a good experience for her, for it enabled her to find her feet in the new country and to learn a little of its ways. The hours were not long but the work was strenuous; with Anna she was responsible for thirty-two bedrooms as well as serving all the meals and doing a good bit in the kitchen.

She went on by bus to Ballarat, staying one night on the

way in Melbourne but not working there. At Ballarat she repeated her experience in Albury; arriving about midday, by three o'clock in the afternoon she was a waitress in the Court House Hotel.

August 25th. It's bitterly cold and wet here. I always thought Australia was a hot country. They've got a Shell map of Victoria in the office and it shows Coombargana as a little spot on a sort of dotted line, near a place called Forfar. It doesn't look as if Coombargana is a very big place and Forfar isn't much to write home about. I looked up Forfar in a tourist guide and it's got one garage and two hotels, the Post Office Hotel and Ryan's Commercial. The Post Office Hotel is the best; it's got eight bedrooms but Ryan's Commercial doesn't seem to have any bedrooms at all.

I've been keeping my ears open to see if anyone said anything about Coombargana, but I haven't heard anything. I think I'll go on at the end of the week.

She left two of her three suitcases in the station luggage room at Ballarat and went out in the bus to Forfar.

August 30th. Well, here I am, and I've come all this way for nothing. Coombargana isn't a village, it's an estate. Apparently it's a terrific place, one of these enormous Western District stations. Fourteen thousand acres, a big house, and God knows how many sheep. The Duncans are one of the big families of the neighbourhood. They've got about twenty men working for them all in houses on the property. Mrs Collins always speaks of old Mr Duncan as The Colonel. I suppose that's Bill's father.

Well, there it is, and now I don't know what to do. That's what Bill meant when he said they had a sheep farm. I wonder if he was afraid of shooting a line?

I've got a job here, so I'll have to stay for a week anyway. I got off the bus and went into the Post Office Hotel and booked a bedroom and had lunch, and after lunch I asked Mrs Collins if she'd got a job for a week or two. I said I was working my way round Australia and going on to Adelaide, and I showed her the letters I'd got from Albury and Ballarat, saying I was a good worker. She said it was the off season so she couldn't pay much, but she'd give me six pounds and my keep if I didn't mind helping out in the bar. I told her I'd never been a barmaid but I was quite willing, only I didn't know the work. So I went down to the bar and Mr Collins showed me how to draw the beer and told me how much it was, and I helped him when the evening rush started. Two men came in on horses about five o'clock, tough-looking types. They were from Coombargana, boundary riders, whatever they may be. They tied their horses up outside like in the movies and came in and had about six beers each, and then rode off up the lane opposite the hotel. I asked who they were, and Mr Collins told me. I asked what Coombargana was, and he told me all about it.

I've been such a fool. I ought to have known that there was nothing I could do for them.

CHAPTER NINE

THE DIARY goes on:

September 1st. I saw Bill's father today. I was sweeping out the bar directly after breakfast and he drove up in a car and got out and came in and asked where Mr Collins was. I said I'd fetch him; he was down the yard feeding his pigs. So I did, and when I got back to the bar Mr Collins introduced me and told the Colonel that I was English and working my way round Australia. He asked where my home was, and I said London. He said he wished more English people would do that.

He's Chairman of the Shire Council, I think, and he was talking to Mr Collins about local matters, something about getting electricity to Forfar and financial guarantees. He's about seventy, I should say, and he doesn't look a bit well, very white. He's got a great look of Alan about him, much more than Bill. He drank one small whisky and water, but refused another.

Alan and Helen are both in England, and have been for some years. Mr Collins told me that, after the Colonel went away. He said that Alan was in Oxford, or had been, but he thought he was in London now. And then he said that Alan had had a crash, flying, towards the end of the war, and had lost both his feet. He came back here after the war and was at home here for a year or two, but they said the accident had changed him a great deal. He didn't make friends or get about much and he was drinking a good bit, and after a time he went back to England. That was several years ago.

The daughter, Helen, went to England soon after the war and married somebody there, and hasn't been back since. Mr Collins said that there had been a younger son, Bill, but he was killed in the war. Coombargana is six miles from here.

Mrs Duncan has arthritis and they don't often see her in the village now. The family would be sort of local squires or something in England, but it's not like that here. When Mr Collins came into the bar to meet the Colonel he said, 'Morning, Dick', as if he and the Colonel were old friends. The family seem to be very much respected in the district, though. Mrs Duncan used to run a Sunday school in Forfar up till about two years ago when she had to give it up because she couldn't get about so well.

I can't get used to the idea of Alan hobbling about on artificial feet and hitting it up. He was such a terrific person in the war, obviously so good at his job and yet so quiet about it all.

September 2nd. There were a couple of foreigners in for dinner, Lithuanians or something. After dinner they sat in the bar, the man drinking gin and water and the woman drinking beer. He was a weedy, poor-looking specimen and the woman the fat, broad-faced, Russian sort of type. When the bus for Ballarat stopped they went away on that, and Mrs Collins was in the bar and she said, 'Well, that's a good riddance'. I asked who they were, and she said they were the married couple from Coombargana. The Colonel sacked them because they were always on the grog. She said they can't keep any help in the house because it's such an isolated place. It's six miles from here, but the nearest picture theatre is at Skipton and that's about twenty miles. They've got an old cook who's been with them all her life but it's a big house and they need more than that, especially now they're getting old. The girls from the village used to work there before the war, but now they all want to be somewhere near the movies and they can get such good wages in the city. Nobody seems to stay at Coombargana longer than a month or two. It's not only Coombargana, all the other big properties are in the same boat. All the money in the world with wool up at its present price, but they've got to do their own housework just like everybody else.

September 3rd. Mr Fox, the postman, was in the bar this

226

evening. He came out from England as a boy about forty years ago, from Beverley, in Yorkshire. We got talking when he heard that I was English, and I told him I was working my way round seeing the country. He said I ought to come out with him on his round; he starts off with the mail at about ten o'clock each morning in an old car and goes to all the outlying properties, getting back here about three or four in the afternoon. He takes the newspapers, too. He suggested I should go with him tomorrow if it was a nice fine day. It seemed too good a chance to miss, so I went and asked Mrs Collins if I could go if I got up early and did out the bar and the dining-room before breakfast. She said I could, so I've set my alarm clock for five-thirty.

September 4th. I've taken a job at Coombargana, as a parlourmaid. I did it on the spur of the moment without really thinking. I rather wish I hadn't now, but it's done and I go there next Friday. It's only for a week or two till they can get another married couple.

I went out with Mr Fox and we called at every house on the way, of course. It's a lovely countryside, rather like Salisbury Plain but on a much larger scale and with fewer houses and villages. All the houses wooden and rather new looking, except the very big properties which are quite different.

We got to Coombargana about half past eleven. It's just like a big English country house with a long drive, stone pillars and iron gates permanently open on the road and an avenue of flowering trees and pines about half a mile long through the paddocks. The house stands by a river in a very beautiful place, though the house itself is as ugly as sin. It's a big rambling two-storied house built of brick I think, rather like a Scotch castle gone wrong. The grounds all round it are lovely and very well kept, acres of daffodils in bloom, and japonica, and camellias in the sheltered places, enormous great bushes of them beside the clipped yew hedges.

We went to the back door and the old cook came out to meet us and took the post. Her name is Annie. She asked us into the kitchen for a cup of tea; apparently this is the usual routine. Mr Fox introduced me and said I came from London, and Annie asked at once if I had met Mr Alan there. The locals all seem very interested in Alan.

While we were sitting at the kitchen table over tea Mr Fox said something about the married couple and asked if they had anyone else. Annie said the mistress was trying the registry offices again but it was very difficult; they could only get the riff-raff to come out into the country these days. She said that for her part she didn't want any more foreigners; she'd rather carry on and do the housework herself with what help they could get from the wives on the place though it was too much for one person. She said the mistress was trying for a Dutch girl, and that might be better.

I liked Annie, and I said I wouldn't mind coming for a week or two myself if it would help them, till they got someone permanent. I can't imagine what made me say that; it just sort of slipped out. Annie was on it like a knife, though. She said that if I meant that she'd go and tell the mistress and she'd want to see me. I started hedging then; I said I could only stay for a week or two because I was going on to Adelaide and I didn't want to let down Mrs Collins at the Post Office Hotel and I'd never done parlourmaid work, but if Mrs Duncan could make it right with Mrs Collins I'd come for a short time.

She said she thought the mistress was in her room still because she stayed in bed till lunchtime this cold, wet weather when she couldn't get out, but she would go and see. She came back and said the mistress was getting up and she would see me in half an hour. Mr Fox had to get on, of course, so we fixed it that I'd stay and have lunch in the kitchen with Annie and he'd call back for me at about three o'clock on the way back to Forfar at the end of his round. He said it would only be two or three miles out of his way to do that.

Annie said I'd better take a walk round the house with her to get an idea of the work before I saw the mistress. She took me first into the dining-room, a big room with a long polished table that I think she said was blackwood, all exactly like a big English country house, very good furniture. Then the hall which is the whole height of the building with a gallery all round it on the bedroom floor, and the drawing-room, all beautifully furnished and with lovely flowers in the bowls. Mr and Mrs Duncan sleep on the ground floor in what used to be the billiard room because Mrs Duncan can't manage the stairs, because of her arthritis. There's a study on the ground floor but the Colonel was in it so we didn't go in there. We took a quick look at the top floor but it's only guest rooms and Alan's room if and when he comes home. Annie sleeps up there over the kitchen, and she showed me the room that would be mine, quite nice and with the most lovely view out across the lawn to the river and the pastures and the hills in the distance. There's a great deal in the house to keep polished and dusted, but so few people it shouldn't be too bad. They've got an electric floor polisher and a Hoover.

Mrs Duncan saw me in the hall, sitting in front of the fire. She's terribly like Bill. She walks with a stick, very lame. She asked me about myself and I told her as little as possible; I said I was working my way round seeing the world and when I'd seen Australia I was going on to South Africa. She asked if I'd ever worked as a parlourmaid before and I said I hadn't but I'd worked in hotels. She asked why I wanted to come to such an out-of-the-way place, and I said that I wanted to see all of Australia and hadn't been able to see a big station property yet. I said I wouldn't be able to stay longer than a week or two till they got someone permanent. She said she'd ring up Mrs Collins and see what she thought about it, and let me know after dinner. She asked if I had any dark dresses because I was in my French-blue jumper and grey skirt, and I said I'd got my dark-blue costume. She said she wouldn't want me to wear light clothes in the dining-room but she didn't want me to ruin my best costume by working in it; she thought she had something that would fit me with a bit of alteration. It looks as though the servants dress in the old style at Coombargana, like in England thirty years ago. I'll probably have to wear a starched white apron or something, over a black dress.

She sent me back to have lunch with Annie in the kitchen and I got Annie to show me how to lay the table in the dining-room. They've got beautiful silver, and it looks so nice upon the polished table. It's all got to be cleaned every week. They had cutlets for lunch, and new potatoes and green peas, and English Stilton cheese afterwards. There was only the Colonel and Mrs Duncan. I asked Annie if they'd like me to serve them with the stuff in the entrée dishes and she said dryly that they hadn't had a parlourmaid who did that for years but they'd like it well enough. So I did it like that for them; they looked a bit surprised but I think they were pleased.

After dinner Mrs Duncan came to the kitchen and asked me to come out into the hall. She said she'd spoken to Mrs Collins and it was quite all right, and I could leave on Friday. I said I'd have to go to Ballarat and get my suitcases and come back to them, and she said they'd pick me up in Forfar when the bus came in. They're giving me eight pounds a week and my keep. The Colonel was there and they both said that they hoped I'd be very happy with them. He said that in the afternoons, in my time off, I could go anywhere on the property and he'd tell the men to show me anything I liked.

Mr Fox came, and I went back to the hotel with him in time for the evening rush at the bar.

She's so terribly, terribly like Bill, it's almost unbearable sometimes.

September 8th. I think I must be crazy to have come here, but here I am. Colonel Duncan sent the foreman, Harry Drew, in to Forfar in a Land Rover to meet me at the bus and I drove out with him. His father came out from Gloucester forty years ago, but Harry was born here. He invited me to tea at his house on Sunday to meet his wife. I said I didn't know what my times off would be, but I'd come if I could and I'd let him know tomorrow.

I took my suitcases up to the room Annie had shown me. I always thought the servants in a big country house must have the whale of a good time and now I know it.

The view from my bedroom is just perfect, the room is very clean and comfortable, and there's a lovely bath-room just for Annie and me, with a shower. There was a dark-grey dress laid out on the bed which fitted more or less. I put it on because it looked as if it had been left there as a sort of hint, rather a broad one, and then I went downstairs to start work. They have afternoon tea on a wheeled tea trolley and Annie showed me how to get that ready, and I wheeled it into the hall and through into the drawing-room. Mrs Duncan was there in a chair before the fire and she showed me how she likes the tea arranged and made me turn round to show her how the dress fitted. It wants taking in a bit at the waist and it's a bit long; I told her I'd have a go at it tomorrow afternoon. I wonder who had it before me.

I laid the dining-room table then and washed up the tea things, and then I came up here to unpack. I've been sit-ting at the table looking out over the river and the pad-docks in the evening light. A man went by just then on the other side of the river riding a horse, at the walk. It's so very, very quiet and peaceful here.

I think I'm beginning to understand more about Bill, after eight years. This is what he was brought up in. This house and this view made him what he was. No wonder he was different to all the other Pongoes. One couldn't help being different, living in a beautiful place like this, not as a passenger but doing a real job of work upon the land. Because it *is* a real job of work — it must be. Twenty-eight thousand sheep don't just look after them-selves and cut their own hair and send it to market for you.

I've got to start thinking of a different Bill, a Bill who was a part of Coombargana. I only knew him as a Marine sergeant in a battledress. That wasn't the real Bill at all; it was Bill in a disguise, and I never knew it though I should have done. The real Bill was a part of all this loveliness.

When I got to that point in her diary I couldn't go on reading for a time. I got up from the table and made up the fire, and then I went over to the window and pulled the curtains aside. It was nearly four in the morning and the moon was setting; in little more than an hour it would be beginning to get light. I opened the window and the cool night air blew in around me; before me lay the paddocks misty by the river in the slanting, silvery light. I stood there thinking how right she had been, how well she had understood. Bill had been a part of all this loveliness.

Both Bill and I had spent our lives at Coombargana and at school till we had gone away to England before the war. We had never thought about our home much, except perhaps to grumble that it was too far away from city life. We had gone away to very distant places and Bill had not returned; I had travelled the world and I had come to realize, in faint surprise, that I had seen no countryside that could compare in pastoral beauty with that of my own home. It takes a long time for an Australian to accept the fact that the wide, bustling, sophisticated world of the Northern Hemisphere cannot compare with his own land in certain ways; I was nearly forty years old, and I was only now realizing that by any standard of the wider world my own home was most-beautiful.

Bill had been fortunate in being born and brought up here, as I had, though we never knew it. In her diary Janet had written that this house and this view had made Bill what he was. Perhaps she had got something there. In the dark night at Le Tirage, within a stone's throw of the Germans, Bill had gone forwards to attach the gadget to the German mines on the lock gates while Bert Finch stayed in support. Perhaps when he worked under water at the wires using up oxygen and so implementing his death, the British Navy had been cashing in on all that Coombargana had put into him throughout his childhood in the Western District.

I closed the window, searched for my pipe and my tobacco, and sat down to the diary again. After the first entries at Coombargana the diary became infrequent, as had happened several times before in the years since the war. I think that means she was contented, with an easy mind; she seems only to have written in it when she was troubled. An early entry, however, seems to be important.

September 13th. There are two photographs of Bill in her bedroom, one that I hadn't seen before of him on a horse, I think by the stockyard here. He's much younger in that one, probably only about fifteen or sixteen. The other is the rather stiff studio portrait he had done at Portsmouth that I didn't like. I've got such a much better one in my case, but of course I daren't put it up in my room here. I haven't heard them say a word about Bill and I suppose that's understandable because it's eight years ago and everything there was to say must have been said. But they talk a lot about Alan.

Everybody here talks about Alan; he's very much in everybody's mind. Annie says something now and then, and Mrs Drew was talking about him when I went to tea on Sunday, and the Colonel and Mrs Duncan say something about him at practically every meal that I can't help overhearing. They all hoped that he was coming home this spring but he's staying in London for another year to get called to the Bar. There's no sign of him getting married, but he does a lot of motor racing.

I think the fact of the matter is that they're all a bit anxious. If he doesn't come back to Coombargana the place will be sold on the Colonel's death, and that means a tremendous upset for everyone connected with it. Annie has been here for forty years, and some of the men for over twenty. They've all got houses on the place and very good houses they are, too – all with electric light from the main generating plant and all with septic tanks. Apparently that's much better than conditions usually are on these country properties. The Duncans have been very good employers. They pay a good bonus after each wool sale so that all the men have cars of some sort. I think that's why they're all so interested in Alan. They want to see him marry somebody and settle down here, and carry on the property.

October 26th. The weather has been lovely while the Colonel and Mrs Duncan have been in Melbourne, warm sunny days, and not much wind. We've had Mrs Plowden in to help us with the spring cleaning, and we've had all the windows open every day, letting the warm wind blow through the house. It's been a lot of work but we've broken the back of it now. They're coming home tomorrow.

Last night after supper we were sitting in the kitchen and Annie started talking about Alan again. She said it was a great trouble to his mother that he hadn't married. She said they hoped that when he came home after the war he'd have taken to one of Helen's friends, but he was very much put out with having lost his feet and didn't seem to want to have anything to do with girls. They all said it was because he was crippled, but Annie herself always thought he'd got a girl in England he was thinking of. She said he never rested till he could get away and back to England, and she thought when he went that they'd have heard he was engaged to somebody in England within six months. But it didn't happen. Gossip of the servants' hall, of course.

I'm terribly sorry for Alan. He sounds rather a lonely person.

October 28th. They came back yesterday. I thought the Colonel was looking better for the change, but Mrs Duncan not so good. Of course, staying in her club and going about shopping in Melbourne she can't look after herself, and she told me this morning she'd had a great deal of pain while she was away, but it had been worth it. I persuaded her to stay in bed all day. This evening I asked her if she'd like me to bring the little table from the study in to her bedroom and lay the Colonel's dinner there so that they could have it together. It's got a good polish on it and it really looked quite nice with the silver and the dinner mats laid out on it just as we do it in the dining-room. It wasn't much more trouble, either.

They had a letter from Alan today. He doesn't write often enough.

There is no mention in the diary that she was pressing to move on to Adelaide, or any mention of another married couple. I think that she was happy in the queer position that she had made for herself at Coombargana, and content to stay on as a parlourmaid indefinitely. I think Dr Ruttenberg in Seattle had probably summed her up correctly; she felt a great need to be of use to somebody, and this was satisfied for the time being. A significant entry when she had been at Coombargana for three months shows her developing relationship with my mother.

December 11th. The Colonel had to go to Ballarat this afternoon to speak at a dinner of the RSL – I think that means the Returned Servicemen's League but I'm not quite sure, so Mrs Duncan had dinner by herself. When I took the coffee in to the drawing-room after dinner she was sitting at her desk turning over a lot of things she'd taken out of one of the little drawers at the side. I put the coffee down beside her on the desk and handed the sugar on the salver, and when she'd helped herself she picked up a photograph and showed it to me and said, 'Jessie, that was my other boy, Willy'. It was a photograph of Bill, of course, standing by the front door with a shotgun and a dog probably when he was about eighteen years old. I couldn't think of anything to say, and after a minute she told me, 'That was taken just before he went away to England, just before the war. He was killed in 1944, doing something on the coast of Normandy just before the invasion.' I'd got a grip on myself by that time, and I said, 'I know, madam. Annie told me. He must have been a great loss to you.' She didn't say anything for quite a time, and then she said, 'Yes. Willy wasn't clever like Alan. He was more of a home lover. If he'd lived I think that he'd have been the one to carry on this place, and Alan would have gone in to Parliament or else into the Department of External Affairs. Willy never wanted to do anything else but come back here and manage Coombargana.' I couldn't stand it any longer, and I said, 'Will that be all tonight, madam?' And she said, 'Yes, thank you, Jessie. Goodnight.' I think I got out of the room without giving myself away to her, but I wouldn't be so sure about Annie. She doesn't miss much that goes on in Coombargana.

*

Another entry reads:

January 5th. We had awful fun today. I'm supposed to get one full day off a week and one half-day, but I've never bothered much about them. I felt I wanted a bit of fresh air and a change though, and yesterday I asked Harry Drew if I could go out rabbiting with them. Old Jim Plowden is the King Rabbiter here and he looks after the rabbit pack, about thirty of the most ferocious mongrels you ever saw. He keeps going after the rabbits steadily all the time, but now they're having a big drive to clean them up and they've got half the men on rabbiting. I drove out with them in the truck up to the hill that they call the Eight Hundred Acre. It's got an awful lot of rabbits in it, or it had last week; I don't think it's got many now. They've been ripping up the warrens with sort of prongs that stick down into the ground behind the tractor and rip down about two feet deep, make an awful mess of the ground but make a mess of the rabbit holes too. Then they work the tractor backwards and forwards to stamp the earth in, and run a great big roller with a lot of things sticking out of it, a sheep's foot roller they call it, run that over the lot.

Where the ground's stony and they can't do that they put in ferrets and chase them out and set the dogs on them as they come out, or shoot them. All the men were armed to the teeth with various sorts of cannon popping off in every direction and having a grand time. I asked Harry if I could have a go and he looked a bit doubtful and asked if I'd ever fired a shotgun, and I said I had, so he lent me his gun. I missed the first two, but then I got the hang of it and bowled over four rabbits in four shots – running, too. It's only a question of laying off enough ahead of them and imagining a ring sight on the gun. The men were very impressed and wanted to know where I learned to shoot, but of course I didn't tell them. We ran out of rabbits then, but on the way home they asked if I'd like a go with a .22 and I said I would. I think they wanted to see if the rabbits had been just a fluke. So they put up a beer bottle on a stone wall and gave me a little rifle and made me try

236

it at about thirty yards. I was just below with the first shot but I got it the second time. I knew I could do it so I told them to put up three bottles in a row and I smashed them in three shots, rooty-toot-toot. I said, any time they wanted anything shot, just get a Pommie girl from England and she'd shoot it for them if they couldn't. They thought that was a scream and laughed about it all the way home.

It was a lovely day. Harry let me clean the rifle when we got back to his house, and I had tea with them. He tried again to find out where I learned to shoot, but I wasn't having any and dodged the question.

After that there are long gaps in the diary of five or six weeks at a time, and such entries as there are are not significant. She seemed to have settled into the routine of washing and cleaning in the house, making the beds and serving the meals. Because neither of my parents are very good on stairs at their age she used to go down to the cellar for my father to fetch up the drinks, and she got to know what wine or cocktails they required when they had friends in the house, and how to serve them. I think her relations with my mother were always those of mistress and maid, but inevitably they became close friends. When the arthritis was painful she could do things for my mother that no one else could do and inevitably my mother talked to her freely about family affairs in the winter months, when few visitors came to the house and there was no other woman for my mother to talk to.

An entry early in the winter is important:

May 6th. It's been bitterly cold today with a dark, leaden sky and a few flakes of snow. They say it's too early for snow to lie, but outside it's as cold as charity. They've got the heating going and the house is warm enough, but I got her to stay in bed till after lunch. I always thought Australia was a warm country, and it was hot enough here in the summer, but it's good and bracing now.

They had great news today, because there was a long

letter from Alan. He's definitely coming home, and they're so excited over it. He's staying in England till September to get called to the Bar, but he's booked a passage sailing from England on October 5th, so he'll be home at the beginning of November.

They're both so happy today, and it was all round Coombargana by the evening. I asked the Colonel if he'd like me to get up a bottle of champagne for dinner and they had that, and Annie made a special effort over dinner for them with caviar to start with and mushrooms on toast to end up – there are a lot of mushrooms in the paddocks now and we can get a basket any time. They had music at dinner for a celebration. Alan's been away five years, but from what they say he's definitely coming home for good now, to get down to work and manage Coombargana. I'm so glad for them.

I'm glad for Alan, too. I haven't seen his letter, of course, but she was talking about him this afternoon when I was helping her get up. She says he's quite made up his mind now that his place is here and he doesn't want to do any of the other things any more, like being a barrister or going into politics. He feels he ought to stay in England till September and finish off what he's begun and get called to the Bar, but he feels that he's too old to start in practice at the English Bar and he's tired of being in England now and wants to come home and settle down. I suppose that was all in the letter. She was saying that he was so restless after the war and being crippled, but she thought he'd got it out of his system. She said she hoped he'd find some nice girl and get married.

It's been a great day for them.

I'll have to move on somewhere else before Alan gets home. He'd be bound to recognize me. I wouldn't want to go much before November because I do think they need someone to look after them a bit, but when Alan gets home everything will be different; he'll be able to do a lot of the things I do for them now. He'll organize things for them, and he'll be able to race around and get some decent servants in the house, not like that ghastly Polish couple that were here before. There won't be any need for me when he comes home. I'll aim to get away a week or two before he arrives.

I'll have to go back to Seattle first, I think, to get hold of Aunt Ellen's money. That should be settled up by now. After that, God knows. I *would* like to get back into the Wrens, if they'll have me. If the armistice negotiations in Korea break down, and it looks as if they will, the war will all flare up again and everyone says it will be much worse than before, and there may be a full-scale war breaking out between America and China, with Russia and England and everyone else joining in. If that happened they'd be bound to want all the Ordnance Wrens they could get hold of.

It's going to be a bit of a wrench leaving this place.

She was to discover as the months went on that it wasn't going to be so easy for her to leave Coombargana. She had made herself too much a part of it.

May 29th. She's been talking for some time of getting Alan's room ready for him, but it seemed a bit early to me. This morning she got up directly after breakfast and wanted to go upstairs, so I helped her with the stairs and then she made me go and get a pencil and paper and the tape measure and she got down to things. There are two big rooms there with a bathroom in between. Alan has got bits of aeroplane in it and some of his clothes there still in the wardrobes and chest-of-drawers, all put away with mothballs. She told me that the other room was Willy's, but she'd refurnished it after the war and now they use it as a spare guest room. I took a look in there this afternoon, but there's nothing in it now to remind anyone of Bill. The view is practically the same as from my room.

She's really going to town over Alan's room. First of all she said it needed new curtains and she made me get the steps and measure up the pelmet and the curtains; she said when she was in Melbourne she'd seen some Italian material in Georges that she thought would do; it cost four pounds ten a yard but it would last a long time. She'll need thirty-eight yards for the curtains. Then she said the carpet wouldn't do at all; it was much too shabby, but it looked perfectly all right to me. There are two up-holstered armchairs there and she wasn't satisfied with those, so we're going to get those downstairs and send them in to Ballarat on a truck to have loose covers made, two sets for each. She's going to get the material for that in Melbourne, to go with the curtains. She wants a new bedspread and new shades on all the lamps. She's going to have all the woodwork repainted and the bathroom re-painted completely.

She wanted to re-paper Alan's room, but I persuaded her not to. There's nothing the matter with the paper and I thought it would make the room look so different for him. I said that half the fun of coming home was to come back to all the things you knew and you remembered, and if she did the wallpaper it would make it look like another room and he wouldn't feel at home. She saw that in the end, and we agreed that the paint should be as much like the old paint as possible, so that the appearance of the room would be the same, but everything clean and nice. I said I'd get a loaf of stale bread and rub down the paper by the electric-light switch at the door where it's got a bit dirty. It's good paper and I'm sure it'll come up all right. She made me measure up the carpet, but she'll have a job to get one big enough. It wants to be about twenty-five feet by twenty. She says that if she can't find anything she likes she can get one made specially, in Bombay.

I totted it all up just for interest; she's going to spend nearly eight hundred pounds doing up that room, I should think. They don't spend anything on themselves in the normal way; they live quite modestly though they spend a good bit on the garden. But she's really letting herself go on Alan's room. It's going to look awfully nice by the time we've done with it.

I stopped reading and stared round the room. There were the new curtains, the new shades on all the lamps, the deep new pile of the Indian carpet beneath my feet, the new loose cover of the chair that I was sitting in, the slightly different

240

appearance of the wallpaper by the electric switch, the gleam of the new paint. I had not noticed any of them.

June 20th. The Colonel placed an order for a new Land Rover today for Alan. Delivery is about two months so it should be here about a month before he arrives. They don't use horses much now, only the boundary riders who go round every day inspecting every fence and every gate and looking to see if any of the sheep are straying or if any of them have anything the matter with them. The Colonel goes everywhere in his Land Rover and he says that Alan must have his own. His feet won't matter a bit then.

I heard them talking about this at dinner, and of course I mentioned it to Annie in the kitchen because there didn't seem to be anything confidential in the fact that they were getting a new motor vehicle upon the property. Everyone will know about it tomorrow. Her reaction was typically Annie. She said, 'Aye, they're getting for him everything the heart of man could desire, saving the one thing.' I asked, 'What's that?' She said, 'A wife.' She's very shrewd.

July 10th. They came back from Melbourne yesterday. I think the prospect of Alan coming home has been very good for her; although it's the middle of the winter and pretty cold she was quite fit and well and told me that she hadn't had much pain; she got up for breakfast this morning, fit as a flea. She told me that she had chosen the pattern for Alan's carpet and cabled the order; it will take about a month to make and she's told them that it's got to get on board a certain P & O boat on a certain date or she won't have it, so it should be here about a month before he gets home. She's got the curtain material and a woman is to come here next week from Ballarat and make the curtains and the pelmets here, staying till it's done. The painters finished last week. She showed me the bedspread and the lampshades; they're awfully pretty.

She told me that when Alan comes home she wants me to look after his clothes, like a valet. She's going to get Mrs

Plowden to come in every morning to do some of the cleaning I do now because she says that they'll be having many more guests in the house when Alan comes home and there'll be a good deal more work, but she wants me to take over Alan's clothes. She's going to show me how to do it and I can practise on the Colonel till Alan comes home. The drill is to lay out the clothes that he'll be wearing in the evening ready for him on the bed at about six o'clock before he goes up to change for dinner; she's going to show me how to put the studs into an evening shirt and how she wants it done. Then when I go up to turn the bed down I collect the clothes that he's been wearing during the day and take them away and brush them and put them away in the wardrobe, looking out for any spots or dirt or loose buttons and doing something about it next day. Nothing's got to go back in the wardrobe till it's been brushed and looked over and put right. The same with the evening clothes; I collect them and take them away to brush when I take him in the morning tea.

I tried to tell her that I wouldn't be here when Alan comes home, but I wasn't ready and I didn't know how to bring the subject up. I'll have to tell her soon, but it's going to be frightfully difficult. I haven't been able to think of any story yet that doesn't mean telling her a whole string of lies, and I'd hate to do that. I'm not sure that I'd be very good at it, either.

I don't know what to do. I *would* like to see Alan again; he was such a grand person and he can't have changed so much. I've been so happy here, I'll just hate going away. I don't know what I'll do if I can't get back into the Wrens. Perhaps I'll be able to go back; the peace talks at Korea don't seem to be getting anywhere. That would be much the best of all. If a full-scale war broke out again I could tell her that I was a Wren on the reserve and I'd got to go back into the Service. That wouldn't mean telling any lies at all, hardly.

July 22nd. I've been wondering if somehow I couldn't see Alan and have a talk to him before he comes home. If I went to Fremantle or something and met him there. He's

242

such a very good sort, he'd advise me and tell me what to do, and he might somehow be able to put things right for me so that I could come back and go on here. The one thing which I couldn't bear is that he should come home and walk into the house and say, 'Hullo, Leading Wren Prentice, what are you doing here? I thought we'd finished with you when Bill got killed.' He wouldn't say that, of course, but that's what it would be like. If I could have a quiet talk with him before he gets home I think I could make him understand how it all happened, and perhaps we could concoct something together that would make it possible for me to go on here. After all, there's no reason why his mother and father need ever know that I had anything at all to do with Bill. Alan would only have to keep his mouth shut, and everything could go on here as usual. Only Alan and I know what Bill and I were to each other. It wouldn't be much to ask him to keep quiet about it. But it's going to take a bit of explaining what I've been doing here at all, even to Alan.

I don't know what to do.

July 28th. The Korean War is over, and they've signed a truce at Panmunjom. There isn't going to be another full-scale war, and I suppose I ought to be glad. But this finishes all chance I ever had of getting back into the Wrens. They won't be needing any more Ordnance Wrens now; they'll be needing less.

I simply can't think what I could do when I leave here; I've got nowhere to go, nothing I want to do. I've *got* to try and think of something.

I laid the diary down, glad for an excuse to stop reading it for a time, and I put another log or two upon the fire. Outside, the sky was starting to show grey.

Viola Dawson had been right about ex-Service people. Janet Prentice, at any rate, had banked upon another war that would solve all her difficulties and bring her back into the full, useful life she once had known. Without it she was lost, because another war had been her main hope since the end of the last one.

I sat down again and went back to the diaries with mounting reluctance. It was a violation of her deepest privacy that I should read what she had written, but I had to know.

August 17th. It's only about six weeks now till Alan sails, and I can't make up my mind what to do. I've been putting it off and trying not to think about it, hoping that something would turn up.

I don't think it would be possible to go to Fremantle to meet Alan on the ship before he gets here. I believe the Colonel's going to fly across and meet him there and fly back here with him. That's what he did when Alan came back before, after the war, and he's talking of doing it again, but I don't think they've decided anything yet. If he did that, of course, it would be impossible for me to meet Alan alone before he got here. I can't help feeling that's the way to tackle it. I know he'd be able to get me out of this mess. But even if the Colonel didn't go to Fremantle, I don't see how I could ask her for a holiday then. They're all counting on me to be here and they're looking forward so much to his homecoming. I don't think I'd have the face to ask for a holiday just at that time. It would look awfully strange, and if they started to get curious and found out that I'd been to Fremantle to meet Alan before he got home it would be worst of all.

Last night I thought I'd better write to Alan and explain things, and I tried to write a rough copy of a letter to send him. But it's one of those things I don't think you can do in a letter. I only met him once, nine years ago, and he probably hardly remembers me. I've been thinking of him as the same person he was then, but everybody here says that he's changed a lot. He's really a total stranger, although he doesn't seem like that to me. He'd get a letter from his mother's parlourmaid asking if he'd mind deceiving his mother when he comes home so that the parlourmaid could keep her job, because the parlourmaid had been deceiving her and living here under false pretences for the last year.

I tried all last night to write a letter wrapping up those

facts and making it sound all right, but I couldn't do it. He's a barrister; he'd see through it at once and get suspicious. I know if I could see him and talk to him quietly before he gets home I could explain how it all happened and make him understand, but I don't believe it's possible to do it in a letter.

The curtains and the pelmets in Alan's room are finished. They look lovely. The carpet's supposed to be arriving at the end of the month. We've got all the furniture piled in the middle of the room and I've been waxing and polishing the floor surround with the electric floor polisher. It's some kind of Tasmanian hardwood, myrtle I think; it's a sort of golden colour with a bit of pink in it. It's starting to look awfully nice for him.

September 25th. Alan sails from England in about ten days' time. I've been drifting, hoping something would turn up, but now I can't drift any longer.

Yesterday morning I was dusting in the hall and when I'd finished that I went through to the dining-room to do the sideboard and the chairs. Mrs Plowden was in the kitchen scrubbing the floor and talking to Annie. They were making a fair bit of noise and they didn't know I was there, and the swing door was open so that I could hear every word they said. They were talking about Alan and a girl called Sylvia Holmes whose people have a property near Hamilton, just speculation based on the fact that he took her to the races six years ago. They're terribly anxious to see him married, and they're always gossiping. And then Mrs Plowden said, 'He might do worse than look in his own kitchen, to my way of thinking'. And Annie said, 'Aye, that's a fact. It wouldn't be the first time that's happened, and it won't be the last.' I went back into the hall. I'm sure they didn't know that I was there.

Well, now it's come out into the open, and I think I'm glad. It's what's been wrong for a long time, this interest that I've been feeling for Alan. That's really what's kept me here in the last months although I wouldn't admit it – that, and the comfortable living of Coombargana, that

I've been reluctant to give up. There are some things about oneself that it's not very nice to wake up to.

All this time I've been kidding myself about Alan. I've been thinking I could go to Fremantle and talk to him like a big brother, and he'd get me out of this jam that I've got in. But it's nastier than that. What I've really been up to is that if I had a heart-to-heart talk with Alan about Bill and all that I've been doing here I could make him fall in love with me, and then I wouldn't have to go away from Coombargana. It's time now to be honest, and that's what I've been intending. Coombargana means ease and gracious living and security and wealth for the remainder of my life. I think that's what I've been reaching out for, really. And I've damn nearly got it. If Alan married me, everybody here would be quite glad.

This isn't a fairy story. This isn't King Cophetua and the Beggar Maid. This is another story altogether, of the Beggar Maid plotting to tell King Cophetua a sob-stuff story so that he would fall in love with her and take her out of the kitchen, and marry her, so that she'd be Queen and lord it over all the other servants, and live in luxury for the remainder of her life. There's no happy ending to that one, not even for King Cophetua because he'd come to realize quite soon how he'd been trapped.

Oh Bill, I can't imagine what I've been doing, how I've got myself in such a mess.

October 10th. Alan sailed about five days ago, and I suppose his ship would be somewhere near Gibraltar now, and coming closer every minute. It docks at Fremantle on the 30th and they're expecting a letter from him to say that he'll be flying home from there. There's only about three weeks now to go.

There's no way out of this one. I'll have to meet him some time, either here or at Fremantle, and now I don't know that it makes much difference which. There's something horrible about me. I know when I meet him I'll be wanting him to fall in love with me, and I've got such good cards to play. But it's all wrong. It's horrible and sordid and wrong, because I'm only thinking of him in that way because I want to stay at Coombargana.

I really did love Bill. I loved him very truly, and I still do. I didn't know his family had all this money. He was just Bill to me. But now I'm playing with the idea of making up to his brother, kidding myself that I could fall in love with him. It's time I woke up to myself. I had a good look in the glass just now, and it's not very flattering. Rather an ugly woman, not so young, who had been genuinely in love with one brother planning to fall in love conveniently with the other brother who is heir to the property. But there's nothing in the mirror to show that the trick would come off. I'd probably just be making a complete fool of myself, as I have been for the last few months.

The worst part is that there's just a tiny fragment of sincerity which makes the whole thing so insidious. I did like Alan when we met nine years ago. I've been looking back through this diary and I see that I thought then that he was something rather terrific. I still think of him like that, and I'd like to meet him again. But that's nothing to do with being in love with him. You can't possibly be in love with somebody you only met for one day nine years ago when you were head over heels in love with his brother.

There's no way out of this one. I can't meet Alan. There's too much intimacy in the explanations that I'd have to make to him to tell him why I'm here at all to make it possible to go on with him here as master and servant, or even to go on as neutral friends. I'd want him to fall in love with me and marry me, I know I would. If he did, I think I'd be unhappy for the remainder of my life, because I'd know it was all phoney and wrong. I'd make him unhappy, too. If he didn't, then there'd be shame and confusion all round, and everything here would be spoiled, and I'd have to go away. And the mirror says that's probably exactly what would happen.

There's no way out of this one.

October 17th. I asked for a day off and went for a long walk alone all round Coombargana today, getting back

247

about six o'clock. It's such a lovely place, and I'm so happy to have seen it all. They're shearing now, finishing on Friday, and everybody's down at the shearing shed in a mad rush. I hardly saw anyone at all, all day.

I wanted a day's tramp to clear my mind and make quite sure that I was doing the right thing, because it's one of those things that you can't undo when once you've done it. It's so permanent. But now I know I'm right. After a year like this I don't think that I'd ever be happy anywhere else but here, and it's not possible for me to stay here any longer now. The only thing I could do now would be to run away, go to Ballarat on some excuse, get on an aeroplane and fly away to England or somewhere and start again. I think I'd rather stay here.

I've got Aunt Ellen's knock-out drops, a whole bottle of them, still. They must be good, because the name was always cropping up in the Seattle papers; they're what all the film stars turn to when they're through. The very highest recommendation. Then all the people in the Junkers will be paid for.

Alan's ship gets in to Fremantle on the Friday, so I think I'll do it on the Sunday night. Everything will be over and done with by the time he gets home on the Saturday, and the excitement of his homecoming will put it all out of their minds. It'll be a bit of a shock to them, of course. I'm sorry about that because they've been so kind to me, but in a day or two Alan will be home and everything will be forgotten. Old people get a bit like children; their griefs don't last very long.

October 23rd. I went walking round the garden this afternoon looking at things and enjoying them, and in the greenhouse Cyril had a lot of azaleas in pots. I picked out a big red one just coming into bloom and took it into the house and asked her if I could put it in Alan's room. She said I could, so I put the flower pot in a dark-blue jar and took it up and put it on his table. It's going to look lovely in a few days' time. I hope they keep it watered.

There the diary ends. The azalea was still upon my table, in full bloom.

CHAPTER TEN

THE FIRE was practically dead and the dawn was light behind me at the window. I closed the diaries, and arranged them in a little pile under the table. I stood up stiffly and reached out for her attaché case to put the volumes back in it, and as I did so her bank books caught my eye. I wondered dully what on earth I ought to do about those, for she had considerable sums of money in Seattle and in England.

When things like this happen there's just nothing to be done about it; even suffering itself is a mere waste of time. I crossed to the window and opened one of the casements, and the cold air came streaming in to the warm room around me like a shower. Before me lay our property, a few ewes in the ewe paddock moving over the wet grass in the first glints of the sun, the river running quietly between. This was the view that she had known and loved, as Bill and I had loved it, all unconsciously. She could have been mistress of Coombargana twice over, but it didn't work out that way.

I turned from the window after a long time, and took my sticks, and went out of my room into the gallery. The house was dead quiet except for the loud ticking of the grandfather clock in the hall; nobody was yet astir. I moved slowly down the stairs, and as I went I wondered a little at the decency of my home, after all that I had read during the night. Even into this quiet place the war had reached like the tentacle of an octopus and had touched this girl and brought about her death. Like some infernal monster, still venomous in death, a war can go on killing people for a long time after it's all over.

I paused in the hall and looked around me, at the flowers that she had arranged, the chairs and tables she must have dusted, the radiogram that she had turned on for my mother when they celebrated the news that I was coming home. I drew a coat on over my dinner jacket and went out on to the lawn, and walked slowly down towards the river bank. From now onwards loneliness would sit with me at Coombargana, in my bedroom with the polished myrtle floor and the scrubbed wallpaper around the electric-light switch, in the dining-room that she had served, and with the rabbit pack. I had been lonely in my home when I had come back from the war in 1946; I should be doubly so now. I had found Coombargana difficult to bear in those days, but with Janet Prentice ever in my mind it would be intolerable now.

I moved along the river bank and sat down on the low stone wall by the trout hatchery, where I had talked with my father only twelve hours before. I sat there for a long time thinking of what lay before me. From there I could see three of the new station houses that my father had built while I was away, and, as I sat there suffering, little signs of life started to appear. A woman came out of one house with a four-gallon oil drum serving as an ash can, and emptied the ashes on a heap in the back yard. A man came out of another house in soiled blue overalls and walked down a path that led behind some trees to the main station buildings, perhaps to start the diesel. The sun grew stronger, and all over Coombargana life began to appear.

I did not know the names of half the people on the property, but they all knew me. The diary that I had been reading made that very clear. Everybody on the property knew all about me, what my interests were, how far I could walk, how much I drank, how long I had been away, what I had been doing in England. All of them were watching anxiously to see what I would do on this my first day back at Coombargana, trying to read the oracle to form their judgement from my first actions whether I was going to carry on the property or sell it, whether they could settle down with their minds at ease about the future or whether they must condition themselves to the probability of change. They knew all about me, yet perhaps they did not know quite all. They did not know that I had been in love with Janet Prentice.

It would be intolerable now to live at Coombargana. But

we had twenty-one people employed on the place, all with their eyes on me and looking for a sign. If I gave up now and went off back to England it would be intolerable again, for Janet Prentice would have had me stay. Only cowards run away because they are afraid of ghosts.

I sat there by the trout hatchery for an hour or more till I grew very cold. Then I got up and I walked slowly through the trees towards the stockyard, thinking of Janet Prentice and of her integrity. I found two men saddling up in the horse yard. I knew neither of their names, but I said, 'Good morning' to them absently. They stared at me curiously and then wished me good morning in return, and I moved on wondering a little at their attitude until I remembered that I was in my dinner jacket still, with an overcoat thrown loosely over it. I went back to the house to change.

Annie must have seen me from the kitchen window coming to the house, for she met me in the hall. 'I have a pot of tea just made, Mr Alan,' she said. 'Will I bring you a cup?' And then she said, 'Mercy, have you not been to bed?'

'No,' I said. 'I didn't go to bed. I found that case.'

'You did, sir?'

I nodded, and then looked her in the eyes. 'Did you know she was Bill's girl?'

She was silent for a moment, and then she said, 'I did not know that for certain, Mr Alan. But I thought perhaps it might be something of that sort.'

I said heavily, 'Well, that's who she was.' And then I said, 'I'd like that cup of tea, Annie.'

'Go on up to your room, Mr Alan, and get changed,' she said. 'I'll bring it to you there.'

I went upstairs and turned on the bath water, and started to undress. She came in a few minutes with a tray of tea and biscuits and put it down upon the table by the red azalea in the blue pot. She glanced at the case on the other table before the dead fire, where I had sat all night, and then she said, 'Did you know her, Mr Alan?'

'I met her once, during the war, just before Bill got killed,' I said. I glanced at her, and then I said, 'This is all something pretty private to the family. I don't want it talked about upon the station.'

'I'll watch that, Mr Alan.'

She went away and I went through to the bathroom, took off my feet, and got into the bath. The benison of the hot water was refreshing, for I was very cold, and as I sat in the warm comfort gradually I came to my senses and the power of reasoning put out emotion from my mind.

As always, Bill was very real to me in that bathroom. Never again would he come striding through the door that led into his room, eighteen years old and impatient to get under the shower. He had become one of the ghosts that haunted Coombargana for me, and now he had been joined by another ghost, standing in her proper place close by his side. They were friendly ghosts, utterly benevolent, but they were ghosts just the same; with all their integrity they could not do the job of work they would have done at Coombargana if they had been alive. In their mute presence they appealed to me to do the job for them.

That ghosts have power nobody can deny, for as I sat there in the warm water they put into my mind the little restaurant known as Bruno's in the Earls Court Road, twelve thousand miles from Coombargana in the Western District. If you want help you will find it there, they told me as I sat in the warm water in a stupor of fatigue, and as they stood beside the bath and told me that, arm linked in arm as they had been nine years before at Lymington, I knew that what they said was true. There was one person and one person only who could take my hand as I walked with the gentle ghosts of Coombargana, who would understand and comfort me, who would not be afraid.

I got out of the bath and went into my room and dressed for my new life. I put on a grey flannel shirt, the brown-green trousers of a grazier, a woollen pullover and a tweed coat. Then I took the case in my hand and went down to the hall.

My father came out of his dressing-room that once had been the gunroom to meet me. 'Morning, Alan,' he said. 'You were up very early.'

'I know, Dad,' I said. 'I didn't go to bed at all. I found a case that this girl left behind, with all her papers in it. I've got a lot I want to tell you before Mother comes to life.'

'We'll go into the study,' he suggested.

We went into his study and closed the door. 'Before we start on this I want to put in a call,' I told him. I picked up the telephone and waited while Forfar got Ballarat and Ballarat got an overseas radio telephone operator in Melbourne. 'I want to book a call to England,' I said. 'It's a London number, Western 56841, Miss Viola Dawson. I shall want about a quarter of an hour.'

They repeated it and booked the call, and I put down the handset and turned to my father. 'Hold your hat on, Dad,' I said. 'I'm going back to England, flying back at once. I don't expect to be there longer than a week or so, and I'll be coming back here then to live for good.'

'For some reason that I haven't fathomed, Alan,' he said dryly, 'with Miss Viola Dawson, I presume.'

I opened the case upon his desk. 'I hope so,' I replied. 'And now I'll tell you why.'

A SELECTION OF POPULAR READING IN PAN

ROMANTIC FICTION

Juliette Benzoni

CATHERINE	35p
CATHERINE AND A TIME FOR LOVE	35p

Kyle Onstott

MANDINGO	30p
DRUM	35p
MASTER OF FALCONHURST	35p

Kyle Onstott and Lance Horner

FALCONHURST FANCY	35p

Jean Plaidy

THE MURDER IN THE TOWER	30p
THE WANDERING PRINCE	30p
A HEALTH UNTO HIS MAJESTY	30p
HERE LIES OUR SOVEREIGN LORD	30p
THE THISTLE AND THE ROSE	30p
THE SPANISH BRIDEGROOM	30p
GAY LORD ROBERT	30p
MURDER MOST ROYAL	35p

Georgette Heyer

SYLVESTER	30p
ROYAL ESCAPE	30p
THE CONQUEROR	30p

Sergeanne Golon

THE TEMPTATION OF ANGELIQUE: Book One *The Jesuit Trap*	30p
THE TEMPTATION OF ANGELIQUE: Book Two *Gold Beard's Downfall*	30p
THE COUNTESS ANGELIQUE I: *In the Land of the Redskins*	30p

HISTORICAL FICTION

Frederick E. Smith

WATERLOO	25p

Jack Olsen

SILENCE ON MONTE SOLE	35p

NON-FICTION

Dr. Laurence J. Peter & Raymond Hull
THE PETER PRINCIPLE   30p
Gavin Maxwell
RAVEN SEEK THY BROTHER (*illus.*)   30p
Dr. A. Ward Gardner & Dr. Peter J. Roylance
NEW SAFETY AND FIRST-AID (*illus.*)   30p
Vance Packard
THE SEXUAL WILDERNESS   50p
Leon Petulengro
THE ROOTS OF HEALTH   20p
Claire Loewenfeld & Philippa Back
HERBS FOR HEALTH AND COOKERY   25p
Miss Read
MISS READ'S COUNTRY COOKING   30p
Paul Davies
THE FIELD OF WATERLOO (*illus.*)   25p
Dr. Haim G. Ginott
BETWEEN PARENT AND CHILD   25p
William Sargant
THE UNQUIET MIND   45p
Ken Welsh
HITCH-HIKER'S GUIDE TO EUROPE   35p

Obtainable from all booksellers and newsagents. If you have any difficulty, please send purchase price plus 5p postage to P.O. Box 11, Falmouth, Cornwall. While every effort is made to keep prices low, it is sometimes necessary to increase prices at short notice, Pan Books reserve the right to show new retail prices on covers which may differ from the text or elsewhere.

I enclose a cheque/postal order for selected titles ticked above plus 5p a book to cover postage and packing.

NAME ....

ADDRESS ....

....